# LOCK 13

*A selection of recent titles by Peter Helton*

*The Chris Honeysett series*

HEADCASE
SLIM CHANCE
RAINSTONE FALL
AN INCH OF TIME *
WORTHLESS REMAINS *
INDELIBLE *
LOCK 13 *

*The Liam McLusky series*

FALLING MORE SLOWLY
FOUR BELOW
A GOOD WAY TO GO *
SOFT SUMMER BLOOD *

*\* available from Severn House*

# LOCK 13

*A Chris Honeysett Mystery*

## Peter Helton

This first world edition published 2017
in Great Britain and the USA by
SEVERN HOUSE PUBLISHERS LTD of
Eardley House, 4 Uxbridge Street, London W8 7SY
Trade paperback edition first published
in Great Britain and the USA 2018 by
SEVERN HOUSE PUBLISHERS LTD

British Library Cataloguing in Publication Data
*A CIP catalogue record for this title is available from the British Library.*


ISBN-13: 978-0-7278-8766-5 (cased)
ISBN-13: 978-1-84751-881-1 (trade paper)
ISBN-13: 978-1-78010-943-5 (e-book)

*All Severn House titles are printed on acid-free paper.*

Severn House Publishers support the Forest Stewardship Council™ [FSC™],
the leading international forest certification organisation.
All our titles that are printed on FSC certified paper carry the FSC logo.

MIX
Paper from
responsible sources
FSC
www.fsc.org    FSC® C013056

Typeset by Palimpsest Book Production Ltd.,
Falkirk, Stirlingshire, Scotland.
Printed and bound in Great Britain by
TJ International, Padstow, Cornwall.

# AUTHOR'S NOTE

All events and characters are fictitious and any similarities to real persons are unintentional and purely accidental. *Lock 13* is not a reliable guide to narrowboating. The Barge Inn at Honeystreet is an excellent pub. I have never been there.

'Three men can keep a secret if two of them are dead.'

Benjamin Franklin

# ONE

S hould you ever wonder (though I don't know why you would) what the average working day of a private detective looks like, try the following. Drive to a strange neighbourhood. Park up in the street. Pick any of the houses – let's say that one over there: the one with the well-kept front garden behind the immaculate box hedge, the new Range Rover Sport in the drive and the two hanging baskets of ivy and ferns beside the north-facing front door. Now watch it. It's not going anywhere, but watch it anyway. Is anyone entering the house? Then take a photograph. Is anyone coming out? Take a photograph. If no one goes in or comes out – just keep watching. Nothing but rubbish on the radio? Eaten all your sandwiches already? Drunk all the coffee in your Thermos? Well, that's a pity because it's only midday and you'll have to sit there for at least another five hours before you could reasonably call it a day's work.

Another day's work might look like this. You get a call from Norfolk & Chance, solicitors, who offer you a quick forty-five pounds to serve a court summons on a person (soon to be a defendant) on behalf of the court. They can't send the papers through the post because the person will simply put them in the bin and pretend they never received them. The papers have to be delivered into the hands of the person so there can be no pretence of not having received them. The papers are called a 'process' and the business of delivering them to the right addressee is called 'process serving'. This means you are scraping the barrel, only to be resorted to if your private-eye cupboard is bare and you're living on toast and quince jam. The problem with playing postie for solicitors and courts is that people will not be over the moon to see you when you arrive on their doorstep or their place of work. They won't open the door. They will vault a fence. They will run away from you, jump into a car and disappear. They will threaten you. They will punch you. Your left eye will be swollen shut for a couple of days and then go through interesting colour changes for the next week or so. And you'll still have to deliver the papers into the person's hands, black eye notwithstanding. Mine is fading now, but so is the memory of the forty-five pounds.

One of the many differences between you and me: most of the questions you tend to ask yourself probably start with 'what' – what to do next, what shall we have for supper, what is that doing on the floor, what do I want, what will the future hold? Most of the questions I ask myself start with 'why'. Why is a talented painter like Chris Honeysett (that's me) wasting his time collecting black eyes or sitting in a classic – some would say decrepit – forty-year-old Citroën DS 21 (the one with the swivelly headlights), doing private-eye work when he should be out there painting atmospheric contemporary views of life in twenty-first-century Britain? Because despite having for many years pursued a successful career in the arts, he never managed to catch it. The few paintings I sell would simply not keep me alive, especially after Simon Paris of Simon Paris Fine Arts has grabbed his fifty-per-cent commission and I have paid the framers. And why on earth private-eye work? I could try to blame having watched too many black-and-white movies with corny dialogues and enigmatic dark-haired women as an impressionable teenager, but in truth I just sort of slithered into it after having, purely by accident, stumbled upon a missing meat inspector who was way past his sell-by date when I found him dangling from a meat hook. It's a long story. It made the papers. After that, complete strangers offered me money to find other things, such as missing relatives (preferably alive but not always) or pets, like iguanas called Knut. And since the police no longer have the manpower to look for missing persons, who else are you going to ask but a middle-aged painter who is so broke he can't afford to say no? After a few successful searches, I gave the thing a name: Aqua Investigation. I live in a rundown old mill house in a little valley to the north-east of Bath, and since I'm surrounded by water and Bath has hot springs, I thought it would be fitting to use Aqua as the name for a business that is mainly founded on hot air and pot luck. It also puts it first in the alphabetic listings. Mostly I work alone, but sometimes Annis helps out.

Annis is a painter, like me. Actually she's a painter very unlike me. She's better-looking for a start and Simon Paris finds her commissions from rich people. Annis turned up uninvited at Mill House a few years ago, when she was still an art student at Sion Hill, stuck her mop of red hair around the doorjamb of the old barn I used as a studio and then managed to insinuate the rest of herself into my life. I let her work in a corner of my studio, but after I kept finding her asleep in front of her easel I gave her a room in the house. And it all went from there. We now also share a bed, but over the years this has never been an exclusive arrangement. My woolly-haired friend Tim and I discovered after a while that we had been sharing Annis's attentions. The fact that this odd and sometimes unnerving arrangement remained in place for so long is testimony to Annis's persuasive charms.

Tim is the third and extremely part-time member of Aqua Investigations. He now works as an IT consultant for Bath University. Tim is an ex-burglar and safebreaker who has gone straight. Or so he says. How he can afford to live in a Georgian flat in Northampton Street and drive a brand-new Audi every two years on what he earns is one mystery I have never been tempted to investigate. While Annis lends her brains when mine give out, Tim is the expert in opening doors and anything to do with computers, surveillance cameras and generally all the gubbins I like using but don't understand. He did teach me how to defeat a locked door, but even with the tools he gave me I always have to make sure I've brought enough sandwiches for the job.

It was the first week of September and it was raining. I didn't mind since I was sitting warm and dry at the Roman Baths in the Pump Room, buttering a scone as the rain ran down the window panes, while the Pump Room Trio played a piece by Haydn I could hum but not name. I was waiting for Giles Haarbottle of Griffins, the insurance company. Over the years Haarbottle has put quite a bit of work my way, probably because it means he gets to leave Griffins' hideous Bristol offices and come to Bath to meet me in places like this one. Aqua Investigations does not have (i.e. cannot afford) an office in town. It's really just a website and phone number, which means I get to meet clients in the coffee house of their choice. Sometimes their choices can be quite revealing; I have met clients in a Michelin-star restaurant and I have met them at Pizza Hut. I have never met a client in a greasy spoon; Bath isn't that kind of place. Haarbottle chose the Pump Room because it reminded him what civilization looked like and I happily obliged. He was late. I had just snaffled my first scone when I spotted him weaving between the tables towards me. Six foot four of hunched middle-aged greyness with enough static in his synthetic clothes to make your hair stand on end when he comes close.

'Sorry I'm late,' he said as he took off his swishy raincoat and set down his leatherette briefcase. 'The train stopped in the middle of nowhere for twenty minutes.'

'You came by train?'

'Have you tried parking in Bath?'

'Good point. I struggled myself today. I usually use the Norton when I come into town; only it's being mended.'

'And what is a *Norton* when it's at home?' he asked, taking a seat and signalling a waitress.

'A Norton, whether it's at home or not, is a classic British motorcycle which is so old you can ride it tax-free and you can park it anywhere. My partner, Annis, owns one and lets me borrow it.'

'Is it insured with us?' he asked painfully.

'No.'

'Good, good.' He ordered a pot of Earl Grey and a cinnamon bun and looked more happily about him at the décor, the Georgian columns and the chandelier, ignoring me and my scone until the waitress delivered his tea. 'How's the painting going?' he eventually asked out of politeness, not having the slightest interest in it.

'Going well enough to keep me in part-time jobs.'

'I'm always happy to put some your way,' he said through a mouthful of crumbs. Eventually, he had gulped enough tea and sufficiently decimated his bun to open his scuffed briefcase. He extracted a thin, crumpled magazine from it and handed it over. It was a copy of *The Angler*. From the cover a grinning man in a baseball cap was looking up, holding a net full of fish. *Catch More Bream*, the caption exhorted me.

'I'm not going fishing with you, Haarbottle.'

'Page twenty-three.'

I turned to the page. He tapped a small red-circled photograph with a long cinnamon finger. 'That's the one. Second chap along – the one with his top off.'

The picture showed two men standing by the water's edge, fishing from a green river bank or lake shore with their rods. It looked as if the weather was hot; bright sunlight shimmered on the rippled water. The topless man was hauling out a rainbow trout. 'Let me guess . . . illegal trout fishing?'

'No.'

'*Uninsured* trout fishing?'

'Don't be daft.'

'A dispute over trout fishing?'

'No, you've had your three guesses. The bloke with the top off is Henry Blinkhorn and he's dead.'

I turned to the cover; it was this month's issue. 'Recently deceased?' I asked.

'Six years ago; died age forty. Drowned on a fishing trip when his boat overturned in bad weather in the Severn estuary.'

'Should have stayed on land. Did well there, by the looks of it.'

'Too well for someone who is supposed to be dead. That picture was taken this year here in Somerset and used purely as an illustration of trout fishing. Someone who remembered the case sent this to us and pointed out that it looks surprisingly like the missing, presumed dead, Blinkhorn.'

'Where exactly was the picture taken?'

'Rainbow Lodge Fisheries, not ten miles from here.'

'You want me to find this chap? We can ask the people at the fishery to tell us if he turns up again, give them the picture . . .'

'They went into liquidation – failed business.'

'We can try other fisheries. Lakes. Ponds, rivers, canals.

You do realize there are thousands of miles of rivers and lake shores from where he could be dangling his rod in Somerset alone?'

He pulled a pained face. 'I'm aware of it. It could be a long job. Prove he's alive. He has been declared dead two years early because his boat capsized in bad weather and that, the widow's lawyers argued, makes it a natural disaster. Especially for us since his life insurance cover amounts to a million and a half.'

I would have given an impressed whistle had I known how. 'Will you pay out?'

'Already had before the magazine arrived.'

'Did you show this to the police?' I scrutinized the photograph. The camera had focused on the angler in front and the topless man was slightly blurred.

'We did.'

'And they told you it's too blurred, you would need more to go on?'

He nodded. 'Almost word for word.'

'I've heard them talk.'

'They said the case would not be reopened and we were clutching at straws.'

'And I'm that straw.'

'Precisely.'

'Clutch away, by all means. Standard clutching rates apply. But what makes *you* so sure it's him?'

Haarbottle drained his cup. 'See that rectangular patch on his chest above his left nipple?'

I squinted at the picture. There was a pale pink rectangle standing out from his sun-reddened chest. 'What is that?'

'We think that is a big plaster. Henry Blinkhorn has a tattoo in that place – some kind of fish. He's obviously covering it up with a plaster because it could identify him.'

'What did this guy do before he disappeared?'

'He ran a lucrative repair and servicing business for office machines. Nationwide. Did very well for a long time but then it went downhill. There's less and less machinery, and businesses just upgrade instead of repairing the old.'

'Who's the beneficiary?'

'His wife, Janette Blinkhorn, age forty-four. No children. Still lives in their well-appointed home here in Bath, one and a half million pounds better off.'

'OK. So the business isn't going well and he wants to spend more time fishing anyway. He arranges to go out in bad weather, fakes his own death and lies low until the payout. That's definitely a long-term scheme. But a million and a half is worth waiting for, I suppose, even if you have to share with Janette, age forty-four, no children. I will get the standard one per cent?'

'If you like.'

'What's that supposed to mean?'

'It's actually two per cent.' Haarbottle pulled a slim, bright yellow folder with the Griffins logo from his briefcase, handed it to me and snapped the case shut. 'You'll find all the necessary details in there.' He rose. 'Stay in touch; I want regular progress reports.' He walked off, recovered his umbrella from the stand near the till and walked out into the rain without paying for his bun. I checked my watch. I had several hours still before starting my other part-time job, teaching a life-drawing class back at Mill House. I waved over the waitress and ordered another coffee. If I found that Henry Blinkhorn was alive and fishing, then two per cent of the payout would net me thirty thousand pounds. Surely I could afford another couple of scones? 'Blackcurrant jam this time, please, and some more clotted cream would be nice, too.'

# TWO

I always dreaded having to teach a class, mainly because of the tedium of it. There were usually about eight or ten students of mixed experience and talent, ranging from those who went to art college thirty years ago to those who, with the best will in the world, would never get into one. Some came for the social side of it, some for something to do between six and nine, some came for the tea and cake provided during the break and only one or two took it seriously. None, of course, took it as seriously as me who had to teach this mixed bag, or Annis who baked the cakes for them, or Verity, the life model, who had to sit shivering between two rattling blow-heaters in our draughty studio.

Mill House lies near the damp bottom of the valley; you reach it via a rutted dirt track that branches off the single lane road that bisects it. At the bottom of the track you turn into the potholed yard of what was once a large grain mill. The mill pond still feeds the stream that runs past the house, but the mill wheel is long gone, mouldering under grass somewhere in the overgrown three acres that surround the house. The courtyard, framed by dilapidated outbuildings and open sheds full of defunct gardening machinery, was once cobbled but now has only one small island of cobbles left; the rest consists of bare earth, patches of perished concrete and weeds. We no longer have any need for gardening machinery; we simply borrow a few of my neighbour's black-faced sheep to keep the grass down. Annis's collection of dents and scrapes that she was fond of calling a classic 1960s Land Rover was parked on the cobbled bit; Verity was also here already, as attested by her minimalist bicycle that had neither brakes nor lights or even hand grips on the handle bars; if it became any more minimalist, it would have to make do with fewer wheels. Perhaps I wasn't paying her enough, I thought as I made my way to the kitchen where I knew I would find the two.

'How does he do that?' said Verity who was sitting at the table. She was a straw-blonde, almost pretty girl with the kind of body that doesn't mind being stared at for hours on end by a dozen people because it knows it has nothing to hide. 'He always turns up the moment the kettle is boiling.'

Annis was standing at the Rayburn, splashing boiling water from the kettle into a cafetière, filling the room with Blue Mountain aromas. 'He's had years of practice.' I lifted the napkin from a large oval dish on the table. Two dozen pieces of lemon drizzle cake smiled sunnily up at me. 'Hands off! Not until breaktime,' warned Annis. 'Verity can have some; she needs sustenance for her forthcoming modelling stint.'

'I find sitting still much easier with some cake inside me,' she agreed and helped herself to a slice, wafting it with an evil smile under my nose on the way to her mouth.

I had poached Verity from a fellow painter who himself had found her in a pub in Larkhall, cadging drinks and scrounging cigarettes (Verity, not the painter) and, seeing that she was obviously broke, paid her to sit for him. She was still obviously broke and I suspected that the four hours of modelling a week, though generously remunerated, were her only income, because I had never before witnessed any girl as thin as Verity eat everything offered to her with such voracious enthusiasm. I suspected that most of her money was not spent on food. I wondered where her parents lived and if they approved of her lifestyle.

'Are you actually from Bath?' I asked her.

'Frome,' she said through a mouthful of crumbs.

'Do your parents still live there?'

She shook her head. 'Died in a coach crash in Italy. Three years ago.'

'I'm so sorry to hear that. Any other relatives?'

Verity swallowed down the cake and stood up to go. 'One aunt. My dad's older sister. She's an ugly old spinster and lives somewhere in Belgium. Haven't spoken to her since I was little. And have no desire to.' She experimentally stretched out a hand towards the dish of lemon cake to see if anyone would protest and, when neither of us did, swiped a slice and with a big grin skipped through the door.

One by one the students arrived and made their way up the meadow to the barn. I called them 'students', Annis called them 'artists', Verity 'punters'. All but one of them were women. I settled them in, made sure each of them had paper and charcoal and an easel to work from, then Verity came, changed in the cubicle I had bodged up for her from lengths of two-by-two and canvas, and the session got under way. We had a full house, the cake and tea during the break were much appreciated and it was a happy bunch of artists, punters, students and model who left Mill House at dusk that night.

So far so good.

The next morning I taught another class at Mill House, this time watercolour. The class consisted of five women and me painting views of Mill House in its setting or of Ridge Farm up the road. In inclement weather we stayed in the studio and did colour theory, colour mixing, wet-in-wet techniques (the roof leaks) and single-point perspective. It had been quite a wet summer so far and by now they knew everything I did. Clouds rolled in from the north but the weather held and another six versions of Mill House were painted, discussed and admired. Two of my older students were so good at watercolour painting that I was convinced they came purely for Annis's baking. Once they had all driven off again in their sensible cars, I got behind the wheel of my utterly impractical DS 21 and drove across to the north side of town.

The grieving widow of Henry Blinkhorn was consoling herself with her £1.5 million payout in the six-bedroom house in Charlcombe Lane where they had lived together until his disappearance five years earlier. It was a large nineteenth-century house built of freestone and called The Chestnuts, of which there were plenty around. The original wall that enclosed the property had been partly removed to allow for a wider gate and a drive to a carport, built far more recently but in a sympathetic style. At the moment it harboured a small but perfectly expensive silver-grey Mercedes. Charlcombe Lane ran along the northern edge of the little valley, and its substantial houses looked disdainfully down on the suburban developments of Fairfield Park in the valley far below.

The lane was shaded by overhanging trees and so narrow that passing places were needed to allow cars to squeeze past each other. This meant that parking up in the road was impossible. My sinister black Citroën was noticeable enough in a busy street; here it would attract immediate attention and block the traffic. I parked it in nearby Richmond Road. Fortunately, I never go far without my folding camping chair and my sketching tools – paint box, collapsible water cup, watercolour sketchbook and travel brushes. What could be less suspicious than a middle-aged watercolourist on a folding chair, squinting and daubing? I had used this disguise before and no one gave me a second glance. (NB: This may be less successful on a rundown council estate.)

I set myself up by the side of the lane with my back to a tree. From here I could just see up the drive of the house and keep an eye on the front door and the car. Several tall trees towering higher than the house made me suspect that a substantial garden lay behind it. I would paint slowly. Very slowly. It goes much against my nature, but if I finished my sketch in half an hour and nothing had happened, then I might end up having to paint the same thing over and over, driving myself mad. I took out my ink pen and started my drawing. I drew every stone in the wall, every stonecrop leaf and flower, the weeds at the bottom of it; I drew the open cast-iron gate and the tiny flecks of rust near the hinges, the entire house, the trailing plants in the hanging basket by the front door, the blank windows reflecting the grey sky here and there. Then I drew every roof tile I could see. A thin line of smoke wafted from one of the chimneys; I drew that. I find cars hard to do but I drew the Merc and then in desperation started filling in the gravel on the drive, one stone at a time. Nothing happened. No one came or left; not a shadow crossed the windows. Perhaps this is why a painter is so eminently suited to this idiotic job: if you enjoy watching paint dry, you're qualified. Then the heavens opened and by the time I had packed up and trudged back to my car I was drenched. It rained all day and the next and I didn't go near The Chestnuts.

The following day it brightened up. Having taught the second watercolour class, I dashed across to Charlcombe Lane. I quite looked forward to the watercolour part of my sketch, as long as I didn't get rained on. But when I got to the house, the Mercedes wasn't there. Widow Blinkhorn was out, presumably spending the money. Not to be put off, I set up anyway and started mixing paint for my sketch and only fifteen minutes later was rewarded with the purring and hissing of a Mercedes engine. Janette Blinkhorn returned. She gave me a curious look and a benevolent smile from behind the wheel as she passed me and turned into the yard. My speculation had been spot on – from the boot she lifted four shopping bags with the logo of Bath's finest supermarket and disappeared inside. I continued my slo-mo painting for another ten minutes before Mrs Blinkhorn reappeared and came over to see what I was up to.

'May I have a look? I hope you don't mind. Oh, you *are* painting my house! I thought you must be.' Janette Blinkhorn was an attractive woman in her mid-forties, with dark eyes and static dark hair that just touched her shoulders. She wore a simple navy-blue knee-length dress, black three-inch heels and a lot of gold on her fingers, wrists and around her neck. Somehow I thought she dressed ten years older than she looked. I noted the 'my house'. If she had her husband hiding in the attic, she might have slipped and called it 'ours'. I didn't mind her looking at the painting at all since that's what they're there for, but it meant that she also managed to take a good look at me which was far less desirable. 'You're very good, I can already see that. All that detail. But why did you pick my house?'

'There's just something about it. I myself live in a modern little house, far too drab to paint,' I lied. 'But when I walked around this bend, I just *knew* I had to paint yours,' I enthused, 'and the name really appealed to me too.'

'Yes, I'm very happy here. I only wish I lived closer to the river. But apart from that, it's perfect.' She nodded and turned back to the house, looking doubtfully up at the sky which was full of dark cloud now. 'I hope the weather holds for you.'

Twenty-odd minutes after Mrs Blinkhorn had gone inside, her hopes were dashed and the first raindrops fell on my sketch. What to do with a wet watercolour sketch is always a problem, but when it rains, doubly so. Before I could even pack half my art materials, it was raining steadily. While I was still grabbing at things, knocking my chair over in the process, the door at The Chestnuts opened and Mrs Blinkhorn emerged with a large black umbrella, rushing to my aid. 'Come inside while it rains – it's only a shower, I think. It'll probably be over in a few minutes.' She kindly held the umbrella over me while I collected my painting gear, then we scooted side by side into the house. 'After you,' she said, 'after you.'

With my bag, drawing board and chair, I clattered into the hall, making grateful noises while trying not to look as though I was registering every detail. The house smelled of a mix of floor polish and Mrs Blinkhorn's jasmine perfume. All my things were quite wet and I was dripping all over the carpet. 'Just leave it all here and come through,' she said. 'I'll make us a nice cup of tea – or coffee, if you prefer. This way. I hope you don't mind the kitchen – I was in the middle of something. I'm Janette, by the way.'

'Chris. It's very kind of you to give me shelter.' From what I glimpsed through the open doors as we passed them, it looked as if her house was furnished comfortably in a flowery style, with framed prints of Dutch still lifes and porcelain figurines at regular intervals. There was no obvious opulence or extravagance on show. The kitchen was a 1980s farmhouse fantasy but was obviously being well used. Terracotta tiles on the floor, wine-red Aga and no microwave – I approved. The kitchen windows looked out over the large rain-lashed garden which consisted of terrace, a sloping lawn, several tall trees, two of them chestnuts, a few flower beds and an ornamental pond with a stone fish spouting water. On the terrace stood an enormous gas-powered barbecue; the rain drummed noisily on its stainless-steel cover.

If Henry Blinkhorn was hiding in this house, surely his wife would not invite a total stranger inside. Would she? As she busied herself with making coffee, I tried to find clues to multiple occupancy – pairs of cups and placemats, for instance, or decaf and regular coffee, gluten-free products next to regular ones – but could see nothing suspicious. I stood by a window while coffee was being procured. 'I like your garden,' I lied.

'I'm not much of a gardener myself, though,' I added truthfully.

'Neither am I,' she said happily. 'I have whatever is the opposite of green fingers. I, erm, have a man to look after it.'

I was going to mention sheep but remembered in time that I had given the impression that I lived in a small suburban house. The coffee was excellent and the rain stopped before I had finished it. What Janette had been in the middle of when she rescued me was spiking a leg of lamb with garlic and bits of fresh rosemary. She smiled at me as she lovingly massaged seriously expensive olive oil into it. Judging by her figure, she probably wasn't going to eat all that by herself, but as she chatted to me about the kind of art she *really couldn't stand* (the Turner Prize, mainly) and about watching *Watercolour Challenge* on television (wasn't it fascinating?), I missed my chance to enquire about her perhaps expecting guests. When I had finished my coffee, I asked to use the bathroom, hoping to find two toothbrushes (note the extreme sophistication of my methods) and was allowed to use the downstairs toilet which gave nothing away except the type of toilet paper she preferred (lightly scented with a flower pattern).

'I'll probably be back sometime soon to finish the sketch,' I promised. 'When there is no rain forecast. Thanks again.'

Walking back to the car, I tried to summarize what I had learnt. It didn't take me long: Janette Blinkhorn was a conservative middle-class meat-eater who could now afford to spend dizzying amounts of money on single-estate organic olive oil. In furnishings, she had average taste veering towards kitsch; she wasn't much of a gardener, wished she lived closer to the river (perhaps Janette fished, too) and she was kind to damp watercolourists. She had a man to look after the garden. Was she going to snaffle the leg of lamb by herself? Have friends round later? I would have no opportunity to find out since I had another life-drawing class to teach.

That day Annis made scones for the tea break, which I find even more torturous to wait for than lemon drizzle cake. Verity arrived later than usual but still managed to cram two of them into her mouth with half an inch of clotted cream and a tottering mound of raspberry jam on top. Halfway through the drawing session the rain returned, this time in earnest, and the forecast was for much of the same over the next three days. It was too wet for Verity to cycle back. Annis was having a serious conversation with someone on the phone, but I managed to wrestle the keys to the Land Rover from her and gave Verity and her bicycle a lift into town. I had done this before but was still no wiser as to where she lived since she was deliberately vague about it and always asked me to drop her off in front of the Bell Inn in Walcot Street; today was no exception. While she locked up her bike outside, a bearded, tousle-haired young man who had watched us arrive through a window came out to greet her. He wore big muddy boots, jeans and a faded waxed hunting jacket with too many pockets. When Verity straightened up from locking up her bike, he planted a kiss on her cheek which Verity ignored and did not return. She gave a quick wave in my direction, then dived through the door into the dry, followed by the bearded greeter. A moment later she appeared near a window, exuberantly greeting a young woman with pink hair, and then I lost sight of her.

The rain had lessened somewhat but not enough to stand outside The Chestnuts hoping to learn more about Janette Blinkhorn's social life. I compromised by driving home via Charlcombe Lane. The lights were on and the curtains drawn at the house but there were no additional cars, motorcycles or bicycles. Perhaps her guest(s) had arrived on foot, been fetched, came by cab or had left already. Perhaps she had shared the leg of lamb with her supposedly dead hubby in the attic. I had a mental picture of her sitting by herself at the kitchen table, with nothing but the bone left, unable to move, burping delicately. There was an outside chance Janette had scoffed the leg of lamb all by herself.

The next day, which was gloriously free from teaching classes, was a complete washout. It was already raining heavily when I woke up. There was an uncharacteristic void in the bed next to me where normally a red-haired Annis, buried under pillows to ward off the advance of day, would either be snoring or demanding to know where her breakfast was. When I eventually found her (Mill House runs over three floors and has cellars), it was on the little covered verandah at the back where there lives a barbecue on which we sometimes allow Tim to incinerate our supper. She was wearing her painting gear and was watching the rain while listening to someone on the phone again. When I went to kiss her good morning, she silently shoved her empty coffee mug at me for a refill. Annis runs on coffee. I myself run on croissants and quince jam, which is another reason why we take different dress sizes. I shoved a couple of croissants in the oven to warm them up, assembled breakfast, brewed Annis-strength coffee and handed her a mug. She was still listening, punctuating her frankly out-of-character silence with attentive grunts and polite utterances like 'I see', 'naturally', 'no problem' and, most worryingly, 'I'd be delighted'.

The rain meant no surveillance on the Blinkhorn residence, and with no classes to teach today. I could theoretically have gone and done some painting of my own. Only I had launched myself into a project I had already begun to regret, and that was to paint a series of views that had started at the house and would eventually take me into the centre of Bath itself, all done *en plein air*, naturally. In my megalomaniac imagination I had seen them hanging all together at a one-man show at Simon Paris Fine Art and naturally all had red dots against them. The reality was that the demands of teaching and the vagaries of the English weather had slowed me so much that I had made very little progress, although I was now completely sold on painting outside. Sitting in the dim studio, with the rain hammering noisily on the patchwork roof and the odd drip from a leak plinking into an empty paint can, I brooded on the distinct possibility that somewhere in Italy or Spain or Greece happy and undoubtedly tanned painters were working in uninterrupted sunshine all day. What I needed, I concluded, was a mobile studio, a painting van perhaps, from which I could work whatever the weather. My gloomy musings were interrupted by Annis, who came in, whistling. *Whistling*?

'You are delighted?' I asked.

'Am I? Oh yes, I suppose I am,' she said dreamily.

'You are "delighted to . . ."?'

'To what?'

'That's what I'm asking.'

'Oh, that. I've got another mural commission,' she admitted.

'*Another* one?' I said accusingly. I hadn't had a commission since I gave up abstract painting, which explained Annis's reticence. 'Not another rock star?' Annis's first mural commission had come about when Mark Stoneking, the sole survivor of the rock group Karmic Fire, wanted to commission *me* to paint a mural in his pool house. But since my style had changed so dramatically, I handed him over to the supremely talented Ms Annis Jordan. She had since been paid a small fortune to paint another mural for an equally rich musician living in the next county.

'This one's a record producer. Reuben Hitchcock.'

'Never heard of him.' Not being a musician, I could not have named a single record producer.

'Another friend of Stoneking's. He went for a swim at his pile and "absolutely loved" my mural. He produced the last two Karmic albums and a lot of others I've never heard of, and he must be rolling in it. He lives in a huge house called Bearwood Hall near Ufton in Wiltshire and wants me to do two murals, no less.'

I stifled a groan born of deep green jealousy, possibly viridian green. 'Don't tell me: he's got two swimming pools.'

'Just the one. He wants one mural in there. And he has an Italianate colonnaded walkway terrace thingy in his garden – forty feet long. He wants another one there. I'll be gone some time.'

'*Gone?*' I said in my best horror-struck voice. '*Gone?*'

Annis furtled about in the back of the studio, dragging a couple of wooden crates into the light. 'Yeah, I'll be staying there; it's too far to commute and he's offered me accommodation. I'll be staying at the gatehouse.'

'Gatehouse,' I mused morosely. 'Why haven't we got one of those?'

'We can't even afford to repair the gate. One of the hinges is knackered. I'll be starting each day with a swim and will get to work straight after breakfast.'

'You'll get wrinkled toes.' Then it hit me. 'What about the tea break stuff? The *baking* stuff?'

'Baking stuff? Haha, *baking stuff*,' she cackled gleefully. 'You'll have to come up with something yourself, I'm afraid.'

'But I don't bake. I cook, you bake – that's how it works.'

'I thought there was more to it than that. Looks like you'll have to extend your repertoire, doesn't it? It's not rocket science. 'Nuff books in the kitchen.'

'But . . .' But I couldn't really think of a but.

'Look, you only have four classes left until the term finishes. The watercolour class ends tomorrow, then one drawing class tomorrow evening, so the same cakes or whatever you decide for that, and then two more drawing classes and the term is finished.' She began clearing her painting table and packing paint supplies into the crates: brushes, large tins and tubes of oil paints, three-litre cans of turps, stand oil and liquin. While my painting kit had shrunk to that of a mobile watercolourist, hers had inflated to that of the mural painter.

'When are you going?' I asked pitifully.

'Tomorrow.'

'You couldn't find it in your heart . . .'

'No, too busy. I still have things to buy in town.'

'What do you need? You can have any of mine.'

'That's kind of you, Chris, but your cozzie wouldn't fit me.'

All thoughts of painting were driven from my mind by the sheer panic the word 'baking' had induced in me. I went back down to the house to consult some of Annis's books on the subject. *Calm down*, I told myself, y*ou're a good cook, so you'll master baking too. Ah*, said the undeceived voice of unclouded memory, *but you started by being a lousy cook and produced a string of disasters before you got the hang of it.*

On our shelves of cookbooks I found a tome called *The Great British Bake Off – Everyday*: *One Hundred Foolproof Recipes*. Foolproof sounded good but there was no guarantee they were Honeysett-proof. I opened it. It started with count-less pictures of baking paraphernalia, in silhouette. Did we have all those? Would I recognize them? What were they all called? This was not reassuring. I turned pages until I got to the recipes. Demerara? Buttermilk? Baking powder? Vanilla pods? Rum? I obviously had shopping of my own to do. And what on earth did 'base-lined' mean? I made a shopping list

as long as my arm and drove into town, spent a small fortune
because I hadn't checked what was already in the house and
came back with enough ingredients to feed every artist in the
county with chocolate cake. Eventually, I produced two uneven,
surprisingly heavy lumps of which I nevertheless felt as proud
as if I had personally given birth to them on the kitchen floor.

Annis stood and looked at the cakes, then at the devastation
in the kitchen. 'Wow, you made them blindfolded.'

'Come and try some.'

'No, no, I'm sure they'll be fine. Don't cut them until
tomorrow.' She ran a finger through some leftover chocolate
icing in the bowl, sucked it thoughtfully and said, 'Mmm,
*unusual.*'

The next morning she kissed me awake, then kissed me goodbye
and deserted me to go and mix with the rich and probably
famous while I had to wait anxiously until it was tea break
time to hear the watercolourists' judgement on my baking
efforts. The verdicts ranged from the polite 'quite interesting'
via the more honest 'a bit heavy' to the encouraging 'not too
bad for your first cake'.

I was a bit more relaxed for the life-drawing class in the
evening. Verity stuffed half a slice into her mouth and then
said something that sounded like 'It's OK'. When she had
done away with the rest of the slice, she added, 'Why don't
you make a Victoria sponge for next time? Victoria sponge is
my *favourite* and they're dead easy to make.' I promised I
would.

So far everything seemed as it should.

The weather had warmed up again so I planted myself outside
The Chestnuts and, in agonizing slow motion to drag it out
as long as possible, started a new pen-and-wash sketch of the
house and the lane. This time a second car stood on the drive
– a small black BMW. It belonged, as I found out after a wait
of ninety minutes, to a blonde middle-aged woman in a twin
set who wore loud make-up and every bit as much gold jewellery as Mrs Blinkhorn, as well as a pearl necklace and earrings.
The two women said goodbye on the drive, kissed the air

beside their cheeks, then the BMW backed carefully out of the drive with Janette Blinkhorn's aid and disappeared down the lane. Janette gave a small wave but did not come over. Nothing at all happened after that, and when it clouded over again, I was glad to pack up and go home.

Victoria sponge didn't require any shopping. In case we had a full house and the students liked it, I baked two. I was generous with the vanilla and very generous with the French strawberry jam and buried them both under an avalanche of icing sugar. Then I had to brush most of it off again so people might recognize them as cakes. Verity had been right: Victoria sandwich is dead easy to make and since it was her favourite I looked forward to her tasting notes. Normally, Verity turned up in good time and 'starving hungry' from her bicycle ride out to the valley, but today her usual time passed and there was no sign of her. The first students arrived. I watched them park their cars in the yard and waved hello from the front door, keeping an eye on the track and my ears pricked for the rattle of her boneshaker, but there was no sign of her. Five minutes after the class ought to have started, I went up to the studio to apologize. 'It appears the model has let us down, I don't know what could have happened. She does have both my phone numbers.' But she had no phone of her own and it was quite possible she didn't have the price of a call from a phone box.

The students were not happy. There is very little you can do in a life-drawing class without a life model. 'You'd better get your kit off, then,' said one woman. I smiled at her but she just raised her eyebrows. 'Unless you want to reimburse everyone their fee? And for me it's a twenty-mile round trip in the car.' There were nods and murmurs of agreement. Oh, no, they were serious.

Now, I'm not so shy that I undress in the dark, but Annis has had plenty of time to get used to my less-than-athletic shape and no longer makes fun of it. Getting my kit off in front of ten strangers, all but one of them women, was quite a different prospect. 'Ah. Right. OK. Erm . . . I'll be getting my dressing gown, then. Won't be a tick.'

My dressing gown was in the laundry basket, I now

remembered, because the back of it had collided with some bright-red and airborne sweet-and-sour sauce (don't ask), so I rummaged around and found one of Annis's insubstantial kimono-style things – pale jade green with a print of golden dragons, made to look like embroidery. It would make me look ridiculous, of course, but a dressing gown was a must. It is a curious convention of life modelling that despite the fact that the model will spend most of the time in the nude, he or she will not emerge naked from the changing booth or room but walk to wherever the pose will be set and then remove the dressing gown. It has to do with professionalism and dignity. I rushed into the improvised changing booth where there was very little room for manoeuvre and changed into the kimono. It was very short on me and did absolutely nothing for my dignity as I stepped out among my students. To give them credit, they didn't laugh too loudly. I turned on the blow-heaters which wheezed and clattered into action, placed a wooden chair we often use to pose the model between them and disrobed. Then I sat down and took up what was meant to look like a casual pose of 'man sits on chair, just happens to be naked'.

'Fifteen-minute pose – someone else will have to keep an eye on the time.' I had taken off my watch because naked with a watch is more naked than naked without a watch. Don't believe me? Try it in a crowded room sometime.

When you are drawing, time is always too short. Whatever the length of the pose – ten, twenty, thirty minutes – you could always do with another five. When you are teaching a class, you move around, observe what people are doing, talk, offer advice and solutions for the students' problems and keep an eye on the time. But when you are trying to sit absolutely still, it is near impossible to construct a measurement of time from the scratching of charcoal on paper, the odd mumblings and sighs. One of the heaters stood a little too close to my left leg but I was determined not to move, while the other's wheezing breath managed to miss me altogether. There are two ways in which humans keep warm: wearing clothes to prevent heat loss or burning energy by moving their muscles. As an artists' model, you can't do either, so if the air tempera- ture is anything less than blood heat, you will feel cold. And,

of course, your nose will itch. Also the back of your right
knee, for some reason. This is a good thing, because it will
help take your mind off the fact that the room has mysteriously
turned arctic and that time has turned to treacle, and the reali-
zation that this pose will never end and that wooden chairs
are objects of torture invented by sadists.

'Is anyone keeping an eye on the time?' I asked casually.

'Yes,' came a voice from behind me. 'Another ten minutes.'

*Impossible*. Apparently, I had only done five minutes of
sitting still. We usually had a thirty-minute pose in the second
half; I was sure I would never survive it. I would freeze solid
or go mad from boredom and start howling and biting people's
ankles. When I was finally relieved from my frozen state, I
announced that we would do a lot of short poses in the first
half. And possibly in the second half too, I said to myself as
I tried to come up with different stances and poses I could
actually hold without my muscles screaming at me.

It was during the last pose before the long-awaited tea break
that I saw a man's face at one of the old sash windows I had
bodged into the wall of the barn. The face looked as if
it belonged to a slightly overweight man in his forties, with
bleached hair and eyebrows. I did not recognize the face and
it appeared at the window slowly, peering through one corner
of it; then it disappeared again. 'Time for our tea break,' I
announced and slipped on my kimono. Whoever had peered
through the window had not come in. I opened the door, still
in my dressing gown, and was just in time to see a man reach
the bottom of the meadow, jog across the yard and get into
the passenger seat of a black Porsche. The car drove off,
disappearing behind the hedgerow along the track, moving
quickly, its engine note receding fast.

Of course, since the drawing classes were available as a
block or as single drawing sessions, someone might have
arrived late, taken one look at my uninspiring nude form and
decided to give it a miss, yet the man had not been carrying
any art supplies and the waiting Porsche did not seem to fit
that scenario. I had no time to worry about it then because I
had to change back into clothes and then run down the meadow
myself to make teas and coffees and fetch the cakes.

'You're quite the one-man band today, aren't you?' said one lady good-naturedly (though admittedly before she had tasted the cake). The fact was that even I could not mess up a Victoria sandwich cake and so I received rather more praise for my baking than my modelling.

The second half of the session felt like an eternity of aches and pains, chill drafts, persistent itches and leaden boredom. But eventually, when I had already given up all hope that it ever would, the session came to an end. 'I hope Verity is all right' was how more than one of the students took leave of the one-man life-drawing experience that evening, and I fervently hoped so too. Trust me to hire a model who has no phone and cannot be contacted.

On Thursday morning, the *Bath Chronicle* landed on my doormat in time for my breakfast. The city of Bath is not exactly a seething hotbed of crime, although it does have its fair share of drug addicts, pickpockets, hotel thieves and marriage swindlers. Any place that attracts a lot of tourists also draws those who will try to take advantage of them, but crime rarely captures the front page of the *Chronicle*. Today was different. *ONE DEAD IN WEDNESDAY'S HOUSEFIRE, Fire Department Suspect Arson*. A piece of croissant suspended halfway to my mouth, I quickly read on. For a few brief seconds my mind had connected Verity's failure to show up with the discovery of a dead body, and I was relieved when I read that the body was that of the young man who had been living in the rented basement bedsit in Upper Weston, a suburb of Bath. Fire investigators had discovered the presence of 'an accelerant'. The fire had been started around four in the morning. My mouth closed around the piece of croissant but the quivering dollop of quince jam jumped off it. I had lost interest in the article, yet, while I scraped jam off the newspaper, one word in the lengthy article seemed to jump out at me. *Porsche*. I returned to the article and found that one witness described seeing a Porsche drive away quickly and noisily from the area around the time the fire broke out, describing it as 'black or possibly dark blue'.

Apart from having enough patience to enjoy watching paint

dry, being of a suspicious nature and having a tiny paranoid bone in my body contribute to my suitability as a private eye. Normally, this is tempered by Annis debunking ninety per cent of my hare-brained theories, but Ms Jordan was at that moment baptizing her new minimalist bathing costume in a record producer's swimming pool, which probably cheered him a lot but was of no use to me at all. And this meant that my little paranoid bone kept on vibrating irritatingly. It was no good telling myself that there must be dozens of black-or-possibly-dark-blue Porsches driving around Bath because I couldn't for the life of me remember ever having seen one of that colour until last night. 'The victim has been named as twenty-three-year-old Joshua Grant,' the article continued and described him as 'unemployed'. But what could an unemployed young man in a rented basement flat in Upper Weston possibly have to do with me?

# THREE

Thick September mists hung in the trees, the sheep that had kept the meadow cropped all summer had been collected and returned to my neighbour's farm, and Mill House lay quiet. I stood breakfasting on crumbly cake at the back door in the kitchen; the kitchen door opened on to the damp and neglected herb garden. I indulged in a moment of picturesque melancholy; summer would soon be over. I had not painted nearly as much as I had hoped and the teaching I had done instead had barely earned me enough money to keep me in paint. Annis had used virtually all her commission earnings on paying off our mountainous debts. This meant I could not afford to let my private-eye job slip. In my mind I called it *The Blinkhorn Affair*, which allowed me to imagine myself as a latter-day Paul Temple who would no doubt soon toast the miraculous solution of the enigma with bottles of vintage champagne. In reality, I usually celebrate with paying bills. One such bill was the last repair invoice for my 1960s Citroën, variously described as 'a fine example of a classic French car' – by me – or 'that Frog rust bucket' – by Jake who keeps the thing on the road. Jake runs his classic (*British*) car restoration business from a farm near Ford (he had originally tried to breed ponies and failed) and over the years he has supplied Aqua Investigations with many of its vehicles, usually so clapped-out that he didn't mind in what state they were returned, if at all. Sometimes, though, he lets me borrow one of the more contemporary cars he has standing around because, as he never fails to point out, an ancient French car in your rear-view mirror is hardly inconspicuous. (He usually adds some insinuation that I am not very bright and a hopeless amateur.) I scraped some money together for the outstanding repair bill and drove to Ford.

There was hardly space to park in his yard, which was nearly as potholed as mine, except that his had the added hazards of car axles, engines on bricks under tarpaulin, empty body shells of British cars so ancient I didn't recognize them, naked chassis, worn-out car seats and doors and bonnets in various states of decay. Next to the workshop rose a hill of discarded car exhausts that would have sent any first-year sculpture student into raptures of delight. The double doors to Jake's workshop, a cement-brick and corrugated-iron barn, stood open. From inside came the sad sound of a starter motor draining a battery in an attempt to start a reluctant engine.

Jake was sitting at the wheel of a curvaceous 1948 Bristol 400 in a pastel shade of green that hasn't been seen on a car body for more than sixty years. The bonnet was up. Below it Jake's mechanic, with white mad-professor hair and the oldest overall in the West, was fiddling with the engine and shaking his head, which he did a lot. It took them a while to notice me. When Jake did, he acknowledged me with a nod, then got out of the car and talked incomprehensible West Country car gibberish with his factotum before eventually turning his critical eye on me. 'Whatever is wrong with your swivel-eyed French chariot will have to wait until the last bill is paid, and I haven't even touched Annis's Norton – that'll need parts made for it, so don't even ask. We're bloody busy up here. Half my regular clients went on some idiotic run down to Cornwall and virtually all of them broke down and then rang me. Some of them still haven't made it back a week later. Bugger me! Is that real money or did you paint it yourself?'

I had successfully interrupted his string of pre-emptive excuses by waving a bouquet of twenties under his nose. 'It's all there. And there's nothing wrong with the DS.'

'Ah, welcome, friend, welcome.' He wiped his hands on his overall before reverently taking the notes from my hand. 'So why are you here? You wouldn't be paying me unless you wanted something.' Jake has known me for a long time.

'Got anything modern I can borrow?' I asked, looking around.

'I've something modern you can *buy*, Chris. You need a bland car for detective work. Driving around in a fifty-year-old Citroën is like following someone wearing a top hat and tailcoat. You get spotted a mile off.'

'I can't afford to buy anything – you're holding my last money. But if this insurance job works out, I might be able to.'

Jake stuffed the money into a pocket of his blue overall, carefully buttoned it up, then scratched at a welding scar on his shiny bald head. 'There is one car I can let you have, but it's not junk so I do want it back in one piece. Took it in part exchange. This way.'

Jake hides anything modern and non-British round the back so as not to offend the sensibilities of the classic car nuts who are his customers. On the strip of concrete in front of a low building that had once been a milking parlour stood a blue Ford Focus RS. 'I like it,' I said.

'Dream on,' said Jake. 'That's Sally's pride and joy. I meant *that* one.' He pointed at a ten-year-old Honda Jazz.

'Oh.'

'Don't go "oh"; it's perfect for a PI.'

He was right, of course. The things were ubiquitous and this one came in a shade of blue so flat and depressing that on a dull day it would be virtually invisible to the naked eye. 'I suppose you're right.'

'I've been telling you that for years. You can leave your Citroën in that space. But I'm keeping it as collateral, so no stunts or car chases.'

I promised.


Of course, a car chase might have enlivened the next couple of days. There was not enough natural cover to keep an eye on The Chestnuts without it becoming obvious and nowhere to park within sight of the place. This meant I was forced to sit in the invisible Honda, parked up in Richmond Road round the corner – since Janette Blinkhorn invariably passed that way whenever she left the house – and wait.

And wait. Eventually, the Mercedes came past and I trailed it all the way to town and into the Waitrose car park. From there I followed Janette past the abbey into the pedestrianized area where she did exciting things like browsing the magazine shelves at WHSmith's, trying on several tops in several clothes shops and dodging *Big Issue* sellers and charity muggers.

When a rain cloud came over and it started to drizzle, she bought a pink umbrella from an accessories shop and walked back towards the car park, with me, umbrellaless, trudging behind. She dropped her shopping bags off at the car, then drank something hot and frothy at the café above the supermarket while playing with her smartphone, before spending a small fortune on two whole sea bass downstairs. Then she drove her purchases home. With the patience of a saint, I parked up again. Late in the afternoon her bejewelled girlfriend drove past me in her BMW, and when I followed on foot after a decent interval, the black car was parked on the drive of the Blinkhorn house. Despite it still being light outside, the curtains were drawn downstairs. Purely out of boredom, I took a photograph and drove home through the rain.

The last day of life drawing before the winter break dawned grey and wet – or so I gathered; I was asleep – and still not a word from Annis. I had deliberately not contacted her, feeling jealous and childish and wanting to see how long it took before she missed me. Quite a while, it appeared. Ah well, she was busy with her new commission. But wouldn't she want to talk about it? Or at least brag about it? As my eyes unfocused over the photograph of a plum cake in *From Gugelhupf to Streuselkuchen*, another bit of childishness crept to the front of my mind from wherever it had been hiding: what about Tim? I had had many years to get over any sexual jealousy, but was I still the first person she shared things with? Did Annis and I have more or fewer things in common? Tim and Annis shared a childish delight in anything Disney, and I knew that when at Tim's place Annis indulged in eating junk food in front of the telly, something she can't at Mill House since I refuse to give room to either (and there's no reception at the bottom of the valley). They go to the cinema together and have been talking about going to Disneyland for years . . .

I found a pretext to call Tim at work. 'How do you find someone if you don't know their address, they don't drive and don't have a phone?'

'You're the detective. Relatives?'

'One aunt who's not in Bath.'

'Then it's personal interests and favourite haunts, I guess.'

I agreed. 'I left it too late for that. My life model didn't show up last time and I've no idea if she'll turn up tonight. Last time I had to do the modelling myself.'

'Ha, I'd have paid to see that. You couldn't persuade Annis to do it?'

*Aha.* 'She's not here. She's doing another mural for a music business bigwig. Didn't she tell you?'

'I haven't spoken to her for ages. Been a bit busy, you know how it is – new girlfriend and all that.'

I nearly dropped the phone into my mug of rich-roast Costa Rican Fairtrade coffee. (I've no idea how we can afford the stuff either; ask Annis.) 'Girlfriend? You have a girlfriend? Why? I mean, since when?'

'Didn't Annis tell you?'

'Not a peep.' Then it hit me. 'Annis knows? And doesn't she mind?'

'Mind? No. "About bloody time" were her words, as I recall.'

'Really?'

'I know. As though she'd just been sleeping with me to help me out, haha. Actually, we haven't been sleeping together for bloody ages.'

'Really? But she spent loads of time at yours.'

'Whenever she feels like telly and a pizza. I must come up and introduce you to Becks; she's looking forward to meeting you.'

'Becks? Is that her name? Trust you to find a girlfriend named after your favourite lager.'

'It's Rebecca.'

'Yeah, I guessed.'

I could hear voices in the background. 'Gotta go and do some work now,' Tim said. 'See you soon, mate.'

*Blimey.* Tim had a *girlfriend.* And I hadn't known. While Annis had. And hadn't even mentioned it. And Tim didn't know Annis was away doing another commission. Perhaps we needed to start a newsletter.

For the rest of the day I felt ridiculously cheery despite the worry about Verity. I made a coffee cake that was so strong on caffeine it would leave my students wide-eyed and sleep-less all night. I waved them in as they arrived in the yard and scooted up the meadow to the studio. But my mood took a dive when again there was no sign of Verity.

'I'm afraid you'll have me as a model again,' I told the expectant artists.

'Did you find out what's wrong with her?' one woman asked.

'I can't get hold of her,' I admitted.

'That's worrying,' another said. 'Young girl like that.'

'Probably shacked up with a new boyfriend,' the only man in the group muttered.

'No, I'm serious,' said the woman. 'She seemed such a nice girl. Can't have been more than twenty. I do wish you'd go and find out what's happened to her. Didn't someone mention you were also a detective of some sort?'

'He is,' another confirmed. 'It was in the *Chronicle* a few years ago. A chameleon called Knut, wasn't it? Such a heart-warming story.'

'An iguana, actually,' I said feebly. Knut had been following me around for years.

'And what about next term?' asked the first woman. 'I'm not signing up for the next term if it's you modelling. No offence, but I only wanted you for your mind, not for your body.'

'I will not be modelling next term,' I promised and went to get my kit off. Definitely not. If Verity didn't get in touch, I would hire another model.

The first part of the session went off all right; I took up a few easy-to-hold poses, and the knowledge that this was the last time I would have to do it made it pass more quickly. It was when I had got dressed for the break and was on my way out of the studio to fetch the refreshments that I bodily ran into a woman who was not on my course. She had been about to knock on the door when I rushed out. We both apologized. 'If you're looking for a life-drawing class, I'm afraid you've left it a bit late – it's the last session this year,' I told her.

'Oh, is it? Actually, I was hoping to find Verity here.' The woman was in her early forties, had short, dark hair and was simply dressed in jeans, walking shoes and a grey top. 'Verity is my niece. I'm a bit worried about her, which is why I came down from Cheltenham to see if I could find her. She called me a few days ago, saying she was living in Bath now, but forgot to give me her address. She did mention that she was modelling for you, Mr Honeysett, which is why I'm here. I hope you don't mind me turning up like this, but I didn't really know what else to do. Verity sounded like she wanted to ask me for money but then changed her mind. She knows I can't really afford to give her money. But I thought I'd come and see if there was anything else I could do for her. She doesn't have any other relatives, you see.'

'Walk with me,' I suggested. 'Got to fetch teas and coffees for the troops from the house.' We walked down the meadow together. 'I'm afraid she hasn't turned up for her last two modelling sessions and we've all become quite worried about her.'

'Oh dear. Do you have an address for her?'

'I'm afraid not.'

'A phone number, then.'

'She doesn't have a mobile as far as I know.'

'A kid her age without a mobile? That's unusual.' She gave me a sideways look as though she did not believe me.

'I had the impression that she was pretty broke. I could only give her so much work here.' I was becoming defensive, feeling that perhaps I should have done more for Verity.

'How did you get in touch with her, then?' she persisted. 'About the modelling?'

'She was introduced to me by a painter friend and turned up punctually to every session. Apart from the last two.'

'I'm not sure what to do next,' admitted the woman. We had stopped near the kitchen door that leads into the herb garden. She looked perplexed for a moment, standing motionless, looking unseeing into the weed-ridden herb beds. Then she pulled herself together. 'Look, if she does get in touch or you find out where she is, would you please call me?' She opened her grey handbag and rummaged for something to write on. She found a till receipt from a petrol station. With a black-and-gold ballpoint pen she wrote down a mobile

number from memory and her name, Christine Rainer, on the
back. I promised to get in touch, stuck the till receipt in my
pocket and nodded reassuringly at her as she turned thoughtfully away. The fan belt on her ten-year-old Polo screeched
as she drove it from the yard. I had been worried about Verity
in a vague kind of way before, but now I knew she definitely
was in trouble. Several things about this aunt did not add up.
Verity had mentioned her aunt only once, to say that they
didn't get on, that she was ugly and that she lived in Belgium.
There was nothing ugly about Christine Rainer. It gave me plenty
of things to think about during what I hoped would be my last
modelling session ever. Either Verity had invented the aunt's
ugliness, failed to mention that they were again on speaking
terms and that she had moved from Belgium to Cheltenham,
or this aunt had only the vaguest knowledge about Verity and
her real aunt.

The next day I again parked up in Richmond Road, hoping
for Janette to come by in her Mercedes. It was warm and
sunny, and I begrudged every minute that I was stuck sitting
in the car, waiting for something to happen. I was resigned to
a long, dull wait. I had prepared well, too, with a flask of
black coffee and all the leftover cake from last night wrapped
in tinfoil. I held out as long as I could before touching them,
since the radio in the Jazz was broken and cake and coffee
were my only defence against the crushing weight of boredom
that made me sink deeper and deeper behind the steering
wheel. *12.30.* After two hours that felt more like five, I couldn't
stand it any longer. I unwrapped the cake, uncorked the
Thermos and poured myself a cup. *12.31.* As I held my brimming coffee cup in one hand and a fat slice of coffee cake in
the other, Blinkhorn's Mercedes whizzed past. In an attempt
to gulp the coffee, I scalded my mouth. Struggling to pour the
coffee back into the flask, I sloshed it over my knee and
dropped half the cake down the side of the seat. I stuffed
the other half in my mouth, chucked everything else into
the passenger footwell and started the car.
    Isn't it surprising how far a Mercedes can travel while you're
having a fight with your lunch? I only caught up with it at the

bottom of Lansdown Road as it waited to turn into Bennett
Street. It disappeared again from view while I had to wait for
uphill traffic to pass, but I could watch her car enter the Circus,
three curved segments of Georgian buildings surrounding a
circular green, beloved by tourists. When I caught up, I could
just make out something silver-grey disappearing up Brock
Street on the other side of the circle. I put my foot down and
immediately braked hard again. A woman, holding aloft a
large white furled umbrella, planted herself in the middle of
the road and started funnelling across a crocodile of slow-
moving tourists who snapped pictures on their mobiles every
five feet as they went. By the time the last one had dawdled
across to the stand of the plane trees in the centre, I had virtually given up hope of catching up with Janette again. I drove
on, zipped up Brock Street, took a right and drove around the
area. Nothing. Then it dawned on me that coming this way
via the Circus made no sense unless your destination was the
Royal Crescent. I turned around.

The centre of the Royal Crescent is taken up by the Royal
Crescent Hotel which looks down on the lawns, trees and
bandstand of Victoria Park and on anyone earning less than
six figures. How will you find it? Look for the pot plants. On
either side of the entrance stands a potted bay tree clipped
into a perfect sphere. Once you have found it, check with your
bank manager whether you can actually afford a room there.
(Or anything at all.) When I arrived, I was just in time to see
Janette's pearl-necklaced girlfriend hand the keys of her BMW
to the top-hatted doorman and disappear inside. The doorman
turned and gestured, and a moment later a young man in
shirt, tie and waistcoat snatched the keys from his fingers and
drove the BMW away to be parked. I left the invisible Jazz
double-parked in the cobbled street and, without a plan, walked
up to the doorman who reacted to my approach with nothing
more than raised eyebrows. 'The lady who just turned up in
the Beemer, is she staying here?'

His eyebrows lowered and contracted in a frown as his eyes
travelled down to my coffee-stained knees and up again, but
he made no answer.

I hadn't really expected to be given details of hotel guests on the doorstep, but I had expected a 'Whatsittoyou?' at least. 'She cut me up back there,' I complained. 'I want a word.' If ever I open a luxury hotel, I'll hire this chap. He was about sixty, probably got paid a pitiful wage, but he exuded dignified contempt while giving no offence. In perfect silence. Perhaps he had previously guarded Buckingham Palace. I changed tack. 'These bay trees real?' I asked.

'They are indeed, sir.'

'Ta.' I snapped off three leaves. 'Cooking rabbit tonight,' I said and made my getaway. I stopped at the butchers, bought a young rabbit and then re-entered the insanity that Bath calls its traffic system. I got stuck behind a sightseeing tour bus going at walking speed down Milsom Street, giving me time for window shopping while breathing diesel particulates. One shop window was crammed with high-end plasma screens, all tuned to the same programme, the lunchtime news. On all the screens the same photograph of a face appeared. I stopped the car. The face disappeared. 'Wait, put that back!' I told the TV screens. 'That's Shaggy Beard and Hunting Jacket.' The face, I was sure, had been that of the chap who had greeted Verity at the Bell Inn. Now the screens were full of images of fire engines, being in turn replaced by the face of DSI Needham, giving a statement outside the scene of the fire. It said 'Live' at the bottom of the screen. My lip-reading skills leave much to be desired, the bus in front of me had moved on and I was being honked at from an impatient driver behind me. The screens moved on to another news item. I drove straight home.

Never let a butcher do anything to your rabbit apart from wrapping it up or he will ruin it by hacking it to bits with a meat cleaver. Take the hind legs off as you would with a chicken – no need to cut through bones – then snap the spine of the beast by pressing down on it. Like asparagus, it will snap at the right place. Then run your knife through it and separate the saddle from the front. Drop the four pieces into a bowl with three bay leaves, a dozen or so juniper berries and peppercorns, splash in some red wine vinegar and glug in half a bottle of red wine. Then sit down and worry about the missing girls in your life (if any).

The appearance of DSI Needham's visage on TV meant that the police were treating the chap's fiery death as murder. While stuffing my face with all the cake I had managed to scrape off the floor of the car, I opened the *Bath Chronicle* and looked up the victim's name again: Joshua Grant. I made a note of the street, too, and drove sticky-fingered across town to Upper Weston.

I found the address in a narrow street of Victorian houses. It was difficult to miss; a uniformed police officer was guarding the outside steps to the basement bedsit where Joshua Grant had died. There were blackened holes where a door and window once sat. The pavement either side of the house was cordoned off with yellow police tape. A forensics van was parked nearby, but there was no sign of DSI Needham's big grey Ford. His Grey Eminence had probably long quit the crime scene and was by now back in his comfortable office at Manvers Street police station. I stood thinking and the police constable stood staring. I knew better than to approach him but did it anyway. 'Needham still around?'

The constable cleared his throat, then asked, 'Do you have information regarding the recent fire here?'

The *recent* fire? How many had there been? 'Any idea who might be responsible, yet?' I carried on.

'May I ask who you are, sir?' he asked sternly.

'By all means,' I said kindly and walked off towards my car. So many unanswered questions. It would have been pointless burdening the constable with my worries; I would go and find Needham and tell him personally.

Detective Superintendent Michael Needham was not a great fan of private detectives in general or of my personal style in particular, but he gave credit where it was due and he had in the past grudgingly admitted that a few of my wild stabs in the dark had skewered the odd culprit that had managed to slip through his own podgy fingers.

The car park at Manvers Street police station was full of police vehicles, but I just found enough room to squeeze the Jazz into a corner. Needham's car was in its reserved space. Over the years I had become familiar with the police station, inside and out. It was a cuboid 1960s carbuncle that urgently

needed to be demolished, but, of course, there was no money
for that so they just kept renovating it on the inside instead.
The lobby had recently been tarted up too, and the lobby was
as far as I got. Sergeant Hayes, the desk sergeant this afternoon, was also not one of Aqua Investigations' greatest
admirers, although less fierce than the superintendent. 'If you
want to make a statement, I'll get a constable to come down.'

'I want to talk to Needham.'

'Well, you can't; he's left.'

'His car's outside.'

'Oh, is it?' He grunted and reluctantly picked up the phone.
When he eventually got an answer, he told Needham I was
there in the same tone he might use when reporting a blocked
toilet. After a lot of *uh-huhs* he hung up. 'DSI Needham will
be down in a few minutes.'

I concluded that if Needham refused to see me in his office,
my popularity had to be at an all-time low. He kept me
waiting for half an hour before squeezing into the lobby
through a side door. Needham could have lost three stone
and you might not even have noticed it, apart from the irri-
tability that came from his sugar cravings and restricted beer
intake. He was carrying a lot of spare weight round the
middle, a briefcase in one hand and the jacket of his suit
over the other arm.

He nodded curtly as he walked past me to the entrance. 'Do
something useful, Honeysett; get the door for me, will you?'

I did. 'Where are we going?'

'*We* are not going anywhere. You wanted to talk to me?'
He made straight for his car.

'If you have a minute.'

He stopped to consult his watch. 'You've literally got about
two minutes.'

I told him about seeing Joshua Grant at the pub and about
Verity disappearing. Needham pursed his lips and silently mulled
it over for ten seconds. 'Just because she stopped turning up
for her modelling job doesn't mean there's a connection. What's
her surname?'

'I think it's Lake.'

Needham gave me an irate look. 'You *think*? You employ

people and don't know where they live and you're not sure what they're called?'

'It's all pretty informal, Mike.' Needham had once, after one-too-many beers, offered first name terms and probably regretted it at leisure; he hadn't used my first name since.

'What you mean is that no one pays any bloody tax. OK, I'll let DI Reid know about the girl . . .'

'Verity.'

'Verity, possibly Lake. OK, if you have any more information, tell Reid.'

'Reid? But Reid hates me.'

'That's true, Honeysett, he does. You made him look like an idiot.'

'He doesn't need much help.'

'I don't have time to discuss DI Reid with you.'

'But why make me talk to *him*?'

'Because he's in charge. I'll be away for a couple of weeks.' He moved off towards his car, blipped his remote and the boot opened by itself. He added his briefcase to a grey suitcase and closed the lid.

'Going anywhere nice?'

'Hendon Police College, two-week course.'

'I didn't think they could still teach you stuff – not at your age.'

'Very little. I'm *teaching* the course, you nitwit.' He got behind the wheel. 'Leave the matter to DI Reid. By all means look for your girl, but don't stray into Reid's investigation – you don't want to give him a reason to make your life difficult. And whatever you do find out, *keep him informed.*' He drove off, blaring his horn at a couple of boys who were too busy staring at their mobile phones to see him come flying out of the station car park. Needham knew that I wouldn't give DI Reid the time of day, so there had been no need for me to point it out to him. I could just imagine what Reid would make of my suspicions. Had I told him that Christine Rainer, who had claimed to be Verity's aunt, had forgotten she lived in Belgium, he'd say that she must have moved. If I told him the two weren't speaking, he would say the two must have kissed and made up. And he'd have simply shrugged if I had

told him that the Montblanc ballpoint pen that poor hard-up
auntie wrote down her name with was worth more than her
car. I knew that because I had once liked the look of one in
a shop window and nearly fainted at the price tag. Of course,
Auntie Christine could have found the biro somewhere and
had no idea what it was worth, but to me she had given off a
faint aroma of money that I had first noticed the moment she
said that she could not afford to lend Verity any. She could
have recently fallen on hard times, said my inner Annis Jordan
critic, but I was willing to bet that she had borrowed the Polo
from her daily.

# FOUR

The only picture I had of Henry Blinkhorn was the slightly out-of-focus specimen provided by Griffins. I called Haarbottle in his office.

'That's the only picture we have of him,' he said. 'We don't keep an album of dead people here.' He sighed in my ear. 'You haven't made any progress, then,' he added in an unsurprised voice.

'These things take time,' I said soothingly.

'Don't I know it. But there's no point in proving that fraud has been committed if all the ill-gained money has been blown in a casino somewhere. I don't care about *justice*, Honeysett; I want the million and a half back.'

'How big would your own bonus be?'

'Let's just say I won't go hungry in my old age. You *are* keeping an eye on his wife?'

'I'm staring at her house as we speak,' I said and quietly eased another piece of bread into the toaster.

'Remind me how much we are paying you for that.'

'Not enough.' Whenever there is the promise of a percentage of the recovered money, the insurance company pays reduced rates – just enough to keep you alive while you do all the hard work. If you draw a blank, then you have worked for very little reward. 'I have actually made contact with Janette Blinkhorn. Undercover, of course. Well, under an umbrella, to be precise.'

'Are you sure she didn't see through you?'

'Absolutely. She invited me in and made me a cuppa.'

'They are crafty people, the Blinkhorns. There's a lot of money at stake. And a lengthy prison term for them if you expose them. I'm not sure I'd eat or drink anything that woman offered me.' He had a point and my stomach contracted when I remembered how willingly I had drunk Janette Blinkhorn's coffee. Just then the toaster noisily chucked out my toast. 'What was that?'

'Glove box keeps popping open. The catch is broken.'

'Perhaps, if the payout comes through, you should invest in a twenty-first-century car. Or perhaps a quieter toaster. Get to work, Honeysett.'

I called the *Bath Chronicle*. That way I could work and butter toast at the same time. The *Chronicle* had run the story when Blinkhorn first went missing, presumed dead. Surely they had a picture of him?

'Must have had,' said the sub-editor. He sounded about sixteen. 'But that was absolutely *ages* ago, wasn't it?'

'It was six years ago,' I protested.

'Exactly.'

'But don't you keep an archive of articles?'

'Yeah, yeah, sure. We digitized a lot of stuff.'

'And?'

'It was before my time, but apparently they got some kids over – school kids, you know? Work experience and that. And they made them scan the stuff? And they chucked half of it in the bin instead because they couldn't be arsed and thought no one would notice.'

'But you did.'

'Too late; the bin men had been.'

I gave in and called Annis. 'I haven't even started on the murals yet,' she said cheerfully.

'Why is your voice echoing? You're not on the loo, are you?'

'I'm in the pool house. It's tropical in here. I spend most of my time in my bathing suit.' It's all right for some, I thought uncharitably, and especially for Mr Hitchcock. 'Reuben and I have been going over my colour sketches but I'm not quite there yet. Honestly, this pool is *huge*. Not quite Olympic, but, yeah, huge. The wall he wants me to paint on is *massive*. Everything here is *huge*. Except Reuben – he's tiny. And practically bald. How did your baking go?'

'The baking was OK; it was the modelling that got to me.'

'Modelling?'

'Verity didn't turn up for the last two life-draining sessions.'

'Draining?'

'Well, it was.' I told Annis the whole story while she sat in tropical silence. I had half hoped to hear reassuring noises from her, alleviating my suspicions, but what I did hear at the end of it was the slurping noise of a straw sucking up the dregs of her drink.

'Sorry, finished another passion fruit drink. There's a button here, and if you press it, five minutes later Reuben's manservant arrives and asks what he can do for you. *He* is not so tiny. Works out, too. In the gym. Next to the pool house.' She sighed wistfully. 'I think you're right to worry about Verity. I tried more than once to sound her out about her background and what else was going on in her life, but she simply ignored it or shrugged it off with some funny remark. It was as though only the present mattered to her. Or perhaps the future. And she did call her aunt an ugly old bat. The aunt was not old-battish, then?'

'No. Extremely well groomed, attractive. Positively un-old-battish and I think she was dressing down for the occasion.'

'What did Needham say?'

'The usual. Keep your nose out, but if you should uncover anything anyway, come and tell us so we can claim all the glory, standing in front of the BBC news cameras.'

'He said all that? Golly. And did he pat you down for your revolver again while he said it?'

I own a strictly illegal WWII army revolver, a Webley .38, which Needham has been trying to take off me for years. It had belonged to a long-dead uncle and came with the house when I inherited it. 'He hasn't mentioned the Webley for ages. And he may not have said all that in so many words, but that's what Needham means. And what's more, he's swanned off to give some lectures, leaving DI Reid in charge.'

'Reid is seriously unpleasant; I'd stay clear of him.'

'That's the plan.'

'I liked Verity. She might be in trouble. Go and find her.'

'I'll try. Does Reuben really have a butler?'

'I don't think you'd call him a butler. But he does say "You rang, madam". He's a sort of factotum – does all sorts for Reuben.'

'Nice for Reuben.'

While Annis no doubt pressed the factotum-buzzer for

another long drink, I stood in my less well-served attic office and studied the Ordnance Survey maps of Somerset and Wiltshire that were fading on the walls. Just for the heck of it, I stuck a coloured drawing pin into Bearwood Hall, where Annis was feeling tropical, and another where I was standing at the bottom of a damp valley. It must be nice to have a house so big that it's marked on maps; you can always find your way home.

Henry Blinkhorn liked to spend his time fishing. His wife lived where they had always lived, which must mean that he had at least one or two favourite fishing haunts nearby. I knew that theoretically they could pack up and slip out of the country any minute now, but I didn't think so. The Chestnuts, I had felt when Janette gave me shelter from the rain, had a solid, permanent feel to it. If next time I went there it stood lifeless with a 'For Sale' sign at the gate, I'd be very surprised (and eggy of face), but taking a punt on the two staying put and staying in touch with each other – or once more getting in touch now that the dosh had been doled out – Henry would be fishing as long as the weather was good, preferably with brand-new snazzy fishing gear bought with the new money. There were plenty of small lakes and trout farms, rivers and canals to dip your rod into in our county alone, all less than an hour's drive from The Chestnuts. I stuck a mackerel-blue drawing pin into the map to mark the Blinkhorns' house and went fishing.

Not really. While I am quite partial to fish in my kitchen, I do not see the point in spending four hours angling for something that takes five minutes to eat. I drove to all the obvious places and showed the magazine cutting to the people who ran fisheries, telling them an unconvincing story about having lost contact with the guy. I couldn't pretend to be an angler for five minutes, knowing nothing about it. I stood about with my binoculars on river banks and canal towpaths, pretending instead to be a birdwatcher while scrutinizing the faces of the anglers and comparing them with my fuzzy photo. Anglers were an odd lot, I concluded. If this was about getting your hands on some fish, I could think of quicker and possibly cheaper ways. And all that gear must cost a fortune. Yet it seemed popular; I was obviously missing the point. And the chances of me catching him this way were extremely slim. I couldn't visit all the rivers, lakes, ponds and canals even just in Somerset. While I was here, he would be fishing elsewhere; while I was there, angling over here. Henry Blinkhorn could be anywhere, happily dipping his tackle into the waters, his face covered in a luxurious growth of beard, unrecognizable except to his wife. Or even to his wife. Perhaps Haarbottle was wrong after all and he had really been sleeping with the fishes these past six years. The possibility of landing a fat cheque from Griffins retreated further the more I thought about it, which meant I was in a grumpy sort of mood when I got home. Then I remembered the rabbit and immediately cheered up again. I tipped rabbit and marinade into a casserole dish, added a good squeeze of tomato paste, topped it up with stock and shoved it in the oven. Soon the house filled with the aroma of cooking, and after sixty torturous minutes I checked on the progress, stirred in handfuls of button mushrooms and cooked it for another hour. The meat was achingly tender, and the aromatic sauce beautifully dressed a mountain of tagliatelle. It was a much happier private eye who left the invisible Jazz standing in the yard and drove his classic Citroën into town.

It was live music night at the Bell. The music hadn't started yet but the HE 109s had set up already; among amps and speakers in a snake-pit of cables on the tiny stage stood drum kit, bass guitar, a keyboard and the largest saxophone I had ever seen. The band were sitting at the bar, easily recognizable by their matching gothic-revival clothing, piercings, messy make-up, multicoloured hair and swastika tattoos. I procured a pint of Guinness and found a seat, sharing a tiny table with a couple of blokes who were sitting with their backs to the stage and were here strictly for the beer. The piped music was loud enough for their conversation to be almost inaudible as I sat back on the bench that ran along the wall. I wasn't here for the music either. This is where I had last seen Verity; that the Bell was her favourite pub in town was the only thing I knew about her for certain, since she had told me so several times and had asked to be driven here if it rained a lot. I had no photograph to show the bar staff. There was a nude charcoal drawing of her that one of the students had left behind, but it was not a good likeness and would have been awkward to unroll in the pub.

I nodded at a few acquaintances – it had been a while since I had come here regularly – and settled in for a waiting game. I'm fond of pubs, but when you have to nurse a single pint all night because you are driving, they lose some of their charm. The band had just moved on to the stage and were picking up their instruments when I spotted Pink Hair at the back of the pub near the toilets. The pub was filling up fast, which meant I could only catch intermittent glimpses of her, but I thought it was definitely the girl Verity had greeted so exuberantly the last time I saw her through the pub window. I told the blokes on my table to look after my seat for me and went over.

Pink Hair was about Verity's age, with a nose ring and blonde eyebrows, and was wearing a fluffy blue top and rainbow nail varnish. It shouldn't have done but it somehow worked for her. She was sharing a table with three people, one of whom was a girl with swastika earrings who dressed completely in darks, had dark hair and dark eye make-up and gave me a dark look as I appeared at their table. The two blokes sitting opposite the girls with their backs to the wall were both mid-twenties, hard of face and stare, and had just drained pints of industrial cider.

I gave the table an all-purpose smile. Just as I took breath to speak, the band decided to start up with an ear-splitting blast. I took an extra breath and shouted over it. 'Hi, I'm looking for a girl called Verity?'

The blokes shook their heads, the dark-haired girl studied her rum and coke, and Pink looked from me to the blokes and back again and shrugged her shoulders.

'Don't know any Verity,' called one of the blokes at the same time as Pink said, 'Don't know where she is.'

I bent towards her ear. 'So you do know her,' I shouted.

'No, not really,' she corrected herself. 'I need the loo.' She got up and disappeared into the crowd that now filled the space between the tables. That left me with the other three who ignored me. One of the blokes picked up their empty pint glasses and shoved off towards the bar, ramming into me as he passed behind me.

Back at my own table, the two blokes there were valiantly defending my seat against a girl whose dress, make-up and swastika jewellery marked her out as a follower of the band, in full swing by now. 'Oh, it's your seat, is it? We can share, can't we?' she shouted and sat down, leaving me four inches of space to park half my behind. The group were playing some kind of gothic neo-punk noise that revolved mainly around the belching bass saxophone, the monstrous horn of which was now only five feet away from me. While the sound was not going to make it into my music library, the group certainly looked interesting. I took out my sketchbook and fineliner and started drawing. No one was ever going to believe the sheer size of this sax. How could anyone have enough breath to wind the thing? But the chap at the other end of it did and blasted it straight at me while I drew him and the whole band. The girl beside me bellowed into my ear that my sketch was great and that she had an art A level. I started the next drawing while taking tiny sips of my beer and keeping half an eye open for Verity. I had chosen a bad day; the HE 109s were obviously popular as the pub had filled up so much that Verity could have wandered in and out without me noticing. I should really have stayed outside and watched the back entrance where smokers came in and out. Just then Pink Hair squeezed through the throng and appeared at my table, carrying empty glasses. She looked over her shoulder back towards her own table which was invisible now. 'Couldn't talk back there. I'm not sure, but Verity is in some kind of trouble. And if not trouble, then some other shit. You're not the first one to ask around for her.'

'Who's been asking?'

She shrugged. 'Couple of people. Posh people.'

'You know where she is? What's it worth?' I handed her a twenty-pound note.

'Make it thirty.'

'That's all I have on me. I'll give you a tenner next time I see you.'

'You might try the traveller site just outside town – you know, the one everyone's complaining about?' She nodded her head back towards her table. 'Those blokes are from there.'

'What about Joshua Grant? Was he a friend of Verity's? Her boyfriend?'

'He thought so. But not really. She kipped at his some nights but she had another guy she fancied at the travellers' camp.'

'What's his name?'

'Sam. He's got a mobile home sort of thing.'

'Do you live out there?'

She pulled a face and shook her head.

'Who set fire to Joshua's place?'

'I don't know. Even if I did . . . I'm not flameproof, you know?' She disappeared with her glasses towards the bar. I was about to go after her when the dark-haired girl appeared and followed her, giving me a suspicious sideways look as she squeezed by. I packed up my drawing gear, drained my pint and trawled through the pub to make sure Verity really wasn't here, then stepped outside.

I breathed a sigh of relief when the door swung shut behind me on the fug and noise. *Getting old, Honeypot*, I accused myself. Impatient as I was to make sure Verity was all right, a dark and moonless night was not a good time to visit a travellers' site. I wasn't sure there ever was a good time, but broad daylight would be my minimum requirement. I went home and sat in the kitchen, listening to the ticking of the empty house, seeking consolation in cold rabbit stew.

For going on to an illegal travellers' site on a rainy September morning, I would normally insist on taking at least one Annis with me for protection. Annis has a persuasive smile, honeycombed voice and a diplomatic turn of phrase, but she also used to play hockey at Cheltenham Ladies' and has quite a kick on her.

The site was not a large affair. The travellers had pitched up in a farmer's field just outside Bath and their camp consisted of twenty-odd vehicles. Quite a few of them were medium-sized ex-coaches; many looked thirty or more years old. There were a few cars and three caravans but only two mobile homes, one of which ought to be Sam's.

The travellers had been here for nearly three months now and it showed. Piles of refuse had accumulated, with plenty of plastic and paper rubbish drifting about the muddy site. A lot of the meadow had been churned into mud. The only amenity of the site was a cattle trough; there were no toilets. These were not Romany travellers; this was a disparate group of nomadic people, most of them under forty, who travelled in convoy, set up illegal camp wherever it suited them, knowing that the eviction procedure would take time. Eviction notices had been served a while ago; I was glad I hadn't been the one hired to serve them.

Sagging tarpaulin had been stretched between some of the vehicles to provide extra shelter and this morning smoke rose from several places and from stovepipes on some of the modified coaches. For the casual observer and on a sunny day, the place might have held an aura of freedom and adventure; on a rainy morning like this, it suggested squalor, poverty, drugs, mental illness and petty crime. There was the occasional whiff of urine and a strong smell from the main pile of festering garbage. Hard living was also evident in the faces of the few people I could see: a young man with shaved head using a hammer to break up wooden pallets for feeding into his tin stove under a bit of tarpaulin; a woman wearing a faded rainbow of garments, washing a protesting child by the horse trough. A dark-haired man with a scrawny drug user's face and red-and-blue tattoos on his bare arms stood leaning against a tiny brown caravan, smoking a roll-up. He followed my squelching progress across the field with an expression of intense hostility. He never took his eyes off me as he knocked on the caravan door beside him. The door opened a crack and the tattooed man pointed across at me. I reminded myself that I was here of my own free will and could run away at any time. I also made a point of reminding myself that I was a slow runner before making for the nearest of the two mobile homes. It was small, built sometime in the last century for the narrow and winding roads of the British Isles. The windscreen was covered in cardboard and bits of black plastic, perhaps in a bid for privacy; the side window I could see had beige curtains drawn. A constellation of six squashed flies decorated the pane from the inside, which appeared not to bother the live bluebottle crawling diagonally across it. The suspension at the rear looked as if it was tired of life and no amount of mud could disguise the fact that the front tyres were practically bald. It was conveniently parked in an enormous grey puddle which was, as I found out, ankle deep. I paused in front of the door, taking a look around. I had seen no sign of Verity's bicycle and didn't have much hope of finding her, but I had a supernatural conviction that I would find her friend Sam inside this mobile shack. Both my boots had sprung a leak and my socks began the work of soaking up the puddle. I rapped a friendly rhythm on the door.

Someone on the inside groaned something that might have been a version of 'What now?' laced with expletives. The groaning came nearer to the door but slowly, taking an age to arrive. Perhaps the caravan was bigger on the inside than it looked from here. The door swung open outwards, missing my careless nose by a whisker. What stood in the opening had once been a young man; now it was a pitiful, crumbly-looking frail thing, hunched over, riddled with self-pity and wracked by nauseating waves of headache. I immediately recognized the tragic hangover-from-hell symptoms and greeted them with quiet delight; he would tell me everything I wanted to know as long as I promised to stop talking loudly about the fried breakfast I'd had earlier.

'Sam?'

'Who, who, who wants to know?' he hooted.

'I'm Chris,' I announced breezily. 'Mind if I come in for a moment?' I asked and advanced on him, closing the door behind me. The curtains were drawn and the interior was dim, which was a mercy. Dickens would have described the state of Sam's home as 'melancholy domestic circumstances'.

He retreated from me as far as the table where he had been sitting, fished a half-smoked roll-up from a full glass ashtray and sucked on it. It had gone out. 'What, what, what do you want? I mean . . .' Sam did not have a speech impediment, but his brain was still so fogged it had left the handbrake on. Standing up for this long became too much for him and he subsided on to the short bench beside the table. He didn't say any more until he had lit his cigarette, filled his lungs with smoke and coughed in one long lung-emptying spasm that ended in a wheeze. 'Are you one of *them*? Leave her alone. Oh, hang on . . . Chris? Are you the arty guy she sat for?'

'That's right, I'm the arty guy!' I said too loudly. He actually winced. 'She's not turned up for the last couple of sessions. I heard she sometimes stayed here.' Though I couldn't for the life of me imagine why. Sam's caravan was an anxiety disorder on wheels. It smelled strongly of ashtray, spilled cider, unwashed feet with notes of stale washing-up water, sour milk and something else I couldn't and didn't want to lay my finger on. The short bunk at the end of the van was covered in something pink and woollen, a tired sleeping bag and a baby-blue blanket with a historic brown stain in the shape of a bolt cutter on it. (No, me neither.) I had no trouble picturing Verity without her clothes on, yet I could not picture her taking her clothes off in this camper van to climb into this bunk. But then what did I know about her?

'I don't think Verity will do any more modelling for you,' Sam said without looking at me, his eyes drifting.

'Oh? Why do you say that?'

'Doesn't need to now. And she's buggered off anyway, hasn't she?'

'Don't know, you tell me.'

'We was going to buy a boat together,' he lamented. He nodded his head diagonally in the direction of the river and the nearby marina. 'But the cheating cow disappeared without even—' A perfunctory knock preceded the door being yanked open. Bare-armed tattoo chap entered with the bald-headed man who had been breaking up palettes; he was still carrying the hammer in a fashion which suggested he didn't want me to miss the fact that he was attached to it. He closed the door behind him. The place suddenly felt crowded and airless. I had no time to count all the studs and piercings, but the chap with the hammer had nose, eyebrows, ears and lower lip pierced, which made the tattooed chap's two nose rings look positively conservative.

'This one of *them*?' he asked Sam without taking his eyes off me. 'You don't give up, do you?' He stepped closer, which wasn't hard to do. That is when I noticed the piece of lead pipe in his belt.

'Whoever *they* are, I'm not one of them,' I assured him.

Sam half rose from his bench but there really wasn't enough room for him to stand anywhere. 'He's not, Mickey, no, he's not one of them.'

'He was asking about her, though, wasn't he? I heard the name mentioned from outside.'

'He's just some other guy she knows,' Sam said feebly.

'Yeah, but he could have been put up to it by them, couldn't he?' said tattoo man. Bald-headed man nodded sagely at this and twirled his claw hammer.

'Verity used to model for my life-drawing class.'

'What, *naked*?' said Mickey, looking from me to Sam. We both nodded at that. 'For money? I don't think she'll do any more of that!' said Mickey emphatically.

'That's what I said,' confirmed Sam. 'Which is why he was just leaving.' The air in the caravan was thick with sweat, testosterone and fear. Sam seemed to be as scared of the two as I was.

'I *was* just leaving,' I echoed.

'Really? I was listening at the door,' said Lead Piping. 'Didn't sound like it. Sounded like you're a nosy git who sticks his nose where it's not wanted. Would you like me to rearrange it for you?'

'He's good at that,' promised Claw Hammer.

'I believe you,' I said and slowly stretched out a hand between the two for the door handle. Neither of them budged an inch. I managed to poke the door open and, with a rather forced 'excuse me', squeezed between them into the open and stepped into the lake of mud. The two of them jumped from the caravan and with their wellies splashed about to maximum effect. They escorted me slowly off the site in a tight frogmarch which was now watched with interest by at least a dozen adults and a few children. 'See?' growled tattoo man into my face. 'They don't like you either. We don't like people coming here uninvited, especially if they ask stupid questions about what's none of their business. Get it?'

'I think I do,' I said, failing to salvage any dignity whatsoever as I strained towards the car which I had wisely left on the road. Never before had the sight of a pale blue Honda Jazz been greeted with more relief. The two did not follow me all the way to the car, but as soon as I had slipped behind the wheel the first stone hit the bodywork. By the time I had fumbled the keys into the ignition and got the engine going, the rear window had a star-shaped crack in it and several stones had hit elsewhere. Wheels spun as I slithered away from the site.

At Mill House there was an answerphone message on the landline; I avoided it. Somehow I felt I had done a day's work already. The Jazz had a couple of dents and scrapes and a cracked window – nothing too substantial. I was sure Jake would expect no less and there was no point in worrying about it now; I would claim 'rock fall' or something on the insurance form. To restore my equilibrium, I went into the kitchen and made pancake batter. I know, I am letting down private eyes everywhere by not downing double whiskies in gritty black-and-white in the middle of the day, but pancakes work much better for me and if you don't have too many of them you can still drive afterwards. I left the batter to rest and went to think the Verity thing over in the big blue comfy chair in the sitting room. The house stood silent, not even a ticking clock anywhere. This was what the house had felt like before Annis who talks and talks, clatters up and down stairs, leaves radios on in bathroom and kitchen, sings and whistles and fills the house with life. Yes, this thick silence was what had pervaded the house before Annis, and I didn't like it.

I shot out of the armchair and fetched the key to the gun locker which is bolted to the wall in the cupboard under the stairs. It contains my shotgun, for which I have a licence, and the Webley, for which I don't. I opened the chamber: six .38 calibre rounds shimmered in the understair gloom. You were not supposed to keep loaded revolvers in your locker even if you had a licence, but since the thing could land me in jail loaded or unloaded, I couldn't see the point in leaving it empty. (What will you say to the intruder – 'Wait a moment while I fetch some ammunition'?) I closed the revolver, made sure the safety was on and took the heavy lump with me into the kitchen. I didn't have a holster for it, which made carrying the Webley awkward. On its first outing, after popping off a few rounds apropos of nothing, I had stupidly stuck it into the waistband of my jeans; I still have the burn mark to prove it. I knew I would not have pulled the gun at the travellers' camp, but I also knew I would have been less scared had I carried it. Whether being scared of scary things is a good or bad thing is debatable but I had come away from Sam's rancid caravan with one firm belief: Verity had somehow attracted the attentions of some unpleasant people, and Lead Pipe and Claw Hammer might not be the worst of them.

I've been making pancakes since the dawn of time but I'm still rubbish at flipping them. So I don't. Which means I'll never get any better at it. Having quickly sautéed some mushrooms and leeks and added some white wine and a dribble of stock, I made two large pancakes, ladled the leek-and-mushroom filling into the centre, added a dollop of crème fraiche and rolled them up. Then I ate them at the kitchen table while focusing on the gun at its centre. The Webley Mark IV is the ugly duckling of the gun world; even the worst gun fetishist would call it unlovely. It was designed purely to kill people at fairly close quarters without fuss. Did I want to carry the thing around and risk a jail sentence if caught with it? I couldn't decide, so I put it in a kitchen drawer as a kind of insane compromise between keeping it somewhere safe and waving it about in the street. Then I called Tim at work.

'The surveillance job I'm supposed to be doing on this Blinkhorn woman, I can't plant myself outside her house without her noticing me, there's nowhere to hide in the lane and what's even more annoying is that the garden can't be overlooked. Any ideas, Tim?'

'Mmm . . . she knows what you look like, too, so you can't blag your way in as a gas engineer either.'

'If the Blinkhorns are con artists, then she'll see through that kind of thing straight away.'

'If she asks you in again, you could try to plant a bug under the kitchen table.'

'I can't sit out there waiting for it to rain and hope she sees me and asks me in. And planting a bug is the last resort. And against the law.'

'Well, that's never bothered us before. In that case, you'll have to fly over the house and hope to see something interesting.'

'What, in a hot air balloon?'

'With a drone, of course.'

'Ah, have we got one of them?' Tim keeps a lot of the technical stuff Aqua Investigations uses at his place (because I would only break it), but I hadn't heard we had a drone.

'*We* do not have a drone, but *I* do and I might be willing – I'm not entirely sure why – to lend it to you. I'll come up tonight and teach you how to use it, and I'll bring Becks – she's been asking to meet you for ages.'

'I'll cook.'

'We'll eat. No rabbit food. I'll bring the beers.'

# FIVE

'I must admit,' said Becks, standing in the kitchen at Mill House with a bottle of red in her fist, 'at first I thought Timmy had made up all that private-eye stuff to make himself look more interesting, but you're the real thing, I looked you up.' Becks – Rebecca Harrington to her Bath Uni biology students – was everything Annis wasn't: she was a head shorter than Tim, blonde, blue-eyed and curvaceous. And obviously in love with Tim, although she appeared to be a little surprised by this and often frowned at him, as though wondering if it could really be true. Tim is a woolly-haired chap full of little contradictions; he lives in a pathologically clean flat full of computers yet has the eating habits of a toddler. 'And' – she looked down into the kitchen drawer where the corkscrew lives – 'you keep a revolver in your kitchen drawer. That's very authentic.'

'Ah yes, sorry about that.'

'No, no, it's quirky, I'm fine with quirky. The whole place is quite, erm . . .'

'Run down?' Tim supplied.

'Full of character?' I said hopefully.

'. . . charming,' Becks completed diplomatically, running her eyes over the multicoloured fingerprints around the cupboard handles, the kettle and the light switch – something painters tend not to see.

She poured herself a glass of wine while I checked on the guineafowl in the oven, then Tim and I grabbed a beer each and headed outside to fly the camera-equipped drone while there was still enough light in the sky. Rebecca watched from the safety of the kitchen door while Tim explained to me in terms a five-year-old could grasp how to control the Phantom 3 drone and how to watch what it saw live on my phone which clamped to the remote. For the first time I could see my little realm at the bottom of the valley from the air, albeit on a tiny screen. Being a bloke, I naturally assumed I'd be quite good at controlling a drone (how hard could it be?) although in the event it took quite a bit of coaching ('not that fast/watch that tree/back a bit/I said back/what did you do that for/it's stuck on a branch') but in the end I got the hang of it.

To be honest, I'm more at home with guineafowl, brandy and a bit of crème fraiche. We ate at the big table in the kitchen.

'And you live here with your partner?' Becks asked. 'Anna?'

'Annis. She's away doing a mural commission at the moment.'

'Have you been together for a long time?'

It was obvious that Tim had mentioned Annis only fleetingly and entirely in terms of Honeysett's girlfriend, and his eyes clearly said 'this is not the time', so I didn't go into details. The past is another country and they do things differently there, I reminded myself. Quite differently.

Since neither biology nor IT is my thing and I never tire of talking about myself, I steered the conversation round to Verity's disappearance.

'Wouldn't the police look for her if she had disappeared?' asked Rebecca.

'You would think so, wouldn't you? But last year a quarter of a million people were reported missing. Police aren't interested unless it's a child under sixteen and the kid didn't pack a bag. If you call to report anyone else missing, you won't even get to talk to a police officer, just the civilian who takes the call, and that's as far as it will go. There's no point even telling them; get yourself a private eye straight away. Can't afford one? Then there's little you can do. Most people turn up again, of course, but about one in ten stay missing. You wouldn't have thought you could disappear in a country with more CCTV cameras than people, but apparently you can.'

'I find that quite reassuring,' said Tim through a mouthful of mashed potato.

'What about parents, relatives and so on?' Becks mused.

'According to Verity, she has one living relative – an aunt

she doesn't get on with. And the aunt turned up here looking for her.'

'Ah.'

I fished the receipt with the aunt's number from my jeans pocket where I had safely filed it away. 'She gave me her mobile number in case I hear anything. But I have a bad feeling about auntie.'

'Evil auntie?' asked Tim.

'Verity said her aunt lived in Belgium and they weren't on speaking terms. *This* auntie claimed she had recently talked to Verity on the phone and that she lived in Cheltenham. She was also making out she was poor when her accessories said otherwise. I'd be surprised if she was anyone's aunt.'

'Being an aunt isn't something you do, you know?' objected Tim, wagging a half-eaten guineafowl leg at me and splattering sauce over the receipt. 'It's something your siblings turn you into.'

'That's odd,' said Becks, frowning at Tim's guineafowl leg and looking very much like a Rebecca for a moment. 'You think something has happened to her, then?'

'Something has happened to a chap she hung out with. He died when someone posted petrol through his letterbox. And everyone who does know her is either cagey and scared or aggressive. One girl I spoke to seemed to be afraid *her* place might get torched if she talked too much. I think there's money involved somehow – perhaps quite a bit of money. I found a very disappointed bloke in a rancid caravan who had expected to be buying a houseboat with Verity and he's now drowning his sorrows in homemade cider. Yeah, I think she might be in trouble.'

'If she was going to buy a houseboat with your caravan chap, perhaps she bought one without him? Whose idea was it – his or hers?' asked Tim.

'Don't know; he didn't say and I'm not sure I want to go back to ask him. I ran into a bit of opposition in that camp. But you could be right. I'll have a look at houseboats when I have time. First I'll have to get some handle on the Blinkhorn thing. If I get a video of activity at the house, I can send it to the insurance company and keep Haarbottle happy.'

'Happy Haarbottle,' said Tim and clinked his bottle of Becks beer against our glasses.

The next morning dawned sunny with a light breeze. 'Ideal flying weather,' I told Annis.

'Happy Honeypot, you can try out your new toy.' I could hear the echo of the pool house down the line. 'It's still a bit misty here, we're not far from the canal, or is it the river? I forget. But it's pretty tropical here by the pool, day and night.'

'Have you done any work yet?'

'A bit. I'm taking my time. So you've met Becks? What's she like?'

We gossiped. I told her everything I knew about Rebecca – what she looked like (serious), drank (Merlot), wore (simple but expensive dress) and drove (minute Mercedes) – and Annis told me about the tiny record producer, his muscle-bound manservant, the gardens, the sauna and the four-course dinners. I hung up, thoroughly jealous of her commission, the pool and her tiny cozzie.

I put the Phantom 3 in the boot of the Citroën and drove to Charlcombe. You are not supposed to fly drones within fifty metres of a house, but if anyone complained, I would feign ignorance of the law, apologize and run away. I parked up a hundred yards or so from the Blinkhorn house and, full of enthusiasm for this new form of surveillance, I started up the drone. The thing took off like a rocket. I tried a few manoeuvres to remind myself of what Tim had taught me, then I aimed at The Chestnuts. It wasn't at all easy to keep an eye on the drone and at the same time follow the footage on the tiny screen of the phone. The sun was bright and I could not shade the screen and fly at the same time, so I squinted into it until, yes, I saw the house. The Mercedes was poking its rear out of the car port and there was her friend's black BMW on the drive. There was no sign of either of them at the back of the house, but there, from under a tree, stepped Mrs Blinkhorn's straw-hatted gardener, pushing a wheelbarrow full of autumn leaves towards the back of the garden. He did not seem to have noticed the drone high above. While he walked away from the house, I let the Phantom 3 sink lower. Perhaps, if I got low enough, I could look into the kitchen window. I aimed at the big barbecue, swivelling about, when two school kids from the nearby Royal High School walked past me. 'What are you doing?' asked one.

'Flying a drone,' I said distractedly.

'Where?' asked the other.

I looked at the kids. I looked up. The drone was out of sight. I panicked. Even though the picture had been steady, the fact that the thing had vanished from sight felt all wrong. 'Up, up, up!' I urged the drone and yanked the stick right back. The Phantom bobbed up like a cork and I was so glad to see it in one piece (especially since Tim had told me three times how much it cost) that I decided to bring it back again straight away and look at the footage I had taken on my computer at home.

On the way to Mill House, however, I calmed down and my confidence returned. I was in a different car and I would not have to go too close to the travellers' site to fly over it and see what, if anything, was going on there on an average day.

With the DS parked up in a nearby passing place on a narrow lane, a few hundred yards from the travellers' camp, I started the drone right beside the car. I was in the shade of a large unkempt hedgerow and this time had a clear picture of what the drone saw on my phone's little screen. Slightly nauseated by the swaying, I went quite high and immediately saw the camp which lay to the right. 'Comin' at yer,' I said aloud, feeling James Bondish and childishly amused at my imagined invulnerability as I flew over to them. It took me a moment to get my bearings since I was approaching from the other side, but once I got my eye in I could see it was all there. Two things became immediately apparent: there was much more to see than last time and the camp was not having an average day.

On the little screen I could make out a red car from the fire department, a police car and a police motorbike. The reason they were there became apparent when I let the drone sink down. Two caravans had been reduced to ashes – or, more precisely, both camper vans. I could see the remains of the axles and engines inside the black oblongs. Both were surrounded by black-and-brown halos where the fire had scorched the ground and baked the mud all around. There was no smoke and no fire engine, which meant I had missed the main event. Police officers in yellow high-vis vests were talking to a group of travellers but I could not make out whether Sam was among them. There was a lot of arm waving and gesturing. I dropped lower and crept closer.

Too close. Being so far away from the drone, I had no sense of how close I was flying to the group and how noisy the little propellers were. They all looked up. The police looked all about them, presumably to see who was flying the thing over their investigation. The motorcycle cop jogged over to his bike which was parked close to the entrance to the field and a moment later started it up, blue lights flashing front and rear. Time to wind in my neck and make myself scarce. In my panic to reel in the drone, I executed some ineffectual aerobatics over the field before I landed it, with a bump, on the roof of my car. I stuffed it unceremoniously into the boot and started the engine. Only I was facing the wrong way if I wanted to avoid the police bike. The lane was narrow. Even where I had parked up in the passing place, it took a six-point turn before I could get away. Of course, my ancient Citroën was no match for any sort of police vehicle built after 1945, which meant my chances of outrunning the bike were always zero; I needed to hide. The bike now had its siren going and it approached fast. A convenient crossroads of narrow lanes offered me a one-in-three chance of evading him. On instinct, I chose to turn left and put my foot down. Perhaps the steering needed seeing to because it felt a little more vague than I would have wished. I knew that driving at this speed was idiotic and that if I met another idiot coming the other way, both my steering and I might end up permanently vague. I could still hear the siren, which was bad news. Was it worth risking a monumental accident just to avoid being told off for flying the thing? What was the worst they could do to me? The police bike appeared in my rear-view mirror. I was just about to slow down and face the music when I met another idiot. Two idiots, in fact. Fortunately, they had already stuffed their Golf GTI into the hedgerow and stood head-scratchingly beside it. There was just enough space for me to fly past once the hapless pair had jumped out of the way. In my rear-view mirror, I watched the bike pull up at the car wreck, having found something more interesting to do (like breathalysing the pair in the ditch). This didn't stop me from constantly checking my mirrors for police cars and bikes, but I got back to Mill House without further incident, as they say.

It became clear to me that there is a difference between being able to fly a drone without crashing it through people's windows and being a good drone cameraman. Watched on my computer, the footage was more than a little nauseating since the drone had never stood still. The first sequence in and above the garden of The Chestnuts really yielded little information. I could see the gardener from above and at a distance pushing a wheelbarrow towards the back of the large garden and then, after a stomach-churning fun-fair swoop to barbecue level, I could just make out the shape of Janette Blinkhorn behind the French window of – presumably – the sitting room. Only a couple of seconds later, as the pilot was being unnerved by a couple of school kids, the drone zoomed high into the air and careered across several rooftops to land by my feet. I sent an email headlined 'Progress report' to Haarbottle and attached the video file, hoping it would make him as queasy as I felt.

The travellers' camp footage started off well and thankfully calmly: a gentle sweep over the hedgerow followed by a steady rise and straight approach, then a slow descent. What had happened there was as plain as yellow pudding: only two vehicles had been targeted – the only two camper vans. All other vehicles looked untouched. That it was arson was likely since they had stood wide apart. And that they had been specifically targeted was obvious since none of the caravans or buses had been touched. Someone had gone in during the night and, knowing only that Sam was asleep in a camper van, had torched both to be certain of getting him. I checked the local BBC website and, sure enough, the fire was the main item, with a picture of the aftermath, a fire engine still in attendance. My eyes flew over the lines of the article to get to the salient points: *No fatalities . . . a miracle no one was killed. . . treated for burns and smoke inhalation at a specialist burns unit . . . arson . . . accelerant, thought to be petrol.*

Journalists and travellers alike naturally wished to portray this as part of the struggle between the travellers and the farmer who owned the field and who had been trying to get them moved on for months. The travellers accused the farmer of having sent 'paid thugs' to set fire to the camp to scare them away. I was certain there were one or two of them who did not believe that for one minute. During an interview, the farmer dismissed it as nonsense, adding grimly yet not unreasonably that if he had set the fires, he'd have burnt down the lot of them.

Downstairs in the kitchen, I switched on the radio and tuned into the awesomely awful Radio Bristol to see if their news bulletins could shed any more light on the matter, but I had just missed the news. Gratefully, I retuned to Radio 3 and started grating an onion into a bowl. Bear with me.

So Sam was alive but had sustained some injuries. I thought he was extremely lucky to have fought his way out of a burning van at all, considering the kind of stupor he seemed to drink himself into at night. The thought of inhaling the smoke from his wretched van made me shudder. Perhaps, I thought, feeling uncharacteristically charitable, the drinking had been a one-off. Either way, I doubted I'd be able to talk to him again any time soon and I also suspected that he would take the attempt on his life as a warning not to get chatty with private detectives.

I peeled and then grated a few potatoes into the same bowl and turned the resulting sludge into a clean tea towel and squeezed all the moisture out of it. But chatty about what? How had a few piss-poor young people at the margins of society managed to upset Porsche-driving people towards the other end of the income scale, enough to become a target for murder? Drugs came to mind, naturally. But two things made me doubt that drugs were involved; I had met many a drug user in my time and Verity just didn't seem the type – in fact, I doubted she even smoked pot. And having been inside Sam's stinking hole of a camper van, I had seen no sign of illegal drug use there either. The other thing, of course, that made the irate-drug-dealer scenario unlikely is that while they are often happy to kill rival drug pushers, they don't normally go around killing their customer base, no matter how much they owe them. They might happily break their legs, yes, but it's all about the money. How much money could a traveller owe anyway?

Having whisked in an egg and seasoned the resulting mix, I dropped ladlefuls of it into a quarter inch of oil in my largest frying pan and watched them sizzle and brown on the stove. There's quite a short list of reasons for premeditated murder. Setting aside sexual jealousy and other relationship nonsense, the list is topped by greed, fear and hatred. Even though there was a connection between Sam in the camper van and Joshua Grant in his bedsit in the form of Verity, their lifestyles were very different. If anyone set fire to travellers' vans out of hatred for their kind, then how did Joshua fit in? Greed seemed out of the question as I could not see anyone greatly profiting from doing away with Joshua or Sam.

There was enough batter for six potato pancakes, which was good because I'm quite capable of snaffling that many in one sitting. I piled them on a plate and sat down with it at the kitchen table.

That left fear. But before I could spend time speculating on what might scare anyone into murdering this lot of unfortunates or even sink my teeth into the first pancake, the sound of car tyres crunching to a stop in the yard supplied me if not with fear then with a definite tingle of apprehension. I went to the window and peered out. From a steel-blue Peugeot 308, which had been parked by the gate so as to prevent any car from leaving, emerged two men. I'd have recognized them as police officers even had I not known the specimen who climbed out from the passenger side. Detective Inspector Reid was a symphony in brown. He had what looked suspiciously like a spray tan, tightly curled brown hair, and he wore a brown leather jacket, tight chinos and brown shoes. DI Reid always reminded me of an Airedale terrier. I had one as a small child, the kind with wheels that squeaked when you pulled it behind you. Since I'm a painter, you can take it from me that his driver was no oil painting either, but at least he had the sense to wear a grey suit, white shirt and black shoes, an ensemble that screamed 'junior officer'. He was carrying an A4 plastic folder. Both were carefully picking their way between the water-filled potholes which pockmarked the yard. I briefly considered not being at home, but with both the Honda and the Citroën in the yard, I was sure Reid was not going to leave without making a nuisance of himself. I decided it was best to get it over with. A loud open-handed policeman's knock summoned me to the front door. Sticking what I hoped was an expression of mild surprise and unconcern on my face, I opened the door to them.

Both had their warrant cards out. 'Mr Honeysett. I'm DI Reid, this is DC Cookson. I've come to have a word,' he said menacingly.

'If it's just the one . . .' I walked back to the kitchen. They were following slowly, dawdling and sticking their noses into doors on the way, so I sat down and made a start on my pancakes, which I like to eat without the aid of cutlery. When the two came into the kitchen, both looked around appraisingly at the colourful mess before taking a chair each at the other end of the long and cluttered table. I lifted the plate towards Reid. 'Want one? They're quite oily; you'd like it.'

Reid pulled a disgusted face. 'What are they?'

'Jewish potato pancakes.'

'What makes them Jewish?'

'I sing "Hava Nagila" while I grate the onions.'

Reid ignored that. 'Where's the drone?' he asked, sounding bored.

'Must be the fridge – it's quite ancient.'

'Don't mess us about, Honeysett, I'm a busy man and I don't have time to waste on nonsense.'

I waggled half a pancake at him. 'You're a busy man but not too busy to come all the way out here to make a nuisance of yourself over a flying toy.'

'Interfering with a police investigation is a serious matter.'

'I'm sure it is, which is why I wouldn't dream of it.'

'You flew a drone straight at two of my officers, then made off from a police vehicle, refusing to stop.' He motioned to

Cookson who whisked a video still from the folder as if it was a magic trick. 'Taken from the solo unit that pursued you.'

'Rubbish. No one asked me to stop, so there was no refusal to stop and no pursuit. The *solo unit*, also known as "motorbike" to normal people, stopped at the sight of an accident. I naturally assumed that was what he was responding to. As for flying at your officers, the drone footage will show that I was never even close enough to annoy them.'

'What were you doing at the travellers' site and why were you flying your drone in an irresponsible and illegal manner? You're not supposed to let it out of your sight or fly it within fifty yards of any dwellings.'

'You really have read up on it. First of all, I never lost sight of it, and, second, I think you'll find "dwellings" does not apply to buses and towed caravans. But I freely admit that I'm not very good at it. I think I'll find a different hobby.'

'We strongly recommend it. Now explain what you were doing there in the first place. You haven't started working for the *Chronicle*, have you?'

I started on another pancake. They really were oily; I had forgotten to pat them dry on kitchen roll. Still nice, though. 'Does the name Joshua Grant mean anything?'

'Chap who got fried in his bedsit the other day. The two fires have nothing to do with each other as far as I can see.'

'That's because you can't see very far if you're busy looking down your nose at poor people's pancakes. Have you arrested anyone for Joshua Grant's murder yet?'

'We're asking the questions, Mr Honeysett. What were you doing at the travellers' camp?'

Could I really eat all six of them? *They're quite nice cold*, I tried to tell myself, *so leave a couple*. I decided to have a fifth and spare one for later. 'There is,' I said attractively through a mouthful of pancake, 'a connection between Joshua and Sam.'

'Which is?'

'Verity.'

'Who?'

'Verity Lake.'

'Oh, hang on; the Super mentioned something when he called. Wasn't she a life model who ran out on you?'

'You could put it like that.'

'I am. And the connection being?'

'She has slept both at Joshua's and Sam's place.'

'She probably slept in lots of beds – yours too, I shouldn't wonder. I've heard you're none too bothered with conventions yourself. A slut who takes her clothes off in front of people. You think she set the fires?'

'No.'

'There you are. The fire at the camp was either set by the farmer – and who can blame him, frankly? – or is down to some squabble between the hippies themselves; you know what they're like – off their heads most of the time.' He stood up and looked about at the mess. 'I do advise you, Mr Honeysett, to be very careful. You don't want this mess to catch fire, do you? You arty-farty types really are a disgusting breed.' His sidekick, who had not said a word so far, had stood up too. I thought they were ready to leave, but they decided to stand on the other side of the table, looking down on me as though deciding what to do next.

'Who else is in the house?' asked the DC. His voice had an unnecessary edge of sarcasm that the question did not warrant.

I had suddenly gone off pancakes and wiped my hands on a tea towel. I felt an urge to invent a guest, preferably one trained in karate, but thought better of it. 'No one.'

'Then whose is the other car?' asked Reid sharply.

'A friend's. I borrowed it.'

He sighed and half turned towards his sidekick. 'You know, we may have to search this place. Long-haired superannuated hippies often have a lax attitude to the law.' Reid started wandering around the kitchen, poking among the baking things I had failed to put away, the open cookbooks and rolls of kitchen foil. Slowly but surely he was working his way towards the drawer where I had chosen to keep my revolver. 'I wouldn't be surprised if we didn't find a few cannabis plants growing somewhere on all this land or, failing that, a bag of herbal stashed away in the house?'

I rose too. 'Are you sure you don't want the last pancake?' I offered. 'Ah, well.' I stuffed it in my mouth and crossed with the plate to the sink, thereby cutting Reid off from the kitchen drawer. He opened a cupboard door instead and peered at the bags and cartons inside, then checked his fingers for paint stains, puffing out his cheeks and giving me a what-*are*-we-to-do-with-you look. I ran water into the sink and collected mugs and plates for washing-up, reaching around the two and herding them away from my gun.

'All right,' said Reid as though he had come to a decision, 'we'll let it go this time. Keep out of this. I don't want to see your ugly mug anywhere near either of these investigations. If I do, we'll charge you with obstruction. Stick with unfaithful husbands and missing persons and you'll stay healthy.' He turned away and left the kitchen.

The DC lingered to throw his weight around. 'We could make life *quite* uncomfortable for you, you know.' He reached into the open cupboard and picked up a carton of Puy lentils. 'I mean, imagine we turned up with a team to search this place for drugs?' He upturned the open packet and let the lentils dribble on the work surface where they sprang away in all directions. 'We'd have to turn *everything* upside down.' He picked up an egg from an open carton and broke it against the work surface. He let the raw egg drop into the mess, then pretended to examine the empty shell. 'We'd have to look inside *everything*. And we usually find s*omething* if we need to. Think about it.' He gave me a smile, wiped his hand on the back of a chair and followed his boss out of the house.

I closed the tap and dried my hands, not being in the mood for washing dishes. I suddenly felt more than a little queasy, and not just because I had wolfed down six oil-soaked pancakes. The warning had been quite clear: stay away or we'll make sure we find a bag of puff at your house. A feeling I had never experienced before spread over me – I began to miss DSI Needham.

# SIX

*Stick with missing persons* had been DI Reid's recommendation for my continued good health and I decided to heed it; Verity was missing and I intended to find her. I wasn't at all optimistic for her continued good health, should she be unwise enough to sleep in anything flammable. I went over and over the all-too-short conversation I had had with Sam. All he had said was that Verity would not model for me again because she 'didn't have to now', that they had been planning to buy a houseboat together but she had disappeared. It sounded to me as though Verity had somehow laid her hands on some money – and it wasn't from her aunt, real or fake – and had decided she was better off without Sam, if indeed she had ever seriously considered a future with him. Had she just strung him along for a place to sleep or had he reasonably expected to share in whatever money she had acquired? Houseboats weren't cheap, I presumed. Sam had asked me, 'Are you one of them?' and the two characters who had escorted me from the camp site had also assumed that I was. Who was 'them'? And did 'they' by any chance drive a dark-blue Porsche?

Since Verity could by now be anywhere in the whole wide world and Sam's remarks were all I had to go on, I would start to look in the one place I knew I would find a houseboat – at the marina on the River Avon.

The marina turned out to be a lot more than just a parking place for narrowboats. It was situated in a basin on the north shore of the river and attached to a caravan park. Dozens of boats were moored there, some beautifully painted, with flower pots and log piles on their roofs; some looked more drab and functional. Not all of them were narrowboats; several were wider boats of varying construction.

The woman at reception, who was obviously in the process

of packing up for the day, nevertheless did a good job at selling me the place. 'We have moorings for over forty boats, not all of them residential. As you might expect in a place like Bath, we provide first-class facilities, both for boaters and caravanners. Electricity hook-ups, diesel and other fuels, there are showers for berth holders, pump-out and chemical toilet facilities, naturally, a water point and we sell bottled gas on site.' She paused after her sales pitch and gave me a questioning look. Perhaps I simply looked too much like a landlubber. 'I'm afraid there is a long waiting list for berths. What exactly were you after, sir?'

'I was wondering whether you sold narrowboats.'

'Of course. We sell new-builds and also act as broker for clients wishing to sell their boats. Were you thinking of a new-build or—'

'I'm not actually looking for a boat. Not to buy. I'm looking for a person, a woman called Verity Lake.' Her eyes widened for a moment but then her face became professional again. 'Did she by any chance buy a narrowboat from here recently?'

'And what is your interest in the young lady?'

'She has gone missing and I'm concerned for her welfare. I'm a private investigator.' With some difficulty, I extracted a slightly bent business card from the lining of my leather jacket to where it had retreated through a whole in my pocket.

She gave it only a cursory glance before dropping it carelessly on her desk. 'I'm afraid, Mr' – she squinted at the card – 'Honeysett, that we cannot give out customer details, whether they are buyers or berth holders. That would be quite unprofessional.' With a decisive push, she closed a desk drawer, then turned off the computer in front of her.

'I understand your dilemma,' I said, trying to look understanding. 'The woman in question may be in danger.'

'Yes, from a man, no doubt. If you are concerned about the girl, I suggest you contact the police and tell them about your worries.'

'Perhaps you are right,' I conceded. 'Thank you anyway. Just one thing . . .'

'Yes?'

'Could I possibly use your toilet?'

She tutted but said, 'Very well . . . erm, you can use the one here.' She showed me through an open door that led to an unlit corridor. 'Second on the left. But please be quick; I'm about to lock up for the day.' She disappeared into a room to the right.

I quietly opened the first door on the left: a broom cupboard full of cleaning products, buckets and mops. Someone had also shoved in a five-foot-tall stack of mineral water in two-litre plastic bottles. The next door led into the promised toilet. I waited inside for sixty seconds and flushed, slipped out and into the cubbyhole next door. Squeezing behind the stack of mineral water and cowering down with an upturned bucket on my head, I felt stupid but – I hoped – invisible to anyone casually glancing inside.

If the conscientious marina people were reluctant to tell me about Verity, then I was even more reluctant to take no for an answer. It was pretty obvious that Verity had at least been here. All I had done was mention her name, but the receptionist had immediately called her a 'young lady', which meant she had at least seen her and recognized her name. If I wasn't discovered, I would wait until the office had closed for the evening and have a snoop in the files.

Earlier, I had strolled along the moorings to look at boats for any sign of Verity and asked the few boaters I saw, but none of those I spoke to admitted to knowing about her. It was a small enough community for at least one of them to have heard of her if she had been a recent addition to the berth holders. I did not really expect Verity to be mooring here if she had bought a boat; the place was too exclusive, and mooring costs ran into several thousand pounds a year, as one boater had told me with something akin to pride.

The bucket I had chosen to wear for my cunning disguise smelled aggressively of some kind of cleaning product, with undertones of blocked drains. Due to the smallness of the space into which I had crammed myself, I could not sit down but had to squat. After about five minutes in the cupboard I was beginning to feel uncomfortable, after ten minutes my ankles were killing me, and after another few minutes my calf muscles joined in. Even worse, I now really did want to use the toilet. Beyond the oddly amplified sound of my own breathing I could hear a distant door and indistinct voices, then footsteps; someone was coming down the corridor. A knock on the toilet door. A few seconds later, the cupboard door briefly opened and almost immediately closed again. 'Must have left while I was turning the drinks machines off,' said the receptionist's voice. 'Honeysomething. OK, I'll lock up. Lots of warm weather ahead, apparently, I'm glad we managed to restock the—' Her voice was cut off as a door closed. All remained quiet. I stayed under my bucket for a while longer to let them walk away from the building, to their cars or boats or wherever they were going. To pass the time, I imagined having a normal life, going to work without a bucket on my head in some place with interesting colleagues, driving home at the end of the day in a newish car with music on the radio, looking forward to a microwaved ready-meal and an evening in front of the telly. *A ready-meal and telly?* I was becoming delirious.

It stayed quiet. After shedding my bucket, I unfolded myself with some difficulty and a rhapsody of groans, then carefully opened the door and peered into the corridor. All was quite dark and still. Half an hour of the cupboard-and-bucket treatment appeared to have aged me considerably; I hobbled painfully into the office with its half-glazed entrance door and two small windows. I could see several lights out in the marina but no movement. The sun had set and I ought to be invisible to anyone out there. The problem was that I could also see virtually nothing apart from the dark silhouettes of the furnishings. I bumped painfully into the corner of the reception desk, then groped my way to the computer and sat down on the office chair. The light from the screen would, of course, illuminate my face, and that wouldn't do at all, which is why I pulled the monitor towards me, covered it and my head with my leather jacket and then furtled around in the dark until I found the power switch. After the darkness of bucket and office, the light was painfully glaring; I dimmed it until it would go no dimmer and hoped not too many chinks of light escaped from my cover. This would definitely be classed as burglary or attempted burglary if I got caught. A ready-meal and telly suddenly didn't seem so bad. How had my life departed this far from the norm?

I found the accounts and clicked on 'Sales'. With an unpleasant warning sound that made me jump, a dialogue box appeared. It was password-protected. What had Tim told me about passwords? Nearly fifty per cent of people use the same twenty-five passwords. The only two I remembered were 'football' and 'password'. Neither worked. I typed in 'boat', 'narrowboat', 'lock' and 'marina'. No luck. I was about to give up when I remembered another one from Tim's list: 'QWERTY'. Bingo. I felt like James Bond. In 'Sales' I went straight to 'Pre-Owned' – I doubted Verity would stretch to a new boat – and slowly wormed my way into the accounts until I found the sale, only three days earlier. Verity Lake had bought a forty-eight-foot Springer – whatever that meant – called *Time Out* for £18,000. The description of the boat included the expression 'in need of updating'. There was a note at the bottom of the page explaining that 'the client' (Verity) bought the boat without commissioning the usual survey because she was 'in a hurry to complete the sale and move on to the boat'. And she had paid in cash.

By the light from the screen I found my business card and pocketed it, then I switched off the computer and put my jacket back on. Having stared at the computer screen from two inches away, all I could see now, wherever I turned my gaze, was an after-image of the accounts page detailing Verity's purchase of the boat.

At last, now I knew where to look for her. The girl was somewhere out there on a boat. If someone was after her and she knew about it, then perhaps a boat was not such a daft idea, especially if no one knew what it was called or what it looked like. Now I knew both, it couldn't be long before I would find her to make sure she was safe.

First, though, I had to get out of the building and the marina. I had imagined that I would simply open a window and climb out, but when I tried, I found that, being ground-floor windows and modern, they were restricted to opening no more than four inches. Even twenty years younger and five stone lighter, I would not have been able to squeeze through the gap. A

Victorian street urchin would have struggled. Upper-floor windows would not have this security feature; sadly for me, there was no upper storey to jump out of – or perhaps just as well, considering my athletic deficiencies. Just on the off-chance and because you never know your luck, I groped my way to the front door. As expected, it was locked. Just as I tried the handle, an elderly couple, both using torches to light their way, appeared around the corner. I quickly ducked down.

'What was that?' I dimly heard the man say.

'What was what?'

'I thought I saw something behind the door. Like a dark figure.' A diffused beam of light moved this way and that as the man played his torch across the door and front window. The light came closer.

'You're always seeing *something*,' said the woman. 'You saw a dead body in the water on Saturday and that was a bin bag full of rubbish.'

The man did not answer. Instead, he stepped close to the half-glazed door and pointed his torch back and forth. I kept very still. He gave a disappointed grunt. 'Too much reflection,' he muttered. 'This glass wants cleaning.'

'Come on, Jack,' said the woman, 'you promised to make lemonade, remember?'

'Comin', comin',' he said soothingly and turned away from the door, leaving me once more in the safety of the dark.

Right now it felt a little too safe. The windows didn't open, the door was locked and the modern double-glazed glass looked difficult to break. By the time I could manage to smash the glass out of a window and climb through it, I might have attracted quite an audience. Moving away from the door, I aimed at the corridor and walked smack into a groin-height photocopier. Having to do all this in Braille might eventually leave me crippled for life. Only when I was inside the corridor did I risk turning on the light on my mobile. On the left were broom cupboard and toilet, on the right one door marked 'Meeting Room'. I tried the handle; it was locked. But there was light at the end of the corridor – a fire door. This would, of course, open if I pressed down on the metal bar, but it would also activate the fire alarm and bring every boater in the marina running towards me carrying jugs of lemonade to douse the flames.

I dialled Tim's mobile number; it went to voicemail which was no good to me. I checked my watch – he would probably be home by now – and called his landline, letting it ring and ring. While the phone rang and I pictured Tim's tiny flat in Northmoor Street, it dawned on me that Tim had a brand-new girlfriend. He might be at her place. Or in the middle of something.

'This had better be good,' said Tim as the receiver was snatched up.

'I can't promise that.' I explained my situation, leaving out the whys and wherefores because I could tell from Tim's impatient 'ahas' and 'rights' that he was unimpressed with the whole thing.

'The fire door is your best bet. Take a run at it and don't stop running until you can no longer hear the alarm bell.' He hung up before I could thank him. I had hoped for a more technical solution, but he was probably right. I pocketed my mobile, took a run at the door and came barging out the other side, narrowly avoiding some wheelie bins, to the ear-splitting noise of a fire bell. I turned right, ducked past some damp shrubs and ran to the marina's gate. Had this been a movie, even a B-movie, then someone would have been waiting for me with a speedboat to facilitate my getaway in style, but since this was a Honeysett production, I found the entrance gate to the marina closed, recently painted to a slippery gloss finish and high enough to present a challenge to the less agile type of burglar. With difficulty, and calling on my large and varied collection of Anglo-Saxon expletives, I clawed my way up the metal gate and slid down the other side, landing with an ankle-jarring thump. As I hobbled to my car, I could hear shouts over the now quieter alarm, but I took Tim's advice and just kept going, scrabbled for the car keys in my pocket and seconds later screeched away from there. The whole thing, I decided, betrayed a certain lack of subtlety and planning.

# SEVEN

Annis agreed. 'Not the brightest tactics, Honeypot. Good result, though. Where do you think she got the money to buy a boat? If people are after her, then she might have pinched it.'

'"Pinched it" may not be the way to describe it. You pinch a Mars bar from a corner shop, but eighteen grand in cash takes a bit of lifting, and if people are being roasted alive, then I suspect it may be a lot more than that.'

'You could be right there. But if she opted for early retirement with other people's dosh, then I'm not sure the boat was such a good idea. If they find out she bought a narrowboat, then they'll find her, surely. It's like the movies where people who need to hide try to do it in a cabin in the middle of nowhere. The place to hide is in a big city where no one notices you turning up.'

'That's what I thought at first,' I admitted, 'but I chatted to one of the boaters at the marina. Apparently, once you're on the water there are three thousand miles of interconnecting canals and rivers you can use, so perhaps it's not so daft. And boats can be repainted and renamed.'

'Renaming a boat is bad luck.'

'Not if you're being followed by a guy with a petrol can and a big box of cook's matches.'

'Point taken. So what's the plan?'

'Find her and warn her.'

'You think she doesn't know she's in danger? Looks like she is running away. Or sailing away.'

'She probably knows about the house fire that killed Joshua Grant in his bedsit, but unless she has telly on her boat or gets the *Bath Chronicle* delivered by owl post, she might have no idea how far they managed to followed her already.'

'And you're going to check three thousand miles of water-ways now to see she's all right?'

'It won't be three thousand miles,' I said optimistically.

'Hon . . .' came the voice of reason.

'Yeees . . .'

'I mean. I liked Verity. She was quite fun, a good model and she said nice things about my cakes, but I thought she was also a bit of an airhead and she obviously must have done something quite stupid.'

'Your point being?'

'My point, as if you didn't know it, is that I think it could be quite dangerous and you're not getting paid to find her. How are you getting on with the insurance thing? Which you *will* get paid for – at least if you get a result.'

I told her about my drone-flying. 'I need to find a new angle on that, but when I sent the footage to Haarbottle, I had an email back saying "Keep up the good work" or something to that effect, so I'm at least keeping them happy until I find out what's going on.'

'Well, try; it's quite a chunk of money.'

'Talking of chunks of dosh, how's the painting?'

'Slow.'

'You sound quite echoey again. You're in the boathouse? I mean, pool house.'

'The pool's big enough to float a boat on. I'm mainly working on the outside mural because the weather is supposed to stay fine for quite a while, which is great for painting *al fresco*. I'll save the indoor mural for a rainy day. I've only done preliminary stuff for that.'

'Preliminary stuff like floating in the pool.'

'Well, it has to be considered from all angles. And I'll have you know I'm up to twenty lengths a day now. It's great – I feel brilliant. I can really recommend it.'

'I'll start digging our pool when I get a minute.'

'Yes, please.'

'What's wrong with our mill pond all of a sudden?'

'Ducks poo in it.'

While Annis was indulging her twenty-a-day habit, I spent the rest of the evening sitting in the armchair by the fire, sipping ten-year-old Laphroaig I had bought in more affluent times, feeling that I had made significant progress that day.

*     *     *

I woke early to warm sunshine. Annis would be in the pool house, no doubt. While I scrambled my breakfast eggs, I imagined the record producer's factotum swimming across the pool in suit and tie, balancing a cafetière of Blue Mountain coffee to a serenely floating Annis, wearing her new bikini, most of which was entirely imaginary. I had absolutely no plan for how to find Henry Blinkhorn, which was, of course, excellent. It left me free to pursue Verity.

It was now four days since she had bought *Time Out* and, I imagined, she could not have got too far on it yet. From the marina where she acquired the boat she could have gone in two directions, downriver towards Bristol where she would hit a dead end as far as navigation with a narrowboat was concerned, or upriver where she was able to join the Kennet and Avon Canal which connected to the rest of Britain's inland waterways. If you wanted to get out of sight, then that was the way you would go.

On the marina's website under 'Boats for Sale', I found Verity's *Time Out* still listed, though with a proud 'Sold' banner at the top. I downloaded the photographs in the description. She was an old boat with a black hull, blue sides and a rust-red roof and foredeck. It had a 'cruiser stern' (apparently) and in the pictures sported flowerpots in the stern and on the roof. There were photos of the interior too – a lot of wood, tired-looking bits of furniture, a galley kitchen and a bathroom tiled with a rose motif. It might have been in need of updating but all the basic facilities were there. There were pictures of the two-cylinder engine, too, which made me even more certain that she hadn't got very far yet; it looked old and rusty.

With the pictures on my phone, so I might recognize the boat, I boarded my Citroën and drove into town. From North Parade Bridge I had a view of the River Avon towards the horseshoe of the weir below picturesque Pulteney Bridge, a postcard shot beloved of the Tourist Board. This was as far as the River Avon was navigable for narrowboats; a few of them were moored opposite Parade Gardens. I did not really expect to find *Time Out* here, right in the heart of Bath, but thought I might feel just a bit stupid if Verity's departure had been delayed for some reason and she was still here, on the

River Avon or the canal as it snaked out from the city. The sunshine had brought tourists and Bathonians out in force. The towpath was so crowded with walkers, roller skaters, joggers and a group of amateur painters with their easels that I had to walk up to each boat to make sure it wasn't what I was looking for. I joined the throng, which was soon thinning out as I left the more picturesque part of Bath behind, and walked all the way from North Parade Bridge to Newbridge, the western end of town, as close to the marina from where the boat came as I dared; *Time Out* was not here.

My feet hurt. You'd have thought that as a PI I'd be used to trudging about but actually most of the job is done sitting in the car or leaning on lampposts. This was more walking than I had done for many years and it had taken me all afternoon. I was developing blisters on my feet, felt parched and starving hungry, and was now miles away from my car. Even while I congratulated myself on having been thorough in my search and satisfied that Verity had really left Bath on her floating refuge, it brought home to me that finding the boat would involve a lot more work than I had imagined. Being too poor to call a cab, I dragged myself to the nearest bus stop and spent half an hour kicking my heels in what the bus company laughably called a 'shelter' until eventually a steaming hot bus took me back to town, but naturally nowhere near to where I had left the car.

When I eventually reached home, my brain had ceased normal operations and flashed only the single word 'tea' in front of me until it could actually smell the stuff. Apart from Laphroaig, tea is still the best private-eye restorative. I drank a pot of it with my feet in a bowl of cold water to try to shrink them to their normal size, while I considered the logistical problems of finding Verity. No roads ran along the canals that would allow me to check what floated on it from the car. Access points to the towpaths were often miles apart. I could, of course, park the car, walk to the next access point, then walk back to the car, but by that method, if I was unlucky, I might have to walk not three but six thousand miles. Without someone to pick me up at the next access point, it would amount to one hell of a fitness programme and take forever and a day. I could conceivably take a cab back to my car each time, but that would cost me a fortune. Would a taxi driver even find the place without instructions from the nearest satellite? I went to bed feeling far less optimistic than when I had started thinking about it. There had to be a better way.

It came to me on waking in the morning: bicycle! Not for nothing did the Honda Jazz have hundreds of litres of boot space: it was made for chucking bicycles into the back. And I knew just where to find one. In the outbuildings. Somewhere. Almost certainly. Or quite possibly.

As forecast, it was another sunny day, perfect for rummaging around in the crud that clutters the sheds and woodwormed remnants of a barn. Dust motes floated thickly in the sunbeams that fell through holes in the roofs. I found no less than four expired lawnmowers, two valve radios, a treadle sewing machine, the engine and rear wheels of a small tractor, an electric kettle with a round three-pin plug (circa 1912), a three-legged stool with two legs, a chest of drawers minus the drawers and about fifty empty paint cans in shades that went out of fashion in the 1960s. All of this was covered in leaves, mouldering canvas, ripped tarpaulin and, above all, dust. I staggered and coughed my way through it until I caught a glimpse of what I was looking for: out from the chaos poked the handle bar and rubber hand grip of a bicycle. I spent five minutes patiently digging it out from the other junk until it was half out, then lost patience and dragged, kicked and yanked until the rest of it was free. I owned a bicycle.

Of sorts. Naturally, it was not the ten-speed mountain bike of my mind (things never are). No, it was a rusted boneshaker with a saddle of cracked leather and hand grips of crumbling rubber which disintegrated as I tried to push the thing to the house. Its black frame was spotted all over with rust. The tyres were flat, of course, and as for the gears – I looked carefully everywhere – it didn't appear to have any. The chain was hanging off and had rusted solid.

Once I had my bicycle standing upside down on the kitchen table, I realized that what I was actually looking at was a typical Honeysett conveyance, only this time I actually knew how to make it go without Jake's help. Having no gears, I quickly decided, was an advantage; no gears meant there weren't any to go wrong, and, anyway, towpaths were all level. It involved a couple of trips into town but by next morning I had a working bicycle with fresh inner tubes, a rust-free chain and a slight wobble in the front wheel, which I decided to find charming. It even had a bell whose chime was clearly audible if you put your ear next to it.

With the rear seats of the car folded down, it fitted easily in the back of the Jazz. Having parked in town, I wheeled the bike through the centre and across Halfpenny Footbridge to start my canal cycle adventure at Lock 7, the first lock on the Kennet and Avon Canal. The bike, when cycled rather than pushed, creaked a little under my weight and had an irregular squeak which even the most generous application of Spanish Extra Virgin had failed to eliminate. The plan was to cycle on the towpath as far as the George Inn at Bathampton, stop for a drink and cycle back to the car, a perfectly manageable undertaking for a perfectly unfit cyclist.

Britain's canals had, of course, been built as the arteries of industry and commerce, transporting every conceivable commodity faster and more cheaply than could be achieved by road. But today and here in Bath you could be forgiven for thinking that the Kennet and Avon had been constructed merely to look pretty. On this stretch the gardens of large Georgian town houses ran all the way to the water's edge and many of the boats moored along here were beautifully painted and well kept. Unfortunately, I was dressed for walking, not cycling, which I soon found out have quite different requirements. The unseasonably warm weather meant that soon I was steaming with the effort of squeaking along. Only a few walkers were about this morning, and whenever I met one, they were forewarned of my wobbling approach by the rattle and squeak of the bike's mechanics. Cycling under bridges, of which there were several, I found quite nerve-wracking as the curve of the interior meant having to cycle close to the edge of the canal to gain enough headroom. The water looked uninviting; Annis would have found things to say about it. I cycled as far away from the edge as possible.

I passed a boat hire company that had boats parked three-deep on the water. From time to time I came upon thickets of brambles. Eventually, I stopped at a veritable wall of them, glad to lift my behind from the uncomfortable saddle for a while, and crammed handfuls of juicy if dusty berries into my mouth. A gusty wind had sprung up which was against me as I resumed my pedalling. The canal cut through Sydney Gardens, a small park beside the Holburne Museum. I needed to duck under two more bridges until I reached a more open stretch I recognized; it would lead me nearly straight to Bathampton where the welcoming arms of the George Inn awaited sweaty private detectives and their rusty steeds.

A smudge of black cloud appeared in the sky, driven towards me by the wind. As I cycled towards it and it swallowed the sun, I realized that instead of checking the weather forecast I had relied on Annis's prediction that a lot of fine weather was ahead, forgetting that she was in the next county. I pedalled faster. Cyclist and rain cloud met halfway to the George Inn. Thunder growled. The heavens opened and a squally east wind chucked refreshing amounts of rain in my face. I stopped to put my jacket back on which I had clamped to the old-fashioned sprung rack, then wiped the wet saddle with my sleeve and resumed pedalling. There were many boats moored on this stretch; most looked shut up, but several showed signs of life: music, running engines or smoke from stovepipes. One looked to me so similar to *Time Out* that despite the different name – *Midnight* – I dug out my phone to compare it with the photos. I found it actually looked nothing like it; I still had to get my eye in where types of narrowboats were concerned.

Pedalling against the wind was turning my little outing along the flat towpath into a struggle. When the first cottages, the humpback bridge and finally the pub rose into view through the thick rain, it felt like the end of an expedition.

The George looks like the archetypal English pub: ancient (it used to be part of a thirteenth-century monastery), covered in ivy and with wood smoke rising from the chimney. It stands opposite the village church and churchyard and has a resident ghost. What more can you ask? After carrying the bike down the few steps to the forecourt, I left it leaning against a bollard, unlocked since I hadn't thought to bring a bike lock. By now the excitement of owning a bicycle had waned to the point where I decided not to be upset if someone made off with it while I was inside.

Inside! Give it twenty minutes of wind and rain, throw in some mud, a damp saddle, protesting knee joints and a runny nose and 'inside' becomes an idea suffused with the promise of shelter, warmth and human comfort. All of which the George Inn was happy to provide to the solvent cyclist. The place was virtually empty, but it was dry, there was a blazing fire despite the warm day and you could barely hear the howl of the wind through the tiny windows and two-foot-thick walls. After handing me a yard of kitchen roll, taking my order for a pint of Guinness and providing me with a menu, the barman remarked on the remarkable wetness of my attire. 'You picked a bad day – thundery showers all day. Supposed to get quite stormy later, too.' When he had finished cheering me up, I sat as close to the fire as was possible without bursting into flame, and while my clothes steamed in the delicious heat, I perused the menu. Which was extensive and took me an entire pint to read through. My problem was that I wanted to eat virtually all of it. Since I found myself in a traditional English country pub, however, I plumped for Asian-Spiced Duck Croquettes followed by the Beetroot, Feta and Horseradish Risotto. Both turned out to be excellent and instilled in me a marked reluctance to leave the fireside just to cycle back to town through the rain. Yet the barman repeated his lugubrious forecast of even worse weather later on, and so I forced my reluctant carcass back out into the rain.

The cracked leather of the ancient saddle had absorbed all the rain water it could and gratefully transferred as much of it as possible to the seat of my trousers from where it progressed by reverse osmosis to my underpants and beyond. It took all but three minutes of towpath cycling to restore me to the sorry state the staff of the George Inn had laboured to cure – wet, aching and grumpy. Imagining Annis floating at this very moment in a tropically heated indoor pool did nothing to cheer me. The wind was at my back now, pushing me along. I got my head down and pedalled furiously. Verity in her narrowboat could have steamed past me wearing nothing but a Victoria sponge cake and I would have neither noticed nor cared. I was the only idiot soul out here, I thought angrily, who hadn't listened to the weather report. With the rain on my back and anger in my calf muscles, I was making short work of the stretch between the George and Sydney Gardens. I had become more confident too and barely slowed down as I negotiated the low bridges, scattering sitting ducks as I did. The bridge in Sydney Gardens, however, had something more solid than ducks under it. Since I had last passed through it, a homeless man with all his worldly goods had taken shelter on the narrow path under its vaulted span. It was the first real test for the bike's brakes. And they were useless. They squealed and slipped as I cycled over the edge of the towpath straight into the canal.

There are two types of 'getting soaking wet': there's the metaphorical one you use when you complain about having been rained on and the literal one when you get immersed in water long enough for your clothes to absorb the maximum amount of water they are capable of holding. The latter requires a completely different set of swear words, which the echoing vault of the bridge magnified while I flailed around in the dark water in a panic, trying to stay afloat while my sodden clothes and shoes weighed me down. As I scrabbled for a slimy hand-hold, the homeless guy tried to help by grabbing me by the hair and yanking on it. It took me a while to find suitable words of gratitude for this. Eventually, I managed to land on the towpath like a wet fish gasping for air.

'Shit, man, you cycled right in!' said the homeless man.

'Nothing gets past you. Thanks for helping me out. For a moment there I thought I was going to drown.'

'Most unlikely. The canal's only four foot deep. You could just have stood up, you know.'

This made me feel even more of an idiot. The homeless guy was probably in his fifties, though the street tends to age people rapidly, so he might have been younger. His name was Dan. He had been on the streets for years and, as I found out, he was well organized. His survival kit included a tiny camping stove with a little blue bottle which hissed under a homemade two-handled cooking pot fashioned from a catering-sized tin of baked beans in which he was heating water. With the sunshine cancelled, I now shivered beside the stove while we waited for the water to come to the boil. When it did, he crumbled an economy chicken stock cube into it and stirred it with a homemade spoon. When he offered me a small tinful of the broth, I was truly thankful and told him so. Despite having a most excellent lunch inside me, it was the economy broth, possibly made with canal water, that slowly restored my will to live, but I realized I would have to move on soon if I didn't want to catch my death. A tiny curve of the front wheel was sticking out of the water, probably buoyed up by the pneumatic tyre. I reached down and yanked the bike out of the water and presented it to the homeless man as a gift. 'Be warned, the brakes are useless.' Then I marched off into town. Rain still fell monotonously. At the railway station it managed sufficiently to disguise the true nature of my muddy wetness for a taxi driver to ferry me to my own car while I left puddles in the back of his. With the heater on full, I steamed towards home and my bottle of Laphroaig. I had some serious thinking to do.

If only I could have stopped shivering and throwing up, it would have made it easier. While probably not a ready source of cholera, canal water is nevertheless not recommended for drinking. I had only swallowed one mouthful but apparently that had been enough to turn me inside out. I spent the night in the bathroom, having got tired of running back and forth between bed and toilet bowl. By mid-morning I successfully held down a piece of dry toast. By the afternoon I could hold down a conversation. I called the Bath Boat Hire Company and asked about renting a boat from them.

'How long did you want the boat for?' asked the friendly voice.

'I'm not really sure.'

'The longest we hire out boats for is a long weekend.'

'Ah.'

'And how many people in your party?'

'It's just me.'

'Out of the question. We never hire out boats to single-handed boaters; too much can go wrong, especially negotiating locks. Virtually all fatal accidents on the canals happen in locks. Just one other person would be enough and we'd be happy to accommodate you.'

So much for my only brainwave all day. I called Annis. 'So I went for a cycle ride,' I bragged, '*and* a swim.'

Once she had stopped laughing, she professed to be deeply impressed with my new fitness regime. 'OK, so cycling is not your thing. How about a monkey bike?'

'What, one of those tiny motorbikes for kids that make you look ridiculous?'

'Precisely. That would work and it would fit into the Jazz. Tell you what, why don't you go up to Jake's, find out whether he has managed to find the parts for my Norton yet and while you're there ask him? He's bound to come up with something. But under no circumstances ride the Norton down the towpath. See if he has a little step-through moped you could use . . .'

'I haven't,' said Jake. 'What's more, it's illegal to ride mopeds on the towpath. The first boater who sees it is going to report you. Anyway, it's just a shortcut to swallowing more canal water. If you are trying to find a boat, what you need is a boat.' He was leaning in the door of his workshop, wiping his hands thoughtfully on a fifty-year-old oil rag.

'I tried to hire one but no luck.'

The day of thunder had passed, the sun was back and everything seemed possible once more. 'Well, as it happens, I know where you could lay your hands on one.'

'With an engine?' I asked suspiciously. 'I'm not rowing up the canal.'

'Of course with an engine; you can't row a narrowboat.'

'A narrowboat? You mean like a houseboat?'

'Indeed. I happen to own one.'

'You? I didn't know you had a narrowboat. In fact, I seem to dimly remember your better half poo-pooing the idea of narrowboats, camper vans, caravans and anything else not connected to the national grid. Not to mention sewage system.'

'All true and well remembered. But I sort of inherited the

thing. Remember last April when they found a dead boater in the canal?'

'Yes, bloke found bobbing in Lock Thirteen. Unlucky for some, as the paper put it tactfully.'

'That was him – that was Neil. Sally and I had met him on our one and only narrowboat holiday in Wales. We didn't really know what we were doing and he was single-handed, so we sort of loosely teamed up, did locks together and so on. And you're right, Sally hated it. Too small, too narrow – I mean, it's called a narrowboat; she should have expected it. Sally is more of a widebeam, if you'll pardon the expression . . .'

'Not sure she would. How about generously proportioned?'

'She'd clout you for that, too. Neil and I exchanged post-cards and emails and chatted about engines. Neil lived on his boat – he was what they call a continuous cruiser, no fixed berth. He'd always ask when we were going to take our next boating holiday. I didn't have the heart to tell him it wasn't going to happen. Anyway, all of a sudden he said he'd had enough of the boat life. He was up north at the time and said he was coming down to see me. Then he started saying he wanted us to *have* the boat. Said it several times. I thought he was going through some kind of bad patch and I'd talk him out of it when he got here, but the day he got here was the day he died. Apparently, he fell off the boat in the lock, knocked himself unconscious on the side of the boat and drowned. Not uncommon, the coroner said. And after all was said and done, and there were no relatives, and they had seen his emails saying he came to give me the boat, the police released it to me. Didn't know what else to do with it.'

'Where on the canal is it parked?'

'*Parked*? You don't park a boat; you moor it.'

'OK, where's it *moored*?'

'It isn't. The canal people lifted it out of the lock. I've got it in storage.'

I looked around at the outbuildings. 'Where?'

'Not here, you daft bugger; it's sixty foot long and we're ten miles from the canal. It's on a trading estate in Bristol.'

# EIGHT

For two days I had to cool my boating ardour while Jake was busy in his workshop. It was the middle of September and we had uninterrupted sunshine and ice-cream weather; the newspapers were full of the usual talk of an Indian summer. I marvelled at it when Jake drove us in his wine-red MK 2 Jaguar to Bristol, windows wide open.

'Did you get to see your boating friend before he died?'

'No, Neil did call me on his mobile, though, only an hour earlier, which made it hard to accept at first that he was really dead. I mean, I know it's stupid but I kept saying "But I only just talked to him", I was that shocked. He was going to tie up below the weir, you know, below Pulteney Bridge – that's what he had been aiming for in all those weeks it took him to come down from the north. He sounded incredibly excited, but not in a good way. A bit hysterical even. And his emails, too, had been a bit weird. "I've got to get off this boat" and "perhaps I'll buy a house in Spain". He had never talked like that before; he had always given us the impression that boating was his life.'

'How did he survive on the canals?'

'Tiny army pension. Got badly injured in a training exercise – invalided out. That's what he lived on. He said the money wasn't enough to keep him alive on land so he lived on the boat. A water gypsy. If you don't have a fixed mooring, you have to move on every two weeks or so. I couldn't bear living like that, without roots or neighbours, but he said he loved it. Which made it so surprising that he wanted to give the boat away and was thinking of moving to Spain.'

'Perhaps the weather up north got to him.'

'Yes, but in one email he talked of buying a house in Spain. What with?'

'Must have had a windfall.'

'He didn't mention it and the police found he was barely solvent. No, it's a mystery. Oh, here we are.'

Jake turned into a sad little trading estate beside the Feeder Canal where nothing much appeared to be happening in or around the corrugated-roofed buildings, several of which had 'TO LET' signs on them. It was hard to believe that we were close to the centre of Bristol; the Floating Harbour was only a mile or so down the road. Between a welding specialist and a signwriting workshop stood three long landlocked shapes propped up on railway sleepers, all narrowboats. Two were partially covered with a multitude of tarpaulins and yellowed plastic sheeting; a third was a mere shell, covered in rustproof paint.

The chap who 'looked after' Jake's boat had a workshop in the same unit as the signwriters, yet I could not quite make out what kind of business his tools, paint pots, work benches, cables and wooden boxes amounted to. His name was Gary. He was a slightly podgy forty-year-old guy wearing a faded orange beanie, denim jeans and jacket, and ancient work boots. He made us tea in mugs so filthy and chipped they would have made Dan the homeless man shiver with revulsion. I just carried the thing around with me without putting my lips to it while we walked up and down admiring the hull of Jake's boat, sixty feet of rust-pitted blackness. It was called *Dreamcatcher*. Jake went all misty-eyed over it.

Gary ran his hand along it. 'Needs blacking again soon, but the hull is in good nick,' he said as though he was trying to sell it to us. 'For a boat of this age,' he added.

'This age', as I found out, was circa forty years. I knocked on the steel hull; it sounded extremely solid. Seeing that amount of steel, which is usually hidden by the water, made it appear very heavy to me. 'How on earth are we going to get it into the water?' I asked.

'Oh, the crane is on its way,' said Gary, checking the time on his mobile. 'Should have been here by now.'

The crane turned into the yard not two minutes later – a huge lumbering black-and-yellow thing with a telescopic arm strong enough to lift a house. It was less than two hundred yards from the storage site to the water of the Feeder Canal but a sixty-foot load hanging from a crane needs a lot of securing and moving very slowly, as I found out over the next

hour and a half of standing uselessly around. Traffic stopped
on the Feeder Road that runs alongside the canal for twenty
agonizing minutes while the crane slowly swung *Dreamcatcher*
over the canal, with Jake standing in the stern of the boat
itself, looking piratical with legs wide apart for balance. The
crane driver knew his business and dropped the boat gently
on to the water. And lo! It floated and it did not sink. I had
already crossed to the other side of the canal via the bridge
at Netham Lock so that Jake could throw me a line. I heaved
on it and found that the enormous boat moved much more
easily than I had expected, considering its size. *Dreamcatcher*,
despite the dippy name, had been painted in classy racing
green, with cream trim and black decks and railings. Jake
clambered along the side and hopped off with another line
and soon had her expertly tied up below the lock-keeper's
cottage. He showed me how to do a rope hitch which allowed
me to tie up and untie the boat quickly. I said 'ah' and 'great'
and 'that's useful' and instantly forgot how he had done it
because I was far too excited. I couldn't wait to get on board.
Of course, I hadn't quite told the truth about my narrowboating
experience when Jake had asked if I had ever been on one,
so when he showed me over the boat, I said 'refresh my
memory' and 'remind me how that works' a lot. He very soon
realized I was completely at sea. So to speak.

'Right, we'll do this stem to stern, or rather the other way
around,' he said, exasperated at my ignorance. 'Just as well it
doesn't take a genius to work a boat. What we're standing on
is the stern deck. You're lucky – not all boats have one. The
railing will stop you from falling overboard every five minutes.
Underneath this' – he stomped his foot on a hatch – 'is the
engine. We'll get to that later. This' – he pointed to a polished
wooden handle about a yard long at the very back of the boat
– 'is the rudder. You push it to the left and the boat moves
right, push to the right and it goes left. These' – he pointed
to a control panel nearby – 'are your controls. I'll show you
those when we start her up.'

At last I was allowed down a few steps into the inside of
the boat. I found I had just a hand's breadth of headroom
above me, and the width, as Jake pointed out, was seven feet

and four inches. He moved about the boat as though he had lived on one all his life. It smelled musty and dusty and the sunlight bounced off the grimy windows. The interior was completely panelled with wood, floor to ceiling. 'Yes, solid oak – that's how they used to do them, not plywood like in the modern boats,' he said proudly. The first area we had stepped into consisted of a two-seater sofa on the left, shelves on the right, followed by a stove with a long stove pipe disappearing at an angle through the roof. 'That's what heats the entire boat. It's very efficient. Burns anything.' Next came the galley. It had everything a kitchen needed, except space. It had a cooker, a small fridge and a Belfast sink. When I idly turned a tap, nothing happened. Jake slapped my hand and closed the tap. 'Water tank is empty, of course.'

There followed a small dining table with two-seater benches to either side, and then a door on the left. Beyond it the corridor was very narrow and quite dark until Jake opened a door on the right. 'Shower and khazi in here. Small basin.' I stuck my head in. Everything in here, including the toilet, seemed to be not quite life-sized and it looked as if the fittings were the 1970s originals. Forward of the bathroom came the bedroom, a queen-sized bed on the left, shelves, a narrow wardrobe and another door, this time on the right. Jake unlocked it and went through; I followed and found myself in a space with steeply sloping sides, a window in each, and a triangular window at the front.

'It's like a loft conversion in here,' I said.

'It's called a cratch. It's where fodder for the horse that pulled the boat was kept. Now with most boats this bit is just covered with a tarp you can roll up but this one has wooden sides.' He undid a couple of bolts on the port side and leant against the wooden slope. The entire side swung up on a hinge. 'You can prop it open and it's like a covered verandah. Neil had it built. Other side opens too. He used to sit and watch birds and things.' He closed and bolted the cratch side and turned to a low double door below the triangular front window. 'Under here is the water tank, and this is where your gas bottles are kept.' He unlocked the gas locker and showed me where the bottles lived and how to switch over from one to the other. 'When the gas runs out, which will happen in the middle of your shower, you'll have to switch bottles. And remember to buy a new one at the next opportunity.'

Back inside, I idly opened cupboards and pulled out the large drawer under the bed. 'What was your friend's name again?'

'Neil. Neil Jenkins.'

'What happened to all his stuff?'

'I think the police got rid of it, but everything that belonged to the boat, so to speak, stayed here. All the kitchen gear and all the things needed to run it.' In the kitchen he opened a cupboard and was rewarded with an avalanche of cheap pots and pans that landed at his feet. He dumped the lot in the sink. Another cubby-hole revealed crockery, and there was a kitchen drawer holding a sad assortment of mismatched cutlery that looked as if it, too, had been bought cheaply forty years ago. From another drawer he produced a hand crank. 'You'll need this,' he said, handing it to me. 'Make sure you don't drop it in the water.'

'Don't tell me I have to start the engine with a hand crank.'

'It's a windlass, you nit, for raising and lowering the paddles.'

'It has paddles?'

'In the locks! To let water in and out! Admit it: you've never been on a bloody narrowboat.'

'True.'

'Any boat?'

'Pedalo, Lake Windermere, 1972.'

'Christ.'

When Jake lifted the engine cover in the back, he squinted down at it and started humming – Jake loved ancient engines – but my own heart sank. Looking over his shoulder, the only thing I recognized was a bank of large black batteries, four in all. The rest could have been an engine or an industrial mincer or a sewage pump for all I knew. Bits of it were furred and corroded metal; other bits were painted in a faintly green colour that used to be fashionable with Soviet car makers back in the 1950s. '*That*,' I said, disheartened by the sight, 'is the boat's engine?'

'It is. It's a diesel engine, made by Lister.'

'I thought they made mouthwash.'

'That's Listerine. Stop mucking about and pay attention. It's a Lister SR2 – remember that, in case you need a part for it or whatever, though they are very reliable. It propels the boat via that shaft down there.'

'How come this engine is so tiny?'

'Because boats float. They used to tow these with one horse, remember? Hence *towpath*. And that was when they were fully laden with coal or whatever. Not only does this little engine power the propeller, it also charges these four batteries. Now, this one' – he tapped the first – 'is your starter battery. It's only to start the engine; it doesn't do anything else. The other three are what's called "leisure batteries". They run everything on board – lights, fridge, water pump, radio, TV, what-have-you. It's all twelve volts.' He straightened up. 'Now for the moment of truth. I had Gary charge the starter battery.' He produced the boat's keys, tied to a lump of wood that had the boat's name burnt into it.

'So they floats if they falls overboard?' I asked.

'Arrr.' Pirate talk had started. He turned the key on the control panel, lights came on, and after a few seconds he turned it further to start the engine. It whirred, coughed, banged and belched black smoke which drifted on the water, then started puttering away like a small tractor. 'Well, shiver me timbers, she's alive. We'll let her run, charge the batteries.' There now followed a lengthy induction into the intricacies of boat life. I listened impatiently while imagining Verity disappearing into the three thousand miles of inland waterways.

I soon learnt that none of the things you take for granted in a house happen on a boat unless you make it happen. The gas for the water heater and cooker came on board in bottles, but if I wanted electricity, I first had to make it by running the engine. There was a solar panel on the roof which worked well in the summer, not so well in winter, but it had been covered by tarpaulin so the leisure batteries were pretty empty. Water had to be taken on at watering points and was moved around the boat by an electric pump. No electricity, no running water.

'What about the toilet? I suppose that goes straight in the canal?' I asked, remembering the taste of canal water.

'Ooooh, no. Dishwater and the water from the shower goes in the canal, but sewage goes into a tank. When it's full, you'll have to pump it out. It's ever such fun,' he promised. He showed me the keys I would need to access water and sewage disposal, and then told me about locks. I must have looked doubtful because he fished out a biro and drew me a diagram on the back of an envelope. I asked a few questions which revealed my lack of understanding. 'All right, all right, I'll get you as far as the Kennet and Avon back in Bath; by then you should have got the hang of it. I hope you've got your credit card polished – the tank's nearly empty. You can refuel at Saltford Marina.'

Jake arranged for Gary to drive his Jaguar to Bath, then, after having checked the boat over, allowed me at the controls. There seemed to be only the one lever. 'How many gears has it got?' I asked.

'Don't be daft. When the lever is upright, like now, it's in neutral. You push the lever forward and the boat goes forward. Push it back and it goes backwards.'

'Where's the brake?'

'Give me strength! Boats don't have brakes! You must think ahead. You slow down in good time, and if you need to stop in a hurry, you go into reverse. In short bursts or you end up going backwards. And remember you can't steer when you're going backwards.'

'You can't? That'll make reverse parking tricky.'

Jake scrunched up the envelope and lobbed it over his shoulder. 'I can see this will take longer than I expected.'

I tried to ask an intelligent question that Jake, with his love of engines, would enjoy answering. 'How many horsepower has it got?'

'About fifteen at full revs.'

'Really? Wow. What's her top speed?'

'About seven miles per hour. Only the speed limit is four.'

'Four?'

'Four. But you're supposed to slow down when you pass moored boats or your wake will make them rock about. And you have to slow down *before* you get to the boats or your wake will still hit them.'

I summarized. 'OK, let me get this straight: I'll be going at four miles per hour?'

'Yes.'

'Slightly less than walking speed?'

'Indeed.'

'But I will have to slow down whenever I see a moored boat?'

'Definitely.'

'Then why don't I walk?'

'You want to walk instead?' Jake asked dangerously.

I pretended to think about it. 'Mmm . . . don't think so.'

'Then go and cast off! And don't let the lines trail in the water!' As soon as I had climbed back on deck, Jake pushed the stern away from the bank, then steered us into the middle of the Feeder and aimed the bow at the lock.

My introduction to the demands of boating was deceptively gentle. The lock-keeper living at the lock-keeper's cottage (where else?) had left the lock gates open. The Avon is tidal but the tide was in our favour, which meant that we could sail straight through. Jake moved the boat gently through the open lock, the sound of the boat's puttering engine reverberating from the brickwork. There was no sign of the lock-keeper. 'And you won't see many of those on your journey,' Jake warned. 'You'll be doing the locks yourself, and I don't mind telling you, it can be quite a palaver if you're on your own.'

'Not to mention dangerous. It killed your friend Neil.' Jake grunted dubiously and kept staring ahead. 'What?'

For a while he did not answer as we encountered a weir, which he gave a respectful berth. We were now on the River Avon, which was far wider here than I had expected. I should have felt elated to be on the move, but Jake's mood had darkened and it was rubbing off on me. 'Here, you take the tiller. Do everything slowly. Yeah, precisely *not* like that – *really* slowly.' I had tried to avoid pointing the bow at a group of ducks and made the boat jink dramatically to the left. I mean, of course, to port. 'Ducks will get out of your way, you nit; you can't run them over. Nice and easy on the steering. It's not like a car where the front changes direction and the arse follows. With a boat, you move the rear and the thing sort of pivots. It's like pushing a pencil around on a table.'

'Aren't we supposed to be on the left anyway?'

'What? No, on waterways you sail more or less in the centre but pass other boats on the right side.'

'Now he tells me.' Being in control of a sixty-foot boat – that's eighteen metres if you're so inclined – and virtually all of it in front of you was as exciting as it was scary.

'You're doing fine,' Jake grumbled. 'It bugged me, Neil dying like that. I mean it worried me. He'd been on the water for nine years, I think. Continuously cruising around. Can you imagine how many locks he must have gone through? Tens of thousands of them. What he didn't know about boating wasn't worth knowing and yet he drowned in a lock.'

'Accidents can happen to anyone,' I said feebly.

'Yeah, but most of them happen to people like you. Neil didn't seem the type. He showed us how to do locks – we did a lot of them together, sometimes side by side if there was room – and one thing he always insisted on was wearing life jackets when doing locks. I thought it made us look like complete amateurs, but he insisted. Not while cruising around but before doing a lock he'd put on his life jacket because if you fall into a lock, with the water surging around you and hardly any space between the boat and the walls, even a good swimmer can drown. And, get this: he said, "What if you fall, knock yourself silly and go in the water? You'll drown before you come to." And that is precisely how he died.'

'Wasn't he wearing his life jacket?'

'No. It was found lying in the boat. On the floor.' In the silence that followed, the engine puttered, ducks paddled near the riverbank. Standing on the deck of the dead man's boat, a feeling of foreboding came over me. At the time I thought it was no more than apprehension about my ignorance concerning canal boating, but I should have listened to it. Looking back on it, perhaps I should have jumped and swum for it.

'Did you tell anyone about this? That he usually wore the jacket?'

'Oh, aye, I gave evidence at the inquest, but the consensus was that Neil was not himself, that he had become mentally unstable or depressed and had begun to neglect things.'

'But?'

'But it still bugs me. Neil was such a happy soul; he really gave the impression that by moving on to the water he had realized his dream and he'd never want anything else. His boat was totally organized, super tidy – Zen-like, you might say – neat like a British army kit laid out for inspection. But when I saw the boat after his death, it looked like a tip.'

'Had the police searched the boat to find any clues? Perhaps that was where the mess came from.'

'Possible, though they don't usually break crockery and just leave everything lying around. If Neil was having some sort of nervous breakdown, then I can't think what had driven him to it.'

'People who live alone can get peculiar. Loneliness can do that.'

'Then make sure you hold on to Annis; you can't afford to get any more peculiar than you are. But Neil didn't feel lonely on the canals. He was a chatty guy, he knew plenty of people on the water. When we cruised with him, he often ran into other boaters he knew, exchanged news, and we'd some-times go to the pub with them. Pubs played quite a big role on our boating holiday – there's loads of them along the canals.'

'That's what I was hoping.'

Once we had steered away from the subject of Neil's death, Jake began to cheer up again. 'That's another thing Sally didn't like about our boating holiday – too many pubs, not enough museums.' He breathed in deeply and sighed contentedly. 'Shame, I could do this all summer – laze about on the canal, cook simple meals or eat at the pub, have a few pints . . .'

'Yes, I look forward to some of that. Sure you don't want to come?'

'Don't tempt me.'

After only half an hour or so on the river I was surprised by how soon the steering of the boat began to feel natural. We encountered little traffic at that end of the river, which meant that once I had snapped out of panic mode, I could enjoy the scenery and the extraordinary lushness of the countryside as we drifted through a nature reserve and past Hanham Green to our left. But even at this gentle speed, it did not take long before my heart sank into my boots when the first lock came into view.

'Hanham Lock is Lock Number One on the Kennet and Avon,' Jake said. 'And we'll teach thee 'ow to use them locks right 'ere, arr.'

We approached the lock, tied up and walked up to it. To say that negotiating locks is a bit of a palaver had been an understatement. Jake was a hard task master. Since I was expected to sail *Dreamcatcher* alone, he just stood beside me, pointing and telling me in pirate speech to 'lift them paddles, open this here gate, arr, like that' and so on until I had the boat in, the lock filled, the upper doors opened and *Dreamcatcher* out again. It wasn't that difficult to understand, just quite a lot of work to progress seventy feet upriver. 'Now if there's no one wanting to use the lock on this side, then go back and close the gates.'

At the time it was still new and interesting and the sun was shining, so I didn't worry. Proud to have done it all by myself, albeit to instructions. The nearby weir scared me a bit, especially after Jake's many predictions of doom should I get too near one, and I marvelled at how people could be so brave to moor so close to it. Or so deaf. There were two riverside pubs that looked tempting, but we had business upriver and puttered on past the Old Lock & Weir and Chequers, which were both doing good lunchtime trade. Tight bends soon tested my navigational, erm, skills. We were going upstream against the current, which meant that to achieve even four miles per hour needed quite a bit of throttle and more careful steering than on the placid waters of a canal. The landscape changed to lush watery meadows on one side and steep wooded slopes on the other. When we got to the next lock at Keynsham, overlooked by another pub and their patrons, Jake made me do everything by myself without comment. A boat had just come out of the lock which meant I could just putter in, make the boat fast, close the gates and raise the paddles with the windlass which, by the way, is a heavy lump of metal – winding paddles up is good exercise. 'There's one thing that can scupper your plans,' Jake warned. 'Dropping your windlass in the water. Without it, you're stuffed and going nowhere. If it happens, you'll have to dive for it. You don't want to have to dive in the river. Or a lock. Or anywhere. So don't drop it.'

I gripped it tightly. 'I'll try to remember.'

Next we stopped at a water point and filled *Dreamcatcher*'s water tank. By now there was enough charge in the batteries to run the water pump and therefore use the loo, which went a long way to endear the boat to me.

I approached the next locks with even greater trepidation, my hands aching from gripping the windlass as if my life depended on it, glaring at the cill markings and getting a lot more exercise than I had bargained for on something that sounded as relaxing as 'river cruise' or 'boating'. Under the twin-arched bridge 211 (they all have numbers, helps you work out where you are), then three more locks before finally we approached Saltford Marina. I had hoped Jake would take over, but he just stood with arms folded and grinned sadistically as I crawled into the marina, expecting to crash into every boat I saw. I landed us at visitor moorings with a bump, a scrape and a groan, lots of backward throttle and apologies, but Jake seemed unconcerned.

The place was large, with sixty-odd boats of all types: white fibreglass yachts, narrowboats and widebeams. As I looked about at the rows of narrowboats moored one next to the other like cars in a car park, I realized that what they saw from their windows was not the lush countryside or the river but the windows of the boat next to them. But we would be here for only a fleeting moment, I thought, until we once more roamed free on the river. It was over an hour later that I stood again at the tiller, weak-kneed, wearing my brand-new blue-and-orange lifejacket and still holding the receipt for my refuelling. '*Two hundred and forty litres*!' I said incredulously, perhaps for the tenth time. 'You could have warned me.'

'Now you've got a full tank, you won't have to worry about fuel again for months; you can use as much electricity as you like – just run the engine. Relax, and get us out of here. I'll have Gary waiting for me with my motor in Bath.'

Seeing the country from the river was so different that I
often lost all sense of where I was. Jake was better at it and
kept up a running commentary for my benefit. 'That bridge
coming up is where the A4 crosses the river. Next up is Bath
Marina in Newbridge and the bridge in question is called New
Bridge, would you believe it? Which it was in the eighteenth
century. You'd think they'd rename the thing . . .'

I was glad we did not have to stop at Bath Marina, the site
of my illicit research. People usually break *into* places; trust
me to break *out* of a place. I instinctively ducked my head as
we passed it. The lock at Weston was Number 6. 'Your next
lock will be on the Kennet and Avon,' announced Jake, as
though we were heading for the Zambezi River after a long
and arduous journey.

The landmarks around me became more familiar, although
not all of them were as good to look at from the back. Neither
of us was in the mood for sightseeing anyway; I was itching
to get properly under way and Jake had given up much of his
day to get me kitted out and show me how to use the boat.
'It's very good of you to let me take out your boat,' I said as
at last we neared the turn-off to the canal. In fact, I had been
wondering, with growing suspicion, just why Jake would
entrust me with a sixty-foot boat which, admittedly, he had
acquired gratis, and then go through the palaver of getting it
back in the water.

'You're sort of doing me a favour,' he admitted. 'Keeping
it parked on the trading estate costs money, and getting a
permanent mooring for it is bloody expensive. I just couldn't
justify the expense, considering wild horses wouldn't be able
to drag Sally on to it, especially since what happened to Neil
in the lock. *Dreamcatcher* is still insured and licensed for
about six months, so having you putter about on it suits me
well and for once you are saving me money. When you get
back, I'll probably put it up for sale. If you don't sink it or
set fire to it. In which case, please make sure you do it properly
and I'll just collect the insurance,' he added.

The shores of the river on either side had been tamed with
a lot of stone and concrete which was not much to look at,
so I nearly missed my exit. Even Jake was a bit vague about

where exactly it was – the entrance to the Kennet and Avon Canal. Unless you are an experienced boater, it looks like a tiny magic door in the wall. This time Jake helped with the lock gates to speed up our progress since he knew what I didn't: as soon as we left the river we had six locks to pass through in quick succession. The first one was much deeper than any we had encountered so far, but it was itself dwarfed by the next one, which was huge. It was cavernous and so deep I thought it was going to swallow us like an enormous wet and algae-covered mouth. The massive gates were so heavy that I struggled to move them at all, which had me worried. 'Are there any more of these?' I asked, pushing backwards and breaking into a sweat.

'Never saw one like it on our entire trip, so I wouldn't worry,' Jake said. I later found out that we were negotiating the second deepest lock in the entire country. The nearby church warned us 'Prepare to Meet Your God', in three-foot-high letters on its roof, which did nothing to lighten the mood as we sweated and worked our way through the locks, though they became much easier and the views prettier. Lock 13, Jake assured me when we reached it, would be the last one for quite a long stretch.

'This is where they found *Dreamcatcher* unattended,' he said, 'and eventually they found Neil's body, barely visible, in that furthest corner there. I wish I had brought some flowers or something to throw in. Though chucking things in a lock is not the done thing, I suppose.'

We went through it in respectful silence after that, while I imagined Neil somehow slipping, falling, knocking himself senseless and tipping overboard, unconscious or semi-conscious in the lock, his lungs filling with murky canal water. I was glad I was wearing a life jacket. Jake had refused to spend money on one for himself just for the day and, rather stingily, I hadn't offered to buy one for him as I was still in shock after having bought enough diesel to circumnavigate the country. I was soon shaken out of my quiet reverie, though, by a phenomenon we had not encountered before – heavy traffic.

Once we had passed the Bath Boat Hire place, which was

probably responsible for overpopulating this stretch of the canal, there were boats everywhere. The forecast for the foreseeable future was for warm and dry weather and a lot of people, for some reason mainly groups of shirtless males, had hit on the same idea: 'Let's hire a boat, get sunburnt and drink our weight in tinned lager!'

I now found myself passing more familiar territory as the canal cut through Sydney Gardens, but we made little progress. The towpath was now busy and there was no sign of the homeless man who had shared his chicken broth with me. There were queues of boats wanting to pass under the bridges and boaters as inexperienced as me were bumping into each other's vessels. One of the boats pumped out some kind of booming dance music at an astonishing volume, though the nine half-naked men that populated the deck and roof of the boat looked too far gone to dance. All of them were pink of face and shoulders and looked exceedingly if brainlessly happy. Eventually, we managed to pass under the bridge where I had come a cropper on my bicycle. I told Jake about it.

'You gave the bike away? That was a stupid thing to do,' was his considered opinion.

'I was a bit disenchanted with the thing. To tell you the truth, it was crap.'

'You'll need a bike on the canal unless you want to take up jogging. Without a bike, you might have to do long treks on foot to get into towns and to and from shops and so on. The nearest bus stop could be miles away from where you find yourself moored.'

'I can't afford to buy a bicycle after, ironically, having bought enough fuel to fill up half a car park of diesel cars,' I complained.

'Yeah, yeah, yeah. I have a solution for that as well. Come up and see me before you set off.'

I was now retracing my damp bicycle journey, only considerably more slowly, and we were heading for Bathampton, along with everyone else, it seemed. We had survived all day on plastic triangles of cheese-and-tomato sandwiches and fizzy pop and were both hungry, but Jake wouldn't hear of going to the George for food. 'I'm taking Sally out for dinner later.

I've arranged for Gary to find us at the café on the other side of the bridge.' We were both tired out and Jake was now impatient to get off the boat. We had to moor quite a way below the George Inn, such was the demand around here today.

The Raft, on the other side of the bridge, was a floating café, a widebeam river barge moored craftily opposite a school full of ice-cream-hungry children. It had tables on board as well as on both sides of the path that ran past it. The place was doing a roaring trade and every table was taken. We armed ourselves with cappuccinos and the last two slices of walnut cake and collapsed on the grass. I hadn't done this much exercise in years.

'Do you good,' was Jake's verdict. 'All that sitting in cars watching people can't be healthy for you.'

We didn't have long to wait for Gary to turn up. In fact, he had got here before us and, not seeing us at the café, had sensibly whiled away the time downing pints outside the George. He did not seem to mind having to play ferry pilot for Jake's car, which made me suspect that either he got paid well or he owed Jake a favour. I already owed Jake so many favours I might one day have to work for him full-time without pay. Gary waited patiently for us to stuff ourselves with coffee and cake, then Jake dropped him at the train station on the way to driving me home.

Perhaps there was something in this exercise lark because I slept exceedingly well and rose full of optimism. Then my muscles woke up too and started up a chorus of complaints. Apparently, I had used groups of muscles that had considered themselves safely retired long ago. I ran myself a bath, added half a bottle of 'moisturizing foam bath' that Annis had carelessly left behind and lowered my creaking body into it until some of the knots in my disgruntled musculature had dissolved. But I could not lie around here for long – no, I had a boat to kit out. I wanted to get back on it as soon as I could; having left it on a forty-eight-hour mooring close to a pub made me nervous as now I felt responsible for the thing, no matter what Jake had said about an insurance write-off. I parked the Jazz and its six-hundred-litre boot space in the supermarket car park and continued to cripple my finances, first in the super-market and then at the farmers' market that was in full swing under the roof of the old Green Park station. I didn't notice the note under the windscreen wiper until after I had loaded the boot and sat behind the wheel. It was a folded-up piece of notepaper, not a flyer, so I got out and retrieved it.

It was handwritten in (expensive) biro. 'Dear Mr Honeysett, I have still not been able to make contact with my niece. If you have had any news of her please call me. Here is my number again.' There followed a mobile number and a signa-ture: Christine Reiner. I retrieved the till receipt on which Verity's 'aunt' had originally given me her number. The number was the same, so was the handwriting, as far as I could tell from just the name and numbers. However, auntie couldn't remember how to spell her own name: on the first note it was 'Rainer', on the new one clearly 'Reiner'. I made a show of carefully refolding the note and putting it in my pocket in case I was being watched. Surreptitiously, I looked about me as I got back into the car, wondering how they had found me here. It was hard to believe that the woman had remembered my car and number plate and then chanced upon it while doing her shopping, especially if she lived in Cheltenham. Or Belgium. It could only mean one thing: auntie had followed me. And, knowing from personal experience just how tedious following people was, if she was bothering to follow me, then she must want Verity badly. For a moment I considered calling the number, pretending I had heard from Verity and sending her on a wild goose chase to the other end of the country, but it struck me as less than fiendishly clever as a plan. It also meant I would have to shake off anyone following me before I stepped on to the boat.

The problem with having your eyes glued to your rear-view mirror is that you don't pay enough attention to where you are going. I had two close shaves and drove smack through a red light, the horn from an irate driver chasing me off the junction; looking back, though, I could see no one else had jumped the lights to keep up with me. Now was the time to shake off any pursuit. For nearly half an hour I drove like an idiot, down tiny streets and up narrow lanes, parking up from time to time to see if anyone followed. Either no one was or they were very good. The third possibility did not occur to me at the time.

Eventually, I deemed it safe enough to drive my purchases to the canal. I staggered back and forth between car and boat until I had thrown it all at the minute galley which disappeared under it. I got the fridge to work and lamented the pitiful dimensions of its ice box, the general lack of storage space and my own idiocy; not only did I have enough fuel for six months, I now had the food to go with it.

Jake was busy. Saturday was a favourite time for owners of classic cars to find things wrong with their ancient chariots and to discover that they had to spend yet another fortune to keep the thing roadworthy. This suited me since it might serve to distract him from the lamentable state of the Jazz's body-work and windows. Eventually, I managed to prize him from his workshop. 'You mentioned a bicycle?'

'Oh yeah, I got it out for you.'

He had. 'But it's pink. And it's a tandem.'

It was, in fact, a pink tandem with black polka dots. He dinged the bell on it, which was also pink. It worked. 'Naturally. We bought it for our own narrowboat trip. And Sally picked the colour.'

'I'll look ridiculous riding that.'

'That's no problem – you always look ridiculous. Anyway, you might make a friend out there. Take it or leave it.'

I took it. I was wheeling the immaculate tandem towards the less-than-immaculate Jazz which I had hidden behind a customer's ancient Austin. 'Perhaps you could ask around about Neil,' Jake suggested lightly. 'You know, see if anyone has an idea what might have changed him like that. People who knew him will recognize *Dreamcatcher*.' Another prophetic remark I would remember later. Jake turned back to his workshop and waiting customers without having noticed the state of the Jazz. I fought with the ridiculously long tandem which took up the whole length of the car and drove it back to Mill House.

*       *       *

As soon as I stood in the quiet sunny yard next to the car, I got an odd kind of feeling and there was no Jake to tell me that it was because I was an odd kind of man. The sun was sinking and there was a pleasant breeze that stirred the grasses in the meadow. The studio barn at the top stood in the shadow of the belt of trees behind it; there was birdsong. And yet I felt as though I had walked into a gunman's crosshairs, and standing still was to invite disaster. I also had the distinct feeling I would feel better with a .38 in my pocket.

The moment I got through the door I knew that someone had been in the house. Or still was. At first I could not tell why, but I practically held my breath until I had reached the kitchen drawer and my hand had closed on the grip of the Webley. If you are susceptible to it, then the seduction of the gun begins the moment you grasp it; it is as though the illusion of safety travels up your arm into your brain. I breathed more easily and began to search the house. In Annis's absence, the kitchen had become the kind of tip where it was impossible to tell if an intruder had turned it upside down. The sitting room looked deceptively undisturbed until I examined the old-fashioned door to the verandah; it had been forced, which wasn't difficult. Quietly and very slowly, I crept through the house, examining every nook, cranny and cupboard where an intruder might have hidden on my arrival. When I was sure the ground floor was clear, I moved up the creaking stairs. I was not in the mood for being jumped, which would most likely result in me shooting several large-calibre holes into the house. I wrenched open the door to the upstairs bathroom and, despite my fear, had to smile – the place smelled as if someone hadn't been able to resist trying out Annis's collection of perfumes and body sprays, which made me think that perhaps my visitor was female, maybe auntie herself. Somehow this lessened my fear, which serves as another illustration of the stupidity of the male brain. I poked the Webley under beds and into wardrobes without a sign of my visitor until I reached my attic office. Someone had taken out their own frustration on the place. It was a tip and for once I was not to blame. Papers strewn about, every drawer pulled out and emptied on to the floor, the computer still on, my email account still showing, the idiocy of 'keep me logged in' clear to see.

Not that auntie had learnt anything about Verity's where-abouts. Very briefly, I wondered whether this might have nothing to do with Verity and those who were trying to find her; could this be to do with the Blinkhorns' insurance fraud? Had Janette found out my real identity, tracked me down and broken in to see what, if anything, I had on the pair? In which case, she should have felt reassured since I had precisely nothing. But it seemed an outlandish career move for the grieving widow and I dismissed that line of thought.

I called Tim at work. I wished I could say that Tim owed me a favour, but I knew that the balance sheet of favours was weighted heavily against me, so I was pleasantly surprised when Tim said, 'Yeah, sure, don't mind house-sitting your place; it'll be like a holiday. Also,' he added more thoughtfully, 'ever since we came for supper at yours, Becks has been saying what a *large* place it was and how *small* my flat is.'

'It's when she starts complaining about there not being much space in the back of your Audi that you want to start worrying. She'll be thinking child seat then.'

'Tell you the truth, I've been thinking child seat lately.'

'Really? Fatherhood?' It felt as if my universe was tilting. For how many years now had Tim, Annis and I celebrated our child-free status and the freedoms it afforded us? 'You're serious about Rebecca, then.'

'Yes.' Another shock to my system. I could not remember Tim ever having expressed an affirmative with 'yes'. 'Yup', 'sort of', 'yeah' and 'uh-huh'. Not 'yes'. This was serious stuff, but I thought I could probably live with it.

Tim promised to spend as many nights at Mill House as he could and make the place look lived-in while I was away. Someone had also been in the studio, although it hadn't been necessary to break in since the sash windows we bodged into the wall are easily opened from the outside. It had been left open. Nothing was missing, which was just as well; have you seen the price of paint? I found myself a couple of wine crates and crammed them with everything a painter might need on a long boat trip and several things he might not: pencils, erasers, Indian ink, dip pens, spare nibs, waterproof fineliners in six sizes, spare waterproof fineliners in six sizes, watercolour box, china palette, plastic palette, tubes of paint, spare half pans of paint, collapsible travel brushes, ordinary brushes, more brushes, gum Arabic (never used) and lifting preparation (ditto). I grabbed another box: sketchbooks, gummed water- colour blocks, loose sheets of watercolour paper (three grades), cartridge pads, gum strip, masking tape, sponges, cotton rags, roll of kitchen towel, jam jars, bulldog clips and rubber bands. I staggered up and down the meadow to the car and back until it was all stowed in what space was left once I had stuffed clothes and bed linen into the corners. You were thinking I had forgotten my collapsible camping stool and my travel easel? Already in the car. I used string to tie down the boot lid as it would no longer shut.

The sixty-foot boat which had, when I first set foot on it, seemed to have all the space a man could need for his few worldly possessions had now turned into a giant jigsaw puzzle where a mischievous soul had thrown a handful of spare pieces into the box. Where was all this stuff going to go? After a two-hour fight with all the things I had unwisely deemed indispensable, I still kept stumbling over this and had to squeeze around that. Couples, I reminded myself, lived on boats this size. People raised children on boats. I was born, as shall become obvious if it isn't already, without a single boating gene in my body.

'Got your mobile?' asked Tim.

'Yup.'

'Charger?' reminded Rebecca.

'Packed.'

'Torch, spare batteries?' Tim probed. 'Toothbrush? Nail file?'

'Packed.'

'Bog roll?'

'Shit!'

'Quite.'

I ran upstairs and grabbed all the spare toilet rolls. Tim and Rebecca had come up after work to drive me to the boat so I could leave the Honda in the relative safety of the yard at Mill House. I had briefed Tim about being followed so he could take evasive action when he drove all three of us and a bootful of extra must-have items to the canal. He embraced this so enthusiastically that it took us an extra half hour to make it to Bathampton.

I saw with relief that the boat was still there. Boats did get stolen, mostly by drunk joyriders after the pub, but *Dreamcatcher* lay peacefully moored near the George Inn. Once we were on the boat, I stuffed all the extra items into the corners – I had added all my favourite cooking gear – knives, saucepans, wok, omelette pan, Turkish coffee pot and cups – and put the revolver in the cutlery drawer. Tim did the honours at the George and with two folding chairs and me on my collapsible painting stool we savoured the balmy atmosphere at dusk on the stern deck, watching the ducks float by while sipping our drinks. People strolling past smiled or gave us enviable looks. I had arrived.

'Very pleasant. I could get used to this,' was Tim's verdict.

But Rebecca's mood was not as carefree. 'Do you think they might come back?'

'Who? Back where?' I asked.

'Back to the house! I worry. You've asked Timmy to house-sit and I worry they'll come back. If you disturbed them when you came home earlier, they might come back and search the house again.'

'Shouldn't think so. I think they were probably done.'

'They are dangerous people, Chris; they killed one poor chap in an arson attack and tried to do away with another. What if they put petrol through *your* letterbox? With Timmy in the house?'

'We've got smoke alarms,' I suggested.

'Fire extinguishers?'

'Not as such . . .'

'If there's a fire, we'll jump for it,' said Tim soothingly.

'We?' asked Rebecca.

'You're staying too, aren't you?'

She gave me an exasperated look that seemed to say *Now*

*look what you got me into*, before she decided. 'Yeah, all right, I'm a light sleeper. But I'll be bringing my own fire extinguisher . . .'

When it got dark and they rose to leave for home, I slipped Tim two keys. 'The Yale key is from the gun locker, the other one from the drawer in the little writing desk where the cartridges are kept. If you hear intruders, use the blue cartridges.' I had emptied the bird shot from half a dozen twelve-bore cartridges and filled them with Arborio rice; less lethal but still devastating at close quarters.

'I'll keep them handy, just in case.'

The two wished me good luck and disappeared hand in hand up the towpath into the night.

The nearest street lamps were few and far between and so far away that beyond the windows all was black. I shut the curtains and closed both doors. The twelve-volt lighting and the dimensions reminded me of old-fashioned train carriages. This was it then: I was on my own on the boat, skipper of the *Dreamcatcher*. I made up the bed and got inside. It felt very comfortable. I turned out the light and lay awake, staring into the darkness, wondering what I had forgotten to bring.

# NINE

'Sugar!' I swore politely as I stood in the galley, because that's what I had forgotten to bring. I liked it in Greek coffee which I had hoped would wake me up on this bleary morning. I had spent a night of interrupted sleep, groping around for the bathroom in unfamiliar surroundings and lying awake for long stretches, listening to the night sounds of the canal's wildlife through the open window in my sleeping quarters. I had finally fallen asleep again just as it threatened to grow light outside and then slept into the middle of the morning. Now I hunted around in all the cupboards and eventually found a mug stuffed with sachets of sugar, pinched from various cafés no doubt by the previous owner. The sugar inside had clumped from the damp but I didn't mind; I liked my Greek coffee *métrio*, with a small spoonful of sugar. When I had warmed a couple of croissants in the oven, I took my breakfast in the sunshine at a small folding table on the stern deck. Croissants to go with my quince jam, I guessed, would be hard to come by in future. They were a mundane thing at home, but here they felt like a luxury and I savoured every mouthful, blowing only a few crumbs to an unimpressed audience of ducks. By the time I had finished my second coffee, it was after eleven and I felt suspiciously relaxed. As I finally started the engine and cast off, a tiny part of my brain was doing a little jig. It was the part that thought my chances of catching up with Verity were so tiny that really what I was doing was embarking on a painting holiday. I spoke sternly to it in a grown-up voice, reminding it what we were here for. It blew me a raspberry.

Having already had a day of boating under my belt, I now felt like an old hand at this as I pushed off from the cut. Wrong again. Immediately, I got beeped at by a narrowboat whose approach I had failed to hear over the sound of my own engine. I hastily reversed out of its way, too enthusiastically as it turned out, and slammed the boat against the mooring, back where I had started. Take number two. I made sure nothing was coming either way. Revs and heartbeat settled at a steady pace as I finally set off. Just on the other side of the bridge, the Raft Café was already doing good business and I passed it extra slowly so as not to upset people's cups of coffee, trying to look as though I'd been narrowboating all my life. A small boy holding a plastic toy in one hand and an ice cream cone in the other stared as I puttered by. I waved. The kid waved back with the ice-cream hand. The ice cream fell off the cone on to the ground. The child's inconsolable wailing followed me for a while as I accelerated away. I put 'waving at children' on my not-to-do-on-a-narrowboat list. I immediately had to slow down again. You need to slow down when passing moored or oncoming boats; traffic was already quite frequent and there seemed to be no end to moored boats around here. I began to understand why the Road Movie is a more successful genre than the Canal Movie: a boat chase at three miles per hour would be nail-biting for all the wrong reasons. Had I done something really stupid by abandoning the road and taking to the water? I passed a boat coming the other way – not a hire boat but a private one with its roof full of logs; the skipper acknowledged me, I smiled back. Nah, this was fine. Verity was not my responsibility. If I found her, I'd make sure she was safe, but it was unlikely I'd ever hear from her again. And I was patently running away from my real job of watching Janette Blinkhorn. Every time I came past anglers, I scrutinized the still figures as I dutifully throttled back, but I could not possibly pretend that this had anything to do with earning money. What those sullen men were hoping to drag from the dark waters of the canal I had no idea. I took deep breaths of fresh country air scented with diesel fumes from my own engine and puttered, smiling, towards bankruptcy.

Eventually, the moored boats thinned out and I achieved something close to the heady top speed of four mph. I may have even broken the speed limit here and there, but the engine note was most pleasing at walking pace. There was very little current on this stretch and the tiller only needed gentle movements to keep the boat in the centre of the water or to move it gently to the right when traffic came the other way.

Ah . . . lovely . . . *nice*. On a sunny September day, what could be better than taking your time, letting the canal make all the decisions and getting nowhere fast? How could this possibly be improved? Why, with a mug of tea, of course. But you can no more make tea while skippering a narrowboat than you could while diving the Great Barrier Reef. Even though you're only twenty feet from the kettle. I pootled on until I got really quite thirsty. Parched. Gasping for a mug of.

Of course, with a car or even a camper van you just pull in at a convenient place and put the handbrake on. Stopping a sixty-foot narrowboat is a trifle more involved. You can't just stop the engine and dive inside to make tea. The boat will move. You'll drift into moored boats or block the traffic. It will do nothing for your popularity ratings. Eventually, I managed to spot a likely place that didn't have a 'Private Mooring' sign on it and gently parked the boat, grabbed the heavy steel mooring pins, the mallet and the stern rope, and hopped ashore. While holding firmly on to the rope, I hammered the reluctant mooring pin into the ground, then tied the boat to it with a granny bow because I had forgotten the knots Jake had showed me, then repeated the operation at the other end of the boat. Great, I had successfully parked and only hit my thumb once. In the galley I put the kettle on and made a mug of tea which I took outside and set down near the throttle. Then I hopped ashore and pulled pins, coiled ropes, stowed pins and mallet and got under way again. I put 'driving off without a mug of tea' on my not-to-do-on-a-narrowboat list. I drank my tea, I puttered along; all was well with the world for ten minutes. Then I needed the loo. This is where you normally call to your shipmate to 'hold the tiller for a moment' while you nip below, but for the single-handed boater there is no such luxury: a call of nature means mooring pins and ropes and mallets and hitting of thumbs, then doing it all in reverse (the mooring bit) and asking yourself searching questions about whether there is anything else you might want in five or eight or ten minutes. No? Then we shall proceed.

The novelty of driving a houseboat around kept me occupied,

and the slowly changing scenery fascinated me. In a car or on a train the land flies past; you have little time to rest your eyes on anything, none at all if you happen to be the driver. On a boat, however, everything happens at a stately pace and trees, wildlife, people and buildings all roll past to be examined at leisure. It was after lunchtime and my stomach was rumbling, but I felt I had not done enough catching up to warrant tying up again and breaking for lunch. Not that there had been much of a chance to moor the boat anyway. I was coming up to Dundas Aqueduct and suddenly the place became busy. For quite a while I had noticed many cyclists on the towpath; now they were coming thick and fast, which made me suspect that there had to be a hire place nearby. Boats were moored nose to tail along this stretch, many of them permanently, judging by the encrustations, as I thought of them, of flower pots, bicycles, log piles and windmills. At last I came into a kind of basin and a wharf with a small crane or two. There were boats manoeuvring and boats queuing, and I realized that I had reached Dundas Aqueduct, which shoots off at a surprising right angle. I couldn't see it from the boat but it was the River Avon and the railway line below which it crossed in a hundred-and-fifty-yard-long channel, only wide enough for a single boat – hence the queue. Eventually, it was my turn and I threaded the nose of *Dreamcatcher*, sixty feet ahead of me, into the mouth of the aqueduct and managed it without ramming anything. Perhaps I was getting the hang of this. The aqueduct also sits astride the border between Somerset and Wiltshire, which meant that for a short moment the front of the boat was in one county while her skipper was still in another one. Another small basin, then a sharp turn right towards Bradford-on-Avon, a small town straddling the river. There were boats moored permanently on this side of the aqueduct too, but eventually the traffic thinned out again. I was threading my way past a double-parked boat and a couple of people in plastic canoes paddling along when an oncoming narrowboat came noisily chugging towards me at twice the normal speed. Loud music was booming from unseen speakers; drunk half-dressed blokes were dancing on the foredeck and the roof. Whoever was skippering it had his forward vision

impaired by dancing figures and too much lager. The canoes
scooted out of my way, but the oncoming boat started to zigzag
and eventually aimed to pass me on the wrong side. I pushed
the tiller hard over and gave it more throttle to avoid crashing
into the boat. One or two of the drunks cheered as I narrowly
avoided their bow while burying my own decisively in the
opposite bank.

The boat chugged away towards the aqueduct and took the
noise with it. The couple in the plastic dinghies, one yellow,
one red, glided almost silently past me and disappeared into
the distance. I put the engine in reverse. The boat didn't budge.
I gave it more throttle. This churned up the water into a muddy
froth but the boat refused to move. Armed with the boat hook
which lived on the roof, I went forward on the outside of the
boat by shuffling sideways on the narrow ledge that runs around
the edge of it. The branches of an overhanging shrub made
my life more difficult than necessary as I poked ineffectually
at the bank, hoping to dislodge the bow, with no effect whatsoever. I shuffled back. Mysteriously, now that I had run
*Dreamcatcher* aground, there appeared to be no more boat
traffic at all, though a few walkers on the towpath opposite
gave me curious looks of the look-at-that-idiot-stuck-in-the-
bank variety. Eventually, from the direction of the aqueduct,
a boat did appear – not a narrowboat but one of those high-
prowed, fibreglass cabin cruisers. It was large and looked brand
new and certainly big enough to give me a tow; it proclaimed
its name – *Free Spirit* – in large swirly writing on the prow.
Only the head of the skipper was visible above his windscreen;
the man wore sunglasses and seemed oblivious to my waving
from the tangle of shrubbery covering my boat's bow. I clambered towards the stern as fast as I could and called, but the
cruiser passed right under my nose without its skipper taking
any notice of my calls and animated waving. There was another
man on board, sitting in the stern, but he was facing forward
and did not look back, oblivious to my hailing them.

I had another go with the throttle, backwards, forwards,
backwards, hoping to get a rocking motion going as you would
with a stuck car, but instead I created a muddy whirlpool that
spread in an embarrassing circle in all directions. I stopped

when a narrowboat appeared from the aqueduct side. I got my waving in early this time and, to make sure it wasn't mistaken for over-enthusiastic friendliness, waved with my boat hook. The approaching boat slowed and with obvious expertise glided to a halt precisely so our two sterns drew level. The entire boat was painted in a dusky purple and was called *Morning Mist*. Her skipper was a man in his forties, dressed, despite the sunshine, completely in black: black jeans, trainers and T-shirt. His nose was long and bent slightly to starboard, below which an eight-inch-long pointy beard compensated for the virtually non-existent hair on his suntanned head. When he opened his mouth to speak, a gold tooth flashed in the sunshine. 'Stuffed it into the bank, have you? How on earth did you manage that?' I started making my excuses, describing the incident and the boat I blamed for my predicament. 'Yup, saw them a moment ago, crashing into the entrance to the viaduct. Pissed as the proverbial. Hire companies simply don't care who they give day boats to. And, of course, they didn't stop?'

'No, neither did the next boat that came along, even though I waved and called.'

'Really? Another hire boat, I suspect.'

'It wasn't a narrowboat; it was one of those cabin cruisers.'

'Oh, a plastic duck – they don't count, a different breed of people,' he said dismissively. 'Don't share our ethos, do they?'

I didn't wait for an explanation as to what this ethos consisted of; instead, I asked, 'So, do you think you could pull me off?'

'Never on a first date.'

'Let me rephrase that.'

'Don't bother. We'll have you out of there in no time. I'm Vince, by the way.' Vince spoke with an educated voice and just a hint of Somerset, and he knew his stuff. He handed me a length of rope and told me to make it fast on *Dreamcatcher*'s bow, then he manoeuvred *Morning Mist* into position. We opened our throttles together, me in reverse, Vince forward, and *Dreamcatcher* slid off the bank to freedom.

'Thanks, Vince, I owe you one. Actually, I was just about to stop and rustle up some food. Fancy it?'

'Smashing idea.'

We moored not much further along behind a line of other

boats and Vince came aboard. He was so tall he could only just stand upright in a narrowboat. He scrutinized every detail of *Dreamcatcher* with a practised eye. 'What's the engine?'

I remembered that one. 'Lister SR2,' I said casually.

'Vintage.'

'Yours?' I asked as though I cared.

'Beta Marine.'

'Oh?'

'Yeah, it's a marinized Kubota engine.'

'Ah yes, of course,' I said. 'Reliable,' I hazarded.

'Totally.' Vince remarked on the workmanship and the solid oak panelling of *Dreamcatcher*. 'Mine's a symphony of plywood and yacht varnish, but that's how they come these days.'

I started by grinding coffee beans in a hand grinder and made a cafetière of coffee. 'Ah, real coffee, eh?' sighed Vince when he sampled it. 'It's all instant on board the *Mist* but I do stop for a cappuccino every once in a while. This is good stuff.' I had taken on board every bean of Annis's coffee collection. 'You don't mind if I smoke, I take it,' he said, indicating my ashtray. 'Yeah, sometimes I tell people I took to life on the water because the canals are the last place on earth where you're allowed to light up.' He took out a tobacco tin, rolled himself a fat cigarette in the blink of an eye and lit it with a brass Zippo lighter.

'You've been living on the canals long?' I asked, rattling my pots and pans.

Vince had a habit of stroking his beard before answering any question, as though he had been asked to consider a philosophical problem. 'Seven years this October. You?'

I consulted my watch. 'Coming up to five hours now.'

Vince spilled coffee into his beard and broke into hysterical laughter followed by a coughing fit. 'Ah, sorry,' he said when he had recovered. 'You had me fooled for a minute. It doesn't feel like a holiday boat; it has a lived-in feel, if you know what I mean, and it's bloody crammed with stuff. So you've only just taken to the water?' he asked incredulously.

Foolishly, I hadn't prepared for this question. It hadn't occurred to me to prepare a cover story and now I played for time while searching cupboards. I couldn't have said why, but I somehow felt reluctant to divulge the whole saga to Vince, no matter how helpful he had been. I could say I was on a painting holiday or I could pretend I was starting life on the water. I compromised. 'I'm trying it out for a few weeks, to see if I like it.'

Vince knitted his brow and looked unconvinced. 'But it's your boat?'

'Borrowed it off a friend.'

'He must be a good friend. And how are you planning to finance a life on the cut, then, if you don't mind me asking?'

Vince appeared to be a better detective than I was, since he would soon know more about me (or the lies I was telling him) than I did about him. I was glad I could point to the pile of painting gear piled up in the front of the boat. 'I'm a painter. Thought I might paint views of canal life.'

'Nice work if you can get it. So where are you heading?'

I *really* should have thought of some sort of story. 'Erm . . . I . . . erm, thought I'd let the canal take me wherever, since I have no idea what's out there. How about you?'

Vince stroked his beard. 'Slowly drifting up north. I'm not in a particular hurry either. This smells good,' he said, changing the subject. 'What are you making?'

'Spaghetti carbonara; I thought it would be an appropriate dish to start with.'

'What, you're making it from scratch?' He abandoned his cigarette and came over to watch. 'It's all tins and packaged stuff with me; I never learnt to cook properly. Used to have a wife for that kind of thing,' he added more quietly. 'But I can afford to eat out quite a bit. Lots of good pub food along the canals,' he added in an upbeat tone.

'You're not poor, then?'

'Evil landlord,' he said without taking his eyes off the cooker. 'I'm renting out my house in Bath to tourists in the summer, students for the rest of the year. I won't go hungry in my old age. I'm hungry now, though. What do you mean, this dish is "appropriate"?'

'Spaghetti carbonara is named after the *carbonari* – coal sellers. Imagine you're a boatman a hundred years ago – no fridges back then. But what goes into a carbonara is wine, garlic, smoked bacon, eggs and parmesan, all of which keep for a long time without a fridge, and making carbonara takes about as long as it takes to boil pasta.'

'Really? Then I want to learn it.' Vince watched my every move as I whisked eggs in a bowl and grated parmesan into it. 'You should be a TV chef with your own show. *The Narrowboat Kitchen* – I can see it now.'

While the pasta cooked, I fried the chopped bacon with a couple of cloves of unpeeled garlic, and doused it with a shot of white wine. I poured the drained spaghetti into the egg mix and stirred like mad, then tipped it into the frying pan with the bacon and gave it a final stir. 'There, done – twelve and a half minutes.'

Vince was wide-eyed. 'OK, I'm impressed now.' We wolfed down mountains of spaghetti as though we had been hauling coal up the canal since dawn. 'You could always open a caff on your boat – this is good grub. I mean you could charge a fiver for this no problem and it took you twelve and a half minutes to do. I'd definitely pay a fiver for it.'

'Any time.'

'Rename the boat *Dreamkitchen*. I can see it now.'

We cast off at the same time and I followed *Morning Mist* and the evil but appreciative landlord Vince up the canal. Another aqueduct at Avoncliff was also teeming with visitors. There was a weir and the ruins of a mill below. I had no idea what the mill used to do, but it seemed insane to have all that water power go to waste instead of making free electricity with it. My own power situation looked rosy; the engine had charged all my batteries, and even if I should decide to park up for a few days, my solar panels would be more than enough to keep my pumps, fridge, hairdryer and radio going. Both my gas bottles were full, so were diesel and water tanks, and the sewage tank was still gloriously empty. There was enough food on board for many a carbonara and there seemed to be no shortage of pubs along this canal. I had a sudden feeling of having run away from school or even of having been set free. No man is an island, John Donne thought (though he had a crater named after him), but I thought perhaps a man could be happy on a floating island, catching dreams in a saucepan. Until, that is, he sees a lock gate looming ahead.

I had worried about doing locks by myself, although thanks to Jake I knew how to do it now, but with Vince going in the same direction we could share the lock and the work. On a sunny day the lock at Bradford-on-Avon attracts a lot of people, or gongoozlers, as Vince taught me to call people who watch narrowboats going in and out of locks, under bridges and through aqueducts. We had to wait for someone coming out before squeezing both our boats in side by side. Vince did all the paddle winding while I stayed on the boat and a couple of helpful onlookers opened the top gates for us when the lock was full. Every other person was recording this momentous event on their mobiles, which brought home to me the fact that you could run (well, sort of) on the canals but couldn't hide since you remained in plain view, at least while the sun was shining. Wind and rain would, of course, swiftly restore a degree of anonymity. Soon after having come through the lock, we passed *Free Spirit*, the friendly cruiser. It was moored along the towpath on the left but nobody could be seen on deck.

Although I was glad to be puttering along with a quasi-companion for a while, it became immediately apparent that not having told Vince about why I was here had one major drawback. Soon after the Bradford lock, we passed a boatyard, Sally Narrowboats, without stopping. Verity on *Time Out* could be in there, using the services, taking on fuel or pumping out her sewage tank. Telling myself that this was far too close to Bath for her to still be lingering there, I shrugged it off and followed Vince. We cruised through the suburbs of Bradford which could be glimpsed here and there, and then out into countryside where we managed to find a temporary mooring late in the afternoon. We were now back in the country, and the only sounds to be heard when our engines finally fell silent were the faint gurgle of the canal, the splashing of a drake on the opposite shore and the lowing of cattle that stood half hidden from view behind a belt of trees.

'Better get an early night tonight, Chris,' Vince told me. 'Quite a few locks to get through tomorrow; we can do them together – saves a lot of work and water.' With that he disappeared inside *Morning Mist* to 'open a can of something'. Whether it was beer or ravioli he had in mind he did not say.

I had always wondered why drinks were measured in alcohol by volume. Now I knew. Being quite partial to a can of something or other myself, I had considered stocking the boat with beer for the journey, but a swift calculation had revealed that I would have to jettison the two-seater sofa in order to accommodate a meaningful amount of it, so I had given my credit card a workout and bought a case of drinkable red wine and a bottle of supermarket Scotch which took up a lot less space while promising the same degree of inebriation. I opened a bottle of red and made a start on it while I cooked myself a simple supper. Vince no doubt would have called it a culinary marvel but I called it lamb in a mushroom sauce with leeky mash and braised red cabbage (from a jar, Polish, very good).

Darkness was gathering outside by the time I had recovered sufficiently from my ill-conceived waste-not-want-not approach to eating mashed potato that I could move again without groaning and thought I'd go and check on the stars. We had made fast on the towpath side of the canal. No doubt there were boats somewhere in the gloom to either side of us but they had sunk into darkness. When I say 'check on the stars', it was a mere figure of speech; I was shamefully ignorant about astronomy and therefore childishly delighted by what I saw above me, without the interference of frankly useless knowledge about what they were called or what superstitious people thousands of years ago thought they represented. God's warm bits, someone once called them, and I preferred to think of them as that. Out here, without a single lamp post to bleach out the night sky, the display was suitably awe-inspiring. It was so dark that without a torch you could easily come to grief or at least get a wet surprise. Just in case, I had left one light on inside the boat. *Morning Mist*, however, lay completely dark and no sounds emerged from the boat when I stood quietly beside it for a moment. Perhaps Vince had taken his own advice about an early night. There was an odd smell in the air, as if from a crowded chicken shed. One minute I could smell it, the next minute the night breeze had carried it off

into the distance. Without any plan other than to walk on solid
ground for a bit, I set off down the towpath towards the very
faint glow that was suburban Bradford. Not even five minutes
into my solitary stroll, my torch, which had been living in the
boot of my car for the past year or two, dimmed. Telling
myself that the starlight reflected on the water would be guide
enough, I carried on for a while until I saw or thought I saw
two swaying lights on the path, still a hundred yards or so
ahead of me. I lifted my dim torch towards them and, as though
in answer, the lights disappeared. Perhaps there was another
boat moored there and the crew had just returned and turned
in. A few moments later my torch dimmed dramatically. I put
Not Leaving Without Spare Batteries on my not-to-do-on-a-
narrowboat list and turned back just as my torch beam became
completely useless. Small noises behind me more than once
made me turn, but I could see nothing that I could marry to
the tiny clicking noises that I thought I could hear from time
to time. I was glad I had left a light on inside the boat because
it told me how much further I had to grope. When I reached
the mooring site, there was still no sign of life on Vince's boat
unless you counted the faint smell of roosting chickens. I stood
very close beside *Morning Mist* and thought I could hear a
gentle snoring coming from a porthole near the rear.

On board *Dreamcatcher*, I locked the stern door behind me,
drew all the curtains, turned on the gas and got into the shower.
If your idea of a shower is to stand for a long time under a
pleasantly hot waterfall for as long as you like, then houseboats
are not for you. Nothing short of shooting holes into it will empty
your water tank faster than a couple of long relaxing showers
every day. The accepted boat routine is: get wet, turn off water,
shiver while you use shampoo and soap, then turn water back on
for as long as it takes to wash it off. I had left the porthole open
for ventilation, and while I soaped myself in dripping unshowering
quietude, I thought I could hear again those clicking sounds I
had heard in the darkness earlier, only closer now. There were
so many new sounds around me that no doubt would become
familiar after a while that I paid no attention. The water pump
whirred into action as I opened the tap and the shower drowned
out all extraneous noises as I finished my ablutions.

Pleasantly tired, I fell into bed in my cabin and dozed off with the window beside me ajar to let in the beautifully fragrant night air. I had no idea what time it was when I woke with a start to complete darkness. It seemed to me that what had woken me was a metallic bang or clank, but whether it had been part of a dream or real I couldn't tell. In my mind's eye I saw a colander slide off the pile of washing-up and clatter into the sink. I sank back on to the pillow with a sigh.

'You stupid moron,' a voice said in an angry whisper a few inches away.

My eyes snapped open. Stupid Moron whispered back a lengthy reply of which I could only make out the last three words: '. . . sick of it.' On the towpath right outside my window, a whispered discussion was going on between Stupid Moron and his accuser. I could make out little from the suppressed conversation apart from some emphatic swear words, followed by a clanging sound as something metallic hit the surface of the towpath.

'How many times are you going to drop that thing? Why not kick his bloody boat while you're at it, shit-for-brains?'

'Stop calling me that.'

'Shit-for-brains.' The faint crunch of four stealthy feet receded quickly down the towpath, soon followed by the unmistakable clatter of bicycles being mounted and ridden off. I sat up to try to catch a glimpse but all I saw were two receding halos of light. Then they were gone and complete darkness had been restored.

I lay back in the dark and thought about it a while. The towpath was being used by all kinds of people for all kinds of reasons, but mainly during the day as there was no lighting at all. Stupid Moron and his friend had left their bicycles a fair way further down the path and then stood making odd noises next to my boat. Which meant they were not there by accident, though the Moron seemed to be accident prone. 'Why don't you kick his boat?' the Moron's mate had suggested sarcastically, not 'the boat' or 'their boat'. In other words, the two knew *Dreamcatcher* was occupied by a man. Did they also know who that man was? If they were just a couple of drug addicts looking for boats to break into, then they would break into a boat obviously not inhabited, which led me to believe that the Moron Twins were next to my boat for a reason. It was a long time before I fell asleep, and if I caught any dreams that night, I did not remember them when I woke to someone knocking loudly on my roof.

# TEN

'**B**reakfast!'
It was Vince, repaying me for supper by bringing over a fry-up of sorts and a mug of tea for me. He watched me eat it while politely blowing smoke from a fat roll-up out of the window. 'We need an early start, so I took the liberty of making you breakfast. You didn't seem like a cornflakes man, so I got the frying pan out. I'm afraid everything I eat is out of tins,' he said in a take-it-or-leave-it tone. The fry-up consisted of warmed-up tinned tomatoes, fried slices of Spam, tinned sliced mushrooms oozing beige water and scrambled egg obviously made from powdered egg which, judging by the taste of it, had come over in the 1940s as part of the Lend-Lease Act.

'Where on earth did you get the powdered egg?' I asked.

'You can still find it if you know where to look.'

'My interest is purely historical.'

'I bought loads of it. Lasts for ages.'

'Obviously.' Even the milk in the tea was powdered. Despite the bizarre nature of the meal, I made myself eat every bit of Vince's kind offering and by the end of the ordeal I felt as though I had gained a valuable insight into the deprivations of the 1940s Home Front.

I followed Vince up the early-morning canal in beautiful light and with only the very occasional civilian on the towpath. There was no sign of the Moron Twins and their bicycles. All Vince had told me about what lay ahead was that today we would go up Caen Hill. Going up a hill in a sixty-foot boat is hard work. 'How are we going uphill?' I had asked. Vince had described it as 'a few locks, we'll do 'em together, less work'. There was little traffic this early, though one narrowboat followed us at a distance. There were several locks to go through before we reached Caen Hill. Each time we passed through one together, the following boat began to catch up

with us but did not seem in a hurry. It was a sixty-five foot
cruiser stern, painted all over in a shade of blue so dark I had
at first thought it was completely black; ghostly pale coach
lines delineated the sides. It was skippered by a man so short
he could barely peer over the top of the roof. He wore a black
T-shirt and black baseball cap, and just as he came close
enough for me to read that the name of the boat was *Moonglow*,
he put on a pair of sunglasses. He kept his boat at a respectful
distance while we negotiated the lock. There were several
swing bridges to go through too, which we left open for the
following *Moonglow*. Even here the dark boat took its time
going through, keeping its distance and failing to close the
bridges after them, even though there was no other boat in
sight. We passed a pub on our right, the Barge Inn, which
looked deserted at this hour apart from one shirtsleeved man
sitting at a table outside, hunched over a mug of something.
He acknowledged my wave with the smallest head movement.
Eventually, I could see in the distance a series of locks. Since
there was no traffic coming the other way, I drew level with
*Morning Mist*. 'This is it, then, is it?' I asked. It looked like
a lot of work.

'Oh, no, this is Foxhangers – just seven locks. Caen Hill is
further upstream. You'll recognize it when you see it.'

'Just seven locks?' I complained. 'How many at Caen Hill?'

'Erm, hang on . . .' Vince did his arithmetic. 'The Caen Hill
flight itself is sixteen locks. With these and the Devizes ones,
it's twenty-nine locks,' he announced brightly.

'It's going to take forever.'

'Yes, I wouldn't make any other plans for today.'

As we made our way through the seven locks at what Vince
told me was called Foxhangers, half of me still wanted to
believe that he was pulling my leg, but after only the briefest
journey we arrived at the foot of the scariest thing I had seen
on the canal so far: a steep hill and locks as far as the eye
could see, reaching up to the blue sky, with a broad path
running beside it on the right. No one had told me that things
like this existed; I had simply assumed that when the engineers
who built the canals came to a hill they would go round it or
tunnel through it, like the railways. Had I arrived here by

myself without warning, I would probably have scuttled the boat and run away.

It was just beginning to get busy, both with boats and walkers and onlookers. The onlookers had their uses. Some enjoyed opening and closing the lock gates, and even children joined in. The locks had side ponds – if they hadn't, only one boat at a time would be able to go up and down – and such vast amounts of water were moved down the hill that there was a pumping station at the bottom sending it all up again. We took turns winding the paddles. By the time we were halfway up the hill, negotiating locks was threatening to become a way of life. It felt to me as though this was what I had always done and would do for the rest of my natural. Looking down the flight, as I had now learnt to call it, I could see *Moonglow* below us, two locks behind, now sharing with another boat. I pointed out our distant followers to Vince.

'Looks like a coffin to me,' was his verdict on *Moonglow*'s paint scheme. 'Perhaps it's an undertaker's. A *floating crematorium*,' he said in a ghoulish voice. 'Get your ashes scattered in Lock Thirteen.'

I did a double take at the mention of Lock 13, but Vince looked in jocular mood and apparently had picked Lock 13, where the previous owner of my boat had died, at random.

Further down, five locks behind, I also spotted *Free Spirit*, the fibreglass cabin cruiser. Vince had nothing but scorn for anything afloat that wasn't a narrowboat. 'See? The thing is so wide the idiots can't pair up – twice the work. And yet there's far less space on their tub than even on a small narrowboat. Huge engine and twin screws at the back, but they can't go any faster than the rest of us. Could, but not allowed. What are they doing on the Kennet and Avon?'

Halfway up, we took a break in one of the side ponds to catch our breath and have a hasty lunch. I boiled spaghetti and stirred red pesto through it. 'I can do packets and jars too, you know,' I told Vince.

'Food preservation is the greatest achievement of mankind,' he assured me. 'I have enough tins and packet food on board to last me for months.'

I imagined the inside of Vince's boat to look like a WWII

grocer's shop, the walls lined with tins of whale meat casserole, baked beans, powdered egg and bottles of Camp coffee. It was then that I realized that Vince had not once invited me to step on board his boat to have a look around it – in fact, I had noticed that whenever he was on board *Dreamcatcher* and wanted to fetch something from his own boat, such as his tobacco tin, he habitually said, 'Stay here, I'll just fetch this and that.' Whenever he was on board my boat, I could detect the faint odour of chicken coup that I thought came from his clothes, since he himself looked meticulously groomed. I imagined that he either kept his clothes in a very stuffy cupboard or else lived with a giant chicken. Now that the chicken had added herself into the mix, my mental picture of *Morning Mist*'s interior had become increasingly surreal. Naturally, I was far too polite to ask Vince to inspect his boat since he clearly didn't want me on board, but I was also enough of a private eye to make snooping round *Morning Mist* at the first opportunity a firm goal of mine.

For the foreseeable future, however, I would be too busy or too tired, it seemed. 'Try to enjoy it a bit more,' said Vince as we resumed our ascent. 'And, of course, once you've conquered Caen Hill, everything else becomes a doddle in comparison.'

'You mean there are no more like these?'

'Nope. A few flights of three or five once in a blue moon, but otherwise it'll be all nice, gentle and relaxing . . .'

We continued our slog through the afternoon with me grumbling quietly and counting and recounting the locks, Vince cheerfully smoking roll-ups while pushing lock gates with his behind, gongoozlers staring into the churning waters and taking pictures on their mobiles. It gave me enough time to brew up a fine head of disdain for the hordes who stood and viewed the world through the rectangles of their telephones, and when I saw a man with a water bottle in one hand and mobile held aloft in the other drop his phone into the lock, I exhibited a distinct lack of sympathy by laughing out loud, which earned me a scowl from the man who stared down into the lock with something akin to despair. As I looked back down the flight,

I could see that both *Free Spirit* and *Moonglow* had kept up with us. In fact, every time I looked behind I saw both skippers look back at me. It was only natural, of course, that they should be looking up and forward, but despite both wearing sunglasses, I acquired a paranoid suspicion that what they were looking at was me.

It was late afternoon when we finally made it to the top of the flight, watched by quite a crowd. Vince had kept my spirits up by promising me that an excellent pub was waiting for us where they 'did great food'. Having experienced first-hand what Vince did to the Great English Breakfast, I fervently hoped that the chef at the pub did not use a vintage Ministry of Food cookery pamphlet as Vince obviously did. We moored not far beyond the Caen Hill locks and marched to the Black Horse with a thirst. Once the barmaid had furnished us with a pint of local ale each, we sat at a wooden table outside in the balmy evening air by the water and perused the food offerings. The menu was simple and so was the language; everything was either 'homemade', 'breaded' or 'grilled'. If it was meat, they grilled it; if it was fish, they breaded it; and if it had even a hint of a vegetable in it, then they homemade it. I chose the Homemade Beef Hotpot while Vince, after less than ten seconds' perusal, picked the Breaded Plaice with Chips and Peas.

We smoked and coughed and drank our beer while waiting for our food. Since having asked what I did for a living, Vince had exhibited no curiosity as to what the rest of my life was like. It seemed as though his chosen world did not reach further than the shores of the waterways and the pubs and shops you could reach on foot from the side of the canal. He talked of nothing much beside boats, and when he did, he would go into such intricate detail that all I could do was nod and try to remember it all since half of the time I had no idea what he was talking about. Electricity mystifies me, and no amount of talk about converters, inverters or alternators has made the slightest difference to that. Other parts of boats were just as mysterious. 'What's a *stern tube*?' I would interject, imagining a torpedo compartment I had not been told about, and Vince would roll his eyes, roll another cigarette and start explaining.

Apparently, Jake had sent me off on my cruise with just enough information to wreck the boat.

'You have to grease the stern tube every day – didn't you know that?'

'What with, an oil can?'

'With a stern tube greaser! You have to give it a half-turn every day to grease the propeller shaft and to stop water from coming in and filling your bilges.'

I was shocked. Apparently, I had bilges that could fill with water because I had missed a few half-turns on the stern tube greaser. Which, presumably, resided in the stern. Near a tube. Vince dug out an interesting collection of horror stories to scare me with, from carbon monoxide poisoning to seized engines via overflowing sewage tanks, and he enjoyed every minute of it. Not even the arrival of the food stopped the flow. The food was edible but then I was so hungry it barely touched the sides, and Vince would have eaten anything as long as it was covered in orange breadcrumbs. He enthusiastically discussed the relative merits of pump-out toilets versus the chemical cassette variety while forking chips and spearing peas on his plate. 'I mean,' he said through a mouthful of green peas, 'who wants to cruise around with a huge tank full of shit under their feet all the time, and then there's the cost. Pump-out cards have gone up again . . .'

I interrupted his scatological discourse with an offer to fetch more beer. As I stood up with our empty pint glasses, I spotted the undertakers from *Moonglow* sitting at a table further along. Both were sitting facing us and both still wore their sunglasses, even though they were now sitting in shade. They sat side by side in front of empty pint glasses, not talking to each other. One was a thuggish-looking bloke with a round face and a coconut hairstyle; the other was in his fifties, with a moustache, a five o'clock shadow and a receding hairline. They sat so still they could have been waxworks. I turned towards the pub and saw that the *Free Spirit* crew were also here, standing near the building and also facing our table, though when I walked towards the entrance, they both moved away. Both were of very similar build, tall, broad, trim, and in their early thirties with identical short haircuts. And both had a sour expression despite the bottles of lager in their hands. Did I tell you about my little paranoid bone? Oh, yes. It was chiming and there was no Annis to tell me that, of course, they were all here, since this was where you went after you had conquered Caen Hill. *Obviously.* I tried to tell myself the same thing, but I'm not quite as convincing as Annis and it went on vibrating. The pub was doing good business and the bar was two deep in waiting customers which gave me time to let my suspicions develop. When I looked back, the thuggish one of the under-takers was now also queuing at the bar. He had his sunglasses pushed up on top of his coconut head and I could see that he had dark rings under his tiny eyes. *Free Spirit* had cruised straight past me when I had grounded the boat but was now forever staying behind me. *Moonglow* had followed us but always at a distance, taking her time and letting two boats ahead of her . . .

When I at last came back to our table with full pints, there was no sign of the Free Spiriters and the remaining undertaker now sat with his back to us. I forgot about them for a while as Vince had found more stories of mayhem and disaster on the waterways with which to worry me. So many of the things he now told me about I had neither heard of nor imagined, and had he warned me of a three-hundred-foot waterfall near Hungerford, I probably would have swallowed it along with the beer. As it was, we swallowed quite a lot of that, having both vowed to have a lie-in next morning after our staircase lock exertions, and it was dark and after closing time when we left the pub. The last people were dispersing into the night.

I was standing by myself near the canal since Vince had run back to use the pub toilet when I felt a sudden urge to hear Annis's voice. I called her mobile and she answered almost instantly. Her work was going *well*, she was working on *both* murals and the weather was just *great*. But somehow she did not sound as exuberantly over the moon as before. The novelty of the swimming pool had worn off, Reuben Hitchcock was hardly there and his factotum, Harry Popik, was really a surly git and did not like being called Pop. 'And he disappears when Reuben isn't here, I've no idea where to, and I have to fend for myself. The nearest shop is miles away and everything's frozen or in tins. If I see another steak and kidney pie, I'll scream. Mind you, when Reuben is here, I get to eat very well, but I haven't seen anyone for days. How's boat life?'

'Strenuous. Must have done thirty locks today.'

'Good for you. You'll lose some weight at last. No sightings of Verity yet? Have you been asking around? No one's seen her?'

'Well, actually . . .'

'Actually?'

'She must have quite a head start on me. And I've sort of been enjoying the boat and I felt like leaving the private-eye thing behind for a while. I'm also a painter, you know?'

'Done any painting?'

'Haven't had time.'

'You've got to do one or the other or preferably both.'

'I know. But it felt quite good not having to explain about what I do or being asked to establish the whereabouts of expensive iguanas.' I heard a noise behind me and turned around. Vince was standing a few paces away, mouth half open, looking at me. He looked quite drunk.

'Where are you now?' asked Annis.

'Moored at Devizes.' Vince was walking away, hands stiff by his side, into the dark, towards our moored boats. 'You're not *that* far away then. Look up Ufton on a map. The canal doesn't pass all that far from Bearwood Hall. Come and visit. You can tell me what you think of the murals so far and I'll introduce you to Reuben.'

'And the swimming pool.' I promised to find Ufton on the map and started walking after Vince towards the boats, along with many others on the towpath. When I got to the boats, *Morning Mist* lay dark and silent and there was no sign of Vince. He had looked drunk and angered for some reason, but he was not staggering so I did not worry he might have fallen into the canal and drowned. As I went to unlock *Dreamcatcher*'s stern door, I found it unlocked. I had assumed I had locked it, but after that many pints I could not be sure. Perhaps, in my eagerness to get to the pub, I had just pushed the door shut and not done it properly. I now locked it from the inside and sat on my bed, asking myself if I wanted another drink. Two minutes and thirty seconds later I was fast asleep.

I woke in a sweat. The morning sun was beating down on the boat and with all the windows closed it was now baking inside. I threw back the covers and sat up, looking blearily out at a duck paddling by. I got up, opening windows as I went, and stood under the shower for a luxuriously tank-draining time until I was awake. Today I would try to sneak a peek at the inside of Vince's boat, I decided, and what better excuse than to knock at his door with breakfast? I'd just not take no for an answer. My hair still damp, I rushed to the galley, hoping to get it done before he was up and about and able to turn me away somehow. Kettle and frying pan on the stove, I softened some onions, whisked eggs with curry spices and scrambled them with the golden-brown onions. Divided it on two slices of bread with a dollop of spicy aubergine pickle on each, unlocked my back door and balanced two plates and two mugs of tea on to the deck. That was as far as I got. The mooring space in front of my boat was empty; *Morning Mist* was gone. On the other side of *Dreamcatcher* a woman was washing the sides of a seventy-foot boat called *Dragonfly* in the sunshine. She was in her mid-forties, with her blonde hair stuffed under a faded blue baseball cap, dressed in white T-shirt, denim shorts and pink trainers. I called to her. 'The boat downstream of me, what happened to it?'

She looked up, sponge dripping with soap suds, bright in the morning sun. 'That one? Left at sunrise; the engine woke me up. Why?'

'Oh, just an acquaintance. We had a few beers last night and I thought I'd wake him with breakfast.'

She dropped the sponge into a bucket and stood with her hands on her hips and her head tilted, squinting against the sun. 'A spare breakfast, eh?'

'Shame to waste it,' I agreed.

We ate at the table on board *Dreamcatcher*. Her name was Sue. 'This is such a blokish breakfast,' she complained, devouring it, 'curried eggs and Indian relish. Not bad, though, but I couldn't eat this first thing. Fortunately, I've had breakfast already. So, you on holiday, Chris?'

I decided to come clean and tell her why I was here and was immediately glad I had because Sue, after telling me I was just like someone off the telly, said, 'I think I saw your Verity, though I didn't get to talk to her. I do remember the name of the boat, though, now you mention it. I thought then that *Time Out* was appropriate because she needed to take time out to learn the rules. We were moored up for the night, just beyond Bradford, me and my husband, Tom – he's gone shopping; you'll meet him later if you hang around. He'll be chuffed to meet a real detective; he watches crime series on telly all the time. Yes, we were sitting on deck, it was such a warm night, especially for September; we had the candle lanterns out and a bottle of wine on the go. It was dark, an hour after sunset at least, when this narrowboat comes up from the direction of Bradford. Got her headlight going on the front and comes steaming past, way too fast. The people next to us were on deck too and they shone a torch at her and called to her. Didn't she know she wasn't supposed to move her boat at night? And I heard her shout back. "Really? Why not?" She had no idea the headlight was only for going through tunnels. Didn't stop either, kept going full tilt and disappeared upstream.'

'When was that?'

Sue thought for a moment. 'About six days ago? Something like that.'

Verity moving too fast and even travelling after dark could only mean one thing: she was getting away from me at a rate of knots, though I hadn't the faintest idea how fast a knot might be. My breakfast musings were interrupted by Sue excitedly tapping the window. 'There's that idiot again!' she exclaimed.

I looked and was rewarded with the arresting sight of a naked chap coming up the towpath. He was a tall, muscular man in his late forties or early fifties. He had long dark hair, a wiry-looking beard and an impressive amount of chest hair that connected via an uninterrupted line with an equally impressive forest of pubes. He was not completely naked since he wore thick walking boots and carried an enormous rucksack on his back. He did not seem to have lost his clothing and didn't display any sign of urgency to get to any. 'You've seen him before? Was he naked then too?'

'Oh yeah, Martin something-or-other. He was even in the *Wiltshire Times* because he got himself arrested for running around starkers. He refuses to wear clothes when he's out and about.' He came past our window so I got a close-up view of his dangling freedom only a few inches away from my scrambled eggs. Just then shouting erupted outside. A man and a woman were hollering, too far away and scrambled to hear the words, but it didn't sound friendly. 'He gets screamed at to put on some clothes wherever he goes,' said Sue knowingly. 'You'd have thought he'd go walking where there are no people.'

When we had finished eggs and tea and went outside, the naked walker was out of sight, but Sue's husband Tom had just returned from his shopping trip. His attire mirrored Sue's exactly apart from his trainers which were grey. 'New to canal life?' Tom asked happily. 'Make the most of any shopping opportunities is my advice.' He pointed at the two big canvas bags bulging with grocery bargains.

Good thinking. I was sure I could cram a few more provisions on to my floating home and followed Tom's directions to the nearest supermarket where I loaded a trolley full of food and beers and even remembered the sugar and the washing-up liquid. When I returned to *Dreamcatcher*, I found that Sue and Tom had also left but at my door lay a packet of chocolate digestives (20% Extra Free) and a note 'Thanks for the second breakfast. Sue.'

Due to my late start and shopping trip, it was now more or less lunchtime and I was hungry again. Annis's hopes that canal life might help me lose a few pounds were dashed when an hour later I tumbled oven chips and piri-piri chicken wings on to a huge plate, added a few tablespoons of coleslaw on the side and reached for the ketchup bottle. I was going to have to negotiate locks by myself from now on and had to keep my strength up, I argued with my invisible accuser. Then I cast off and left Devizes behind me, moving ever further east.

By now I had become completely used to the pace at which narrowboats moved. I did not fret when I had to drop my speed due to anglers or moored boats, and after the news that Verity had been seen speeding away from Bradford a week or so earlier, I also came to terms with the thought of never catching up with her. All of which meant that, until I had a new idea about how to prove that Janette Blinkhorn's fishy husband Henry was alive, I might as well go easy on the guilt and enjoy myself. And I began to enjoy myself.

If you are looking for Essence of England, then the Vale of Pewsey should do you (other quintessentially English land-scapes are available), especially if you have the leisure of looking around it at less than walking speed. Dotted with villages, dimpled with gentle hills, criss-crossed by hedgerows and the canal, fringed with trees and encroaching vegetation, snaking through it. Half of the time I was drifting through a jungle that allowed no views other than that of wildlife, a deer springing away at my approach, a kingfisher dive-bombing the water, a bird of prey circling high under a blue sky and, closer to my floating home, a grass snake swimming in the margins, whether for food or pleasure was hard to tell. When I could see further than the jungle fringes, the views were as rural as an abstract artist-turned-landscape painter could wish for. If I was no longer chasing Verity, why didn't I stop standing three feet from my boat's diesel exhaust and park the thing somewhere in the sunshine? Somewhere with a view? I had once more managed to completely lose my bearings, as though Devizes had simply been a strange dream and now I was back in a world where I could not name any of the villages and hills I saw. Out here my quietly puttering fifteen-bhp engine was the noisiest thing for miles, with very little competition from a tractor here and there, pulling a trailer across a field in the hazy sunshine. Roads and bridges appeared in front and passed out of view behind on the canal, and if I had thought to bring a map of the network, the numbers on the bridges would have told me where I was and what I was looking at. Naturally, I hadn't. Being preoccupied with my new and deli-ciously vague plans and standing in glorious autumn sunshine had the effect of putting my little paranoid bone to sleep. Since leaving Devizes behind, I had drifted along even more slowly than usual with the result that several boats overtook me where the canal was wide enough. While again making polite way for a hire boat in an unseemly hurry, I saw *Free Spirit* crawling into view far behind. Once more the fibreglass cruiser was behind me and it wouldn't have surprised me if they had the undertakers in tow. Had I been driving along in a car and seen the same two vehicles in my rear-view mirror, I'd have just put my foot down for a bit and taken a few left and right turns to see if they were following me, and, if so, tried to shake them off, but on a canal that's rarely an option. I had just passed a winding hole where I could have turned around and travelled back towards Devizes to see what would happen, but apart from not being quite sure what the procedure for turning a boat around was, all that unexpected and frankly undeserved September sunshine was making me lazy. I decided to stop somewhere and moor up for a bit and let them pass me instead and so lay my ridiculous doubts to rest. I was just passing another picturesque village and looking out for a good place to stop when I heard angry voices and shouts from the towpath. The towpath was quite busy this morning with walkers, cyclists and boaters and some kind of bottleneck had occurred, with several people crowded into the space between two moored boats. As I drew up to the place of the commotion, I saw that it involved two couples, several children, two cyclists and a naked man. Several people were yelling at once, the loudest one a burly man who had shouted himself bright red in the face. He wore a white T-shirt and dark-blue shorts, making him look like a walking Union Jack. He was shouting into the naked man's face while two women, holding on to bawling children, backed him up by interjecting obscenities. The naked man, with his rucksack on his back and his hands slack by his side, seemed to be saying nothing. From what I could hear, the language of the offended strollers was a great deal more obscene than the mere presence of the unclothed man. Without warning, Union Jack took a swing at the naked man, who staggered back towards the water's edge. Now one of the other men sprang forward and kicked out at him, connecting with a thigh and propelling the naked man backwards into the canal.

He went under immediately, pulled down by the weight of his
luggage. I had throttled back and turned *Dreamcatcher* towards
the place where he had gone under. The people on the towpath
were still shouting; the young cyclists looked shocked. The
naked man's head bobbed up. I could see he was struggling
to free himself from his rucksack. When *Dreamcatcher*'s stern
drew level, I threw the engine into reverse until the boat had
stopped, then reached out towards the struggling man with my
boat hook. He thrashed around in the water, ignoring it, perhaps
uncertain whether I was friend or foe. At last I got the hook
under a strap on his rucksack and heaved both it and the man
towards the boat. When finally he realized that I wasn't trying
to drown him, he struck out with his legs and after some
scrabbling, heaving and pulling, I landed a wet naked chap
and his soggy possessions on the stern deck where he lay
panting and flapping for a moment like a fish out of water.
The people on the towpath weren't finished, however, now
shouting that I should have left 'someone like him' to drown.
I made a couple of succinct internationally recognized hand
gestures which prompted the other man to lob a stone in my
direction. It overshot. He reached for another but one of the
women pulled him away. This was the second time in so
many weeks that people had lobbed rocks at me. Since when
had we become a nation of stone throwers? I put the engine
into forward gear and drew away with my catch into the centre
of the canal.

   The man, whose name was, as Sue had rightly said, Martin,
disentangled himself from his rucksack. 'Thanks for helping
me out. I thought I was a goner this time.'

   'This time?'

   'Yes, I got chased off a jetty into Blagdon Lake once. I
can't swim. Not even without my rucksack.'

   'Perhaps you should take swimming lessons.'

   'Can't,' he said, laboriously untying the soggy laces on his
wet boots. 'They don't allow naked people into swimming
baths. People wearing synthetic bits of garment dyed with
toxic chemicals are fine, of course.'

   'Do you go everywhere naked?'

   'Pretty much.'

'Why?'

'Because that is how we were born and I dislike clothes and I claim the freedom to not wear any. Being naked is not a crime.'

'No, I suppose not. But aren't there rules about that sort of thing?'

He had managed at last to take off his boots. His feet were several shades whiter than the rest of his body. 'If you really want to know, I'll tell you,' he said with a sigh. 'Mind if I sit on this?' He opened up one of the two folding chairs I kept on the stern deck. 'All right. It's an offence under Section Sixty-six of the Sexual Offences Act of 2003 to expose your genitals in public with the *intention* of causing alarm or distress.' He recited this in a voice that suggested this was not the first time he had had to explain the legal side of public nudity to someone like me who was vague about the law. 'It is also an offence to harm the morals of the public. Do you think I'm harming the morals of the public?'

'Hard to imagine. I, for one, feel completely unharmed.'

'I've been in prison for this, you know? Even though it isn't a criminal offence to go naked in public, they have thrown me in jail. For doing something the rest of God's creation takes for granted. You don't put clothes on other animals, so why should I be forced to?'

'But if it's not criminal, then how come you got jailed?'

'The only way they could jail me was by turning me into a criminal first.'

'How did they do that?'

'They gave me an anti-social behaviour order, the handy ASBO. If they cannot force you to live by their rules, they give you one of those and breaking the ASBO *is* a criminal offence. For the rest of sixty million Britons, it is not a criminal offence to walk around naked, but for the one person who actually wants to, it is. I am the only man in Britain for whom being naked is a crime.'

'Then why not pack it in and wear clothes? Or only go naked where no one sees you?'

'Because my rights as a human being are at stake. Everyone's rights. If they can criminalize something that isn't a criminal

offence to specifically punish one individual, then they can
tailor-make criminal offences for whatever *you* believe in. And
that is why I can't back down. By going naked I am defending
your rights as well as mine.'

'I hadn't looked at it like that. That puts it in a different
light.'

He looked across at me, still dripping from his hair and
nose. 'It does, doesn't it? I must say most people don't give
me a chance to explain myself. Except, bizarrely, police officers
and lawyers and judges. They get paid to listen to you, and
then they persecute you. And they get paid for that too,' he
said in a dry, bitter voice.

That reminded me. 'I think you should empty your rucksack
and dry that out; it must weigh a ton with all that water it
soaked up. You can spread your stuff on the roof. But not on
that thing there – that's the solar panel.'

'Oh, all right. You sure you don't want to put me down on
the towpath again? I can look after myself, you know. I'm
used to confrontation.'

'But you can't swim. And now your rucksack has soaked
up half the canal it would sink like a stone. Where were you
heading, anyway?'

'Erm' – he looked up for a moment as if to get his bearings
– 'east.'

'Where do you sleep? I mean, you can't get into B and Bs,
can you, or are there nudist B and Bs?'

'If there are, I haven't heard about it. No, I have a pup tent
and a sleeping bag.' He pulled both from his voluminous
rucksack and unrolled the sleeping bag which glistened with
moisture. A tiny camping stove and cooking pots came out
next; rain cape, socks and, presumably for unforeseeable
emergencies, underpants and a pair of jeans. 'I was hoping to
get to the campsite beside the Barge Inn; it's not far from
here. They know me there.'

'You're probably hard to forget. You mean they don't mind
you being naked there?'

'As long as I pitch my tent at the edges somewhere. They're
very laid-back around these parts.' He spread out the sodden
contents of his rucksack on the deck and the roof. His leather

wallet, stained dark with canal water, yielded one solitary ten pound note which he weighed down with a plastic cigarette lighter on the warm deck.

*Dreamcatcher* ambled along while I enjoyed the views for a couple of hours, without a single lock interrupting our lazy progress. I told him about my plans to moor up and do some painting.

'What do you paint?' he asked.

'Anything if it stands still long enough.' It was late afternoon. A lot of cyclists had been whizzing past us, tinkling their bells to shoo aside the walkers.

Martin knew the area well from previous ramblings and pointed out the landmarks for me: the Knoll, Clifford's Hill, All Cannings. 'Salisbury Plain is that way.' He pointed south.

After another hour Martin announced that the Barge Inn and campsite should come into view soon. What also came into view was a long line of moored boats. 'There's always a lot of boats parked here,' Martin assured me.

We passed at least a dozen narrowboats, most of them continuous cruisers by the looks of it. They are easy to spot. Large piles of uncut tree branches, wheelbarrows, plastic drums and big lumps of this and that covered with faded tarpaulin adorn many of them, while holiday boats normally make do with the odd flower pot. *Dreamcatcher* had not yet acquired any encrustations apart from the pink tandem chained up on the foredeck. I was chugging past the line of boats, hoping to find a gap into which I could insinuate my boat, when I spotted *Free Spirit* behind us, now close enough to see the two crew on deck, one with a large pair of binoculars trained on us.

I pointed them out to Martin who had suddenly ducked down. 'They've been following me for days,' I said. The one with the binoculars was now ostensibly scanning the trees to the north of us. 'Do you think they could be twitchers? Bird watchers?'

'Them? Doubt it. They're police.' Martin was squatting on the deck, shielding himself with his empty rucksack, clearly frightened.

'*What*?' I stared back hard at the following pair. 'How do you know they're police?'

'Watch it, mate, there's another boat coming,' Martin called.

In my consternation I had forgotten the boat needed steering and *Dreamcatcher*'s bow was aiming point blank at an approaching boat whose skipper was parping his horn to let me know what he thought of it. I threw the tiller over and managed to miss the other boat by the width of a coat of paint. The chap on the other boat gave me an exasperated look as he passed and called, 'Bloody Sunday boaters!' and then he saw Martin in his birthday suit and added, 'Weirdos!', parping his horn a few more times. When I looked over my shoulder again, *Free Spirit* was falling behind. It looked as though they had stopped. I went dead slow myself and turned to Martin. 'What do you mean, they are police? How do you know?'

'I walked past their boat two nights ago and they stopped me and gave me a hard time. They started pushing me around and insulting me, just for the fun of it. They didn't say they were police straight away, but when I started defending myself, they whipped out their IDs. Then they pushed me around a bit more.'

'Do you remember their names?'

'No.'

'What rank were they – do you remember that?'

'Detective something-or-other.'

'You sure it said "detective"?

'Yes, but that's all I remember.'

'You didn't see what force they belonged to?'

'What force?' He looked puzzled.

'Yes, you know, Devon and Cornwall, Avon and Somerset . . .'

'Oh, Avon and Somerset. Are they coming closer? They said if they caught me again, they'd make sure I go back inside. Back to jail. They knew who I was.'

I looked behind. 'I can't see them at all now. They've probably moored up at the end of the line of boats.' *Free Spirit* was wide and tall but much shorter than a narrowboat and could probably even turn around without the need of a winding hole. 'You're out on parole?'

'Yes. They can put me back inside anytime they like.'

'Damn.' I was having a much stranger day than I had planned

for. 'So, with you being naked on the deck of my boat, I am allowing you to commit a criminal act?'

'I suppose so. You're an accessory. Even with your clothes on. I'll get off as soon as you park up.'

'Don't be daft.' I passed the Barge Inn. It was a slightly dour building set at a right angle to the canal, but add a pub sign and a beer garden to any building and people are inclined to be quite forgiving of any architectural shortcomings. A few patrons stood or sat outside enjoying the early-evening sun as it sketched tree and boat shadows across the quiet water. I found a mooring place just a stone's throw from the pub, though I hoped that we were done with stone throwing for today. While Martin fingered his laid-out possessions and returned them to his rucksack in order of relative dampness, I was preoccupied with the revelation that *Free Spirit* appeared to be crewed by two police officers. It was not beyond the realm of possibility that they were just on holiday together, or even that they were a loving couple on holiday together, with massive binoculars to watch the birds and the occasional naked man. While wearing sunglasses. Only I could not get a single fibre of my being to agree with this hypothesis. *Free Spirit* had let pass too many opportunities to overtake me since I grounded *Dreamcatcher* near the aqueduct. There they had come on me unawares because of the tight corner, but since then they had been careful to stay far behind yet never out of touch. But why would the police be watching me, and in such unorthodox fashion? I only had two things on my books and one of them, the dead-man-fishing Henry Blinkhorn affair, had been poo-pooed by the police, according to the insurance company, and I was clearly not doing my job.

That only left Verity. I had told both DI Reid and Needham about Verity and they had dismissed any suggestion that there was a meaningful connection between her and the dead body in the burnt-out bedsit or the arson at the travellers' camp. Or had they? Needham had been unenthusiastic but not dismissive – it wasn't really his style. I tried to recall what he had actually said. *By all means look for your girl, but don't give Reid an excuse to make your life difficult.* Or something to that effect. But then he was off teaching and in his absence it was the delightful DI Reid who was in charge. It was Reid who had dismissed the idea that Verity was connected to the arson attacks. So if Needham was away teaching and Reid had no interest in Verity, then who were these two boating coppers hanging on my extremely slow tail? CID, no less, if Martin remembered the detective thing on their warrant cards rightly.

Martin meanwhile had stuffed his possessions back into his rucksack; half of it still hung over the sides because he was going to give it some more airing at the campsite. 'Well, thanks, Chris, for pulling me from the canal,' he said by way of farewell, getting ready to jump on to the towpath.

'Wait a second. From here the camp site is on the other side of the pub. If the police have moored up, they might be coming down the towpath towards the pub and you'd run smack into them.'

'What can I do about it?'

The obvious suggestion – that he put some clothes on – died on my lips. 'How do you survive? Financially, I mean.'

He looked puzzled for a moment at this turn of the conversation. 'I retired early. I have a tiny pension. And I own a studio flat in Bridgewater which is paid for. I get by.'

'Still, can't be easy on a tiny pension.'

'Can be a struggle sometimes.'

'How would you like to do a job for me?'

He looked even more suspiciously at me. 'What *kind* of a job?'

'I'm a painter – you can model for me.'

He snorted, uncertain as to whether I meant it. 'Don't you have to be a pretty girl to be an artist's model?'

'No. Just more or less human,' I said, speaking from experience. 'I need to keep up my drawing skills and models are difficult to find.' I didn't have to pay Verity for the last few sessions so I thought I might as well spend the money on Martin. It might save both of us from trouble tonight.

'What's the pay like?' he asked. I told him the going rate. He was impressed. 'What, per hour? Just for sitting still? Yeah, OK, I'll do it. Though why you would want to draw someone like me is beyond me. When do you want me to start?'

'Now. Are your jeans dry? Then put them on.'

'Put them on? I thought artists' models had to be naked?'

'Sometimes. But it's drawing clothed people I need to prac-
tise. What I want to sketch is people doing ordinary things,
like eating and drinking. Get your kit on and we'll go to the
Barge Inn. You can pose for me in the beer garden with a pint
and some food in front of you. A couple of hours should do
for a start.'

'Will I get to eat the food, too?'

'Eventually.'

He rummaged around in his rucksack and pulled out his
slightly damp jeans and a pair of underpants. 'The things I do
for money,' he mumbled as he pulled on his clothes.

While naked, he had looked wild and slightly deranged; the
addition of jeans and T-shirt made him look like any other
ageing hippy who came to the Barge Inn. The inside of the
pub had, according to Martin, recently been done up. 'It used
to have terrible artwork everywhere.' The new look was darkly
atmospheric, the lighting soft, with dark wood furniture and
floors. The place boasted a huge array of beers, some local,
and when we were eventually served by the slightly harassed-
looking barman, we bought two and went outside into the beer
garden, Martin carrying the menu, while I was lugging my
drawing and watercolour gear. We were lucky to find a table
that had just been vacated by a group of cyclists. The beer
garden sported a rack for parking and chaining up bikes as
well as a dumpy-looking monolith. 'Fake,' Martin assured me.
'But you can see the white horse from here, and that's not
fake at all.' He pointed it out and I could just glimpse the
enormous Alton Barnes White Horse where it had been carved
into a distant chalk hill a couple of hundred years ago. The
pub seemed to do good business, though the staff who served
food did wander about with a lost expression for a long time
before matching dishes with waiting customers. The clientele
were a mixed bunch, consisting of cyclists, walkers, boaters
and people from the camp site. You get a lot of hippies come
here too. The place is surrounded by stuff they go in for,
Stonehenge isn't far and there's crop circles popping up, so
you get the UFO believers and people looking for some sort
of mystic experience. As if on cue, an otherwise completely

normal-looking man in his fifties started walking around the fake standing stone with what looked like a bent wire coat hanger, probably looking for cosmic energies.

I had brought an ambitiously large sketchbook and a bulging bag of art materials. After having looked through the sketches that were already in the book, mostly of the landscape between Mill House and Bath, Martin seemed relieved, having assured himself that I was a bona fide artist and not just after his clothed body. I told him to stay exactly how he was sitting at that moment, with both arms on the table behind his pint of ale, and started my first sketch. Drawing people is among the more nerve-wracking things you can do with a pen. If you draw a tree or a street scene or a landscape, everyone accepts your view of it, but draw an actual person and you'll be fiercely judged on your ability to render the likeness; only botanical art is scrutinized more closely. It helps if your specimen doesn't move about. Martin's idea of sitting still did not quite match mine. He fidgeted and scratched himself as though wearing clothes really was a chore for him. I had my back to the canal while he sat facing it, with his eyes nervously scanning everything that moved. After about ten minutes he was visibly sagging a little under the weight of immobility. 'Can I take a drink of my beer?'

'Sure, I drew that first.' I was drawing with a dip pen and India ink, planning to use watercolour over the top once dry. I drew Martin and his pint, the pub building behind him, and was just reaching for my watercolour box when Martin lifted his pint again.

'The coppers are here,' he murmured, hiding his mouth behind his pint. His eyes and eyebrows semaphored that they were on his left. I pretended to rearrange myself on the bench with my sketchbook until I had them in view. They were standing on the edge of a disparate group of drinkers outside the pub – all the tables were taken now – and failed to look casual in a way only police officers can. Now that I knew they were CID, I naturally thought that everything about them screamed 'Police!' – from the way they pointedly kept their heads turned elsewhere while staring through their sunglasses at us to the slightly awkward, freshly ironed clothes and polished black shoes that I thought did not go with a boating holiday and pints of cider. They looked to be of equal height, about six foot, and both had short-cropped hair, which was fashionable among police officers to make themselves look tough (and to avoid having their hair pulled by suspects resisting arrest). They wore black T-shirts which still had creases from where they had been folded and black chinos which looked brand new and which no one in their right mind wore with regulation black police shoes. The slightly slimmer of the two, who seemed to have virtually no eyebrows, was vaping furiously from a red e-cigarette. I sketched a little cameo of the pair in a corner of the page.

'You are not scared of them?' asked Martin.

'Beginning to be.'

'What are they after, do you think? Are they following you? Have you done something?'

'No, my conscience is clear.' I thought for a moment about the revolver in the cutlery drawer but I forgave myself. 'No, but I also sometimes do a bit of detective work and they might be keeping an eye on me. Just why, though, I haven't figured out yet. But I will.' I turned away from the pair again, feigning indifference. I was getting hungry and Martin said he was, too. I dispatched him inside – well, he was working for me – with some money to order us fish and chips twice and more pints of beer while I got my watercolours ready. It took him a long time to fight his way back through the crowd with our pints.

'They're now sitting two tables away,' he said. 'So what kind of detective work do you do?'

'Oh, the usual, insurance fraud, mis pers . . .'

'Miss Perrs?'

'Missing persons – boring stuff like that.' I wasn't even going to mention iguanas. 'Now get back into your pose; I'm ready to do the colour.' I unstoppered my water container and opened my twenty-four-colour paint box.

Martin sat still again in roughly the same way as before, his restless eyes following my paintbrush as I mixed colours in my palette, darting furtively towards the police officers and sliding mournfully over his pint of beer. Eventually, I spotted a man in black jeans and trainers and a blinding white shirt walking about with two plates of fish and chips. I waved him over. 'You ordered fish and chips twice?' I nodded. Then he spotted the paints. 'Oh, it's you – you've finally made it, have you? We expected you three days ago; I'd almost given up on you. Rang you a couple of times but no answer. What kept you?'

'The boat journey took longer than I had hoped,' I said experimentally while wracking my brain as to how the chap could possibly have been expecting me.

'Oh, you came by boat? You didn't mention that. Slowest transport on earth. Why didn't you come in and make yourself known if you're here at last. You'll start tomorrow, will you?'

I gave up trying to figure it out. 'I didn't make myself known because I don't think I am who you think I am. Who do you think I am?'

'Sam Gower. You're not Sam Gower? The painter?' He nodded his head hopefully at the paints on the table. 'Come to paint the pub?'

'No. Chris Honeysett the painter.' His arms sagged with disappointment. 'Why don't you put those plates down before any more chips drop off?'

'Oh, I'm so sorry.' He set down the plates and let two sets of cutlery roll on to the table. Martin, released from his pose, grabbed the cutlery and started eating while looking up at the disappointed man.

'You were waiting for a chap to paint your pub? Not with emulsion, I take it?'

'No, no, he does paintings of people's houses, to hang on the wall. I wanted him to do one of the pub. I'm John, by the way. I'm the new manager here. I wanted to surprise my wife with a painting; she loves watercolours. She's away visiting our son in Australia at the moment but she'll be back in four days and it looks like Mr Gower has let me down.' He put his head to one side to get a better look at the sketch of Martin, which included part of the pub building behind him. 'You're very good, I must say. Can I have a look?' The few dabs of colour I had managed to put down so far had dried so I handed him the sketchbook. 'I like these a lot,' he said. 'I think they are better than Gower's, from what I've seen on his website. Are you moored up here? Will you be around for a bit?' I nodded with a mouthful of haddock. 'You wouldn't be interested in doing a painting of the pub, would you? With the beer garden in the foreground, the standing stone and everything? In four days? I'd pay you of course. Gower charges four hundred. Unframed, that is.' I pulled a face as though needing to think about it. 'And we'll feed you, lunch and dinner, and I'll throw in a few beers.'

'I'll start tomorrow.'

'Do you think you have enough time?'

'It's a bit tight but it can be done.'

'Oh, that's wonderful – such a relief. I thought it wouldn't happen after all. I'm really grateful.'

'I'll do some preliminary drawings tomorrow and let you look them over, see which you like best, then do the painting based on that.'

'Excellent. Is your name really Honeysett?'

'Yes.'

'It's just the village here is called Honeystreet. It was meant to be – that's obvious.'

'I can see that. Is there any ketchup?'

'Of course, be right back.'

Martin looked impressed. 'So this is how you make your money.'

'Very rarely,' I admitted, but he looked at me as though I had conjured wads of banknotes out of thin air. With the parlous state of my present finances, of course, a few hundred pounds plus free meals and drinks for a couple of days was a very welcome development, as was the eventual arrival at our table of every conceivable condiment, from ketchup via tartare sauce to mustard, just in time to anoint my last five chips with it.

In the fading evening light I finished the drawing I had started. Martin pronounced it excellent. 'No one's ever painted me before. Tell you what, instead of paying me, do you think I could have the painting? You bought me food and drinks, too . . .' I was more than happy with this currency arrangement and carefully eased the painting out of the sketchbook.

I had feared that now his stint of wearing clothes for me was over, he might strip off immediately at the table, but he walked off with the rolled-up painting to his tent fully dressed.

When I casually looked about me, I found that the Free Spiriters had disappeared. As I packed up my painting gear and stood up, I realized that I had probably not counted my pints as closely as I should have. Normally, this would not have overly worried me, but my mind was windmilling with theories all the way down the pitch-black towpath towards *Dreamcatcher*. It didn't help that I hadn't thought of bringing my torch. Several of the vessels along here lay completely dark and silent. I padded along towards one boat that showed a dim light behind one curtained porthole and from there moved on towards a wooden butty that sported a single ghostly solar-powered lantern that illuminated virtually nothing but itself and faded as I approached, but I knew *Dreamcatcher* was moored not far beyond it in the darkness. As I passed into the gloom beyond the butty's glimmering lantern, I heard a sudden commotion in front of me, and muffled swearing followed by receding footsteps of at least two people, moving rapidly away from me without the aid of torches, which was unusual on the towpath after dark. Overhead, clouds had been moving in all evening and by now there were only a few stars in the sky to help me find the silhouette of my boat, clatter on board, get the door unlocked and myself inside. There was nothing to suggest that what I had heard had anything to do with me or even *Dreamcatcher*, but I made doubly sure of the doors and windows anyway. Then I built little teetering towers of pots, pans and crockery behind both doors which would crash to the floor if they were opened from the outside.

# ELEVEN

I t was mid-morning when I awoke to the engine sound of a hire boat chugging too fast past the moorings, sending *Dreamcatcher* rocking and swaying and my pots-and-pans alarms crashing down, proving that they would be one hundred per cent effective if triggered by an intruder. This cheered me enough to jump out of bed, take the revolver from under the pillow and return it to its home in the cutlery drawer. Having collected my pots and crockery from the ends of the boat and reinstalled them in the galley, I toasted two slices of bread under the grill and then buried them under a mountain of fried onions and mushrooms and a poached egg dusted with cayenne pepper and celery salt. Then I carried it with my mug of black coffee up on deck.

Warm sunshine was drying up the moisture from an earlier shower, and already there was traffic on the water and cyclists and walkers on the towpath. What had felt sinister and unsafe in the darkness of the previous night now looked joyful and benign. We had successfully turned what was once an industrial highway – where boats heavily laden with stone, coal or agricultural produce were drawn on long ropes by horses – into a holiday destination and playground, delicately scented with diesel fumes. And I had been commissioned to paint the Barge Inn. My breast swelled with pride as I drove from my mind the sensible objection that I had more or less ditched a job that could net me thirty grand to end up painting a pub for four hundred. At least I was going to enjoy this job and, most importantly, Annis was no longer the only one with a commission. I called her to let her know. 'Free food and drink, too.'

'But no swimming pool. And you do realize I get paid ten times as much.'

'Yes, but you have to paint twenty times as big.'

'How's the rest of canal life?'

'Full of little oddities.' I told her about Martin, the naked walker.

She had heard of him. 'He's not as mad as the papers make out. And there are bigger oddities. I think I'm being followed.'

'*You're* being followed? You're supposed to be doing the following.'

'I know. But it appears someone is also following the follower. Two chaps on a cabin cruiser are keeping an eye on me, and last night I found out they were police.'

'The rozzers are following you in a boat?'

'I think so.'

'Sure they're police?'

'They flashed their warrant cards at Martin. Perhaps they want to find Verity after all and think that I might be on to something.'

'If Needham wanted the girl found and thought you could do it, he would either ask you to do it or tell you to keep out of it. I don't think he would have you followed.'

In the light of day, some of my paranoia evaporated. 'They could just be on holiday together,' I admitted, 'but they refuse to overtake me. I moor up, they moor up.'

'You'll be at that pub for a few days. If it turns out they stay put too, then perhaps it's time to get worried.'

'You're right. For all I know, they may have moved on already.'

I didn't tell Annis about the night noises or what I thought had been blokes on bikes, possibly trying to break into the boat the other night, nor did I mention the floating coffin that was *Moonglow* which also seemed to have followed me, for the simple reason that I had forgotten all about them. As it turned out, I shouldn't have.

The pub was open. True to his word, as soon as he saw me setting myself up in the beer garden, John came outside and asked me what I wanted to drink. He wiped the bench and table dry for me and furnished me with a pot of coffee. 'Can you make sure you get the standing stone in? My wife adores that thing. Cost a fortune to stick that there, but the punters love it. She would have liked a whole stone circle, but you can't imagine the price of stone. Stonehenge must have cost a fortune to put up. Anyway, I can see you want to get started so I'll leave you in peace.'

For a long while I just sat and studied the house and adjacent buildings, drank my coffee and made friends with the rather uninspiringly utilitarian edifice. I decided not to romanticize it but let it speak for itself and concentrate on the varied stonework, the shrubs and picket fence along the front to soften it. I fitted the standing stone into the front left as though I was sitting close to it. Then I counted the panes on the sash windows (helps to avoid embarrassment later), measured the distances between all the features with a pencil and outstretched arm (this makes you look daft but it works) and started the first sketch. There were a few people in the beer garden and more were arriving towards lunchtime, but the natural reserve of the British public meant that I worked undisturbed for two hours. I had nearly finished the first draft when someone did come up to speak to me. A thick-set man in his mid-fifties stood behind me and to the right, just close enough for him to see over my shoulder and for me to be aware that every pen stroke was being watched. He remained perfectly quiet until I had stopped drawing for a while and only spoke when he saw me screw the lid back on the ink bottle.

'That's amazing how you do that straight with ink, without first doing it in pencil,' he said. He came closer. He wore a straw hat that failed to shade a very large nose, which went some way towards explaining the redness of it in an otherwise untanned face, its paleness accentuated by a pair of sunglasses. He looked faintly familiar, but right now I could not place him.

'It's just a preliminary sketch,' I explained. 'I've been commissioned to paint the place. I'll be using a pencil when I come to do the painting, to make sure I get it absolutely right.'

'You do commissions, do you?' he asked. 'Are you any good at doing boats? I mean, sorry, silly thing to say, I'm sure you must be, the way you dashed this off.'

I was slightly miffed at the 'dashed off' since I had been working solidly for two hours, but I decided to take it as a compliment nonetheless.

'You wouldn't be interested in doing our boat? Not a painting – just an ink drawing like this. How much do you normally charge?'

The 'normally', you should note, is always the opening of a client's negotiations, where he naturally assumes that you will charge him less than you do 'normally', since his is a special case. The way to counteract this is to name a price in excess of what you do normally charge, which then allows you to give him a generous discount. He thinks he got a bargain and you know you haven't been taken advantage of, though not for want of trying. 'I charge a hundred and ninety pounds for an ink sketch this size and four hundred and fifty for a watercolour.'

'Will you be around for a while?'

'A couple of days at least.'

'I'll talk it over with my partner,' he said and disappeared. It took me a full five minutes to realize that he was one of the *Moonglow* crew, and I had just told him I'd be here for two more days. Did it matter? Perhaps I was wrong to include them in my boating paranoia.

I showed the manager my sketch. He seemed delighted with it but made a few suggestions. Could the standing stone be more prominent? And could I leave out the security camera and the burglar alarm? After a very acceptable lunch of home-made this and locally sourced that, I set to work again on my second preliminary sketch. This time I had more of an audience as the place filled up and people stopped to peer at my sketch while carrying their drinks past my table. The second sketch took a little less time, yet it was after five when I packed up my gear and headed back to the boat where I basked in the evening rays on the stern deck.

So far canal life had turned out less idyllic yet more rewarding than I had expected. I thought I could now understand why people decided to spend all their life on the canals, which made me think of Vince, who had been helpful and friendly and then suddenly disappeared without a word. I recalled the way he had looked at me that night – drunk, yes, but fear or anger also came to mind when I thought about it. I had been talking on the phone at the time. What had Vince overheard that might have spooked him enough to steam away at the crack of dawn? Having found and lost my boating mentor, this soon made me feel uneasy again, though merely about the mysterious workings of the boat itself, and since I wasn't going anywhere at the moment and the sun was keeping my batteries topped up, I decided to worry about my police escort instead. Were they still here?

After sunset I ventured down the towpath in the direction of Bath to check if I had reason to worry. I didn't have far to go to confirm it; in a long line of narrowboats, the white cabin cruiser stood out even in the fading light of the evening. I could have saved myself the bother; when I returned to the pub, I found them already there, sitting morosely opposite each other in front of pints of something or other. Perhaps it was time to turn the tables on them. After having ordered poached trout (a safe bet because it is difficult to ruin), I carried my pint of Guinness to a table where I could observe my observers and began to stare at them as though they were the most fascinating specimen of manhood ever to grace a beer garden. Tonight, though, they both wore shirts and ties. The evenings were getting chillier now and all three of us were wearing leather jackets, only I suspected that on theirs the pockets didn't have huge holes in them, allowing things like cigarettes and lighters to disappear into the lining, which periodically makes me look as if I'm having a seizure when I hunt for them. But apart from that, I was Mr Cool. And they pretended not to notice. Just as a girl came wandering into the garden carrying my supper, the thinner of the Spiriters put down his e-cigarette to answer his phone which was playing a hectic dance tune. He spoke into the phone, then both of them looked towards the road and abandoned their pints on the table.

A burgundy Bentley Continental had arrived. The driver was opening the doors for the two officers who were a good head taller than him, then he drove them sedately away into the night. There were no other passengers; someone had sent a car for them. With my phone's camera I took a pot-shot at the disappearing car, hoping to catch the number plate; there were ways of finding out who owned the wheels. No doubt boats too were registered in someone's name somewhere, but I had no idea how to find out who owned *Free Spirit*, while Jake had a contact at the DVLA, a classic car nut, who would occasionally exchange owner details of cars for a bottle of vintage champagne to stick in his hamper when he took out his vintage Rolls Royce Corniche for a Sunday run in the Wye Valley.

The trout was very acceptable, cooked simply and served with a tiny sprig of curly parsley coyly covering its glassy eye. I took my time over supper, drank two more pints while wondering what to do next. The Bentley's number plate was fuzzy but readable. I sent the picture to Jake, together with fulsome praise for the boat and a promise to pay for his contact's champagne in exchange for the registered owner's name. That done, I went back to *Dreamcatcher* and changed into dark clothes. I had made up my mind: it was time for a bit of breaking and entering. Tim, who used to do it professionally before going straight, had taught me how to defeat several types of lock, mainly because he no longer wanted to do it himself, even when, as I (often) told him, we were on the side of the angels. The lock-picking kit Tim had bequeathed me came in an elegant leather pouch and in itself counted as 'going equipped', which was enough for a custodial sentence; together with the unregistered Webley, it could land me behind bars for quite a while. I opened the kitchen drawer and looked down at the revolver for a minute before closing the drawer again, leaving the gun where it was.

Despite having been a private detective for longer than I care to admit, I have never quite managed to pull off a casual stroll when I am obviously up to no good. As I made my way *casually* down the towpath by the light of a young moon, I felt as though a neon sign was flashing above me, spelling 'UP TO SOMETHING'. My arms refused to swing naturally with the rhythm of my walk, and my eyes darted guiltily here and there, having forgotten how to look innocently out of my head. I walked past the beer garden, where several tables were still occupied by drinkers from the boats, the village and the camp site. I tried whistling tunelessly, which made it worse. Having forgotten to bring gloves on this trip, I took with me a pair of (clean) socks, like a part-time drug-addict burglar, because I had no intention of leaving my fingerprints on a boat used by the police. Of course, I was aware that these days advances in forensics mean a sneeze is enough to give your presence away, but then I had planned to get on and off the cruiser without them knowing that I had been there, a feat that should be perfectly achievable as long as I didn't try to bake a cake in their galley. I met two torch-carrying people along the towpath, probably boaters heading for a quick drink at the pub before closing time; we exchanged polite mutterings of 'Evening' as we passed each other. I did not use my torch and instead made do with moonshine.

*Free Spirit* was no longer at the end of the line of boats; the darkened shapes of two more narrowboats lay beyond it. Since I was trying not to use my torch, I swung on board the cruiser without the aid of a gangplank and nearly tripped over a coil of rope on the deck. I felt my way past the boat's wheel and engine controls down four steep steps to the cabin door. The Yale lock was one I was familiar with, and even in the deep gloom at the foot of the stair, I managed to select the right lock picks. The hardest thing is having enough patience not to leave scratches on the lock that show a break-in has occurred. I had learnt patience because I was rubbish at lock picking and was prepared to be there a while, but the mechanism was worn out and I had no problems getting inside. I closed the door behind me and stood in complete darkness. The place smelled aggressively of body spray or aftershave with an undercurrent of fried sausage. Pointing the torch downwards, I turned it on. The boat had four portholes at the side and two windows at the front. I was relieved to see that all of them were tightly curtained. Being used by now to the long and narrow layout of my narrowboat where the saloon is followed by the galley, dining area, toilet and shower and finally the cabin, I was surprised at how on this boat everything seemed to be crammed into the same place. Two bunks on my left were covered in discarded clothes and open holdalls. A banquette and table were barely large enough for two people to eat at the same time. Behind the door opposite the bunks, I found a toilet and hand basin; the door next to it revealed surely the smallest shower cubicle afloat, packed to the bulkhead with supermarket shopping bags resting on ripped-open boxes of cheap lager. Tucked in one corner was an unopened bottle of blended Scotch. I opened it for them – they would probably blame each other – and took a couple of fortifying swigs. It was surprisingly acceptable, so I took another couple of swigs just to be sure. I closed the door and let the torch beam travel over the rest of the cabin. There was a galley of sorts which consisted of a stainless-steel basin crammed full of empty beer cans and two gas rings buried under dirty pots and pans from which rose the smell of burnt sausages. What from the outside looked sleek, contemporary and imposing turned out on the inside to be every bit as tragic as a cheap fibreglass caravan from the 1970s. A grey upholstered bench at the very front of the cabin was covered with various papers, some handwritten, some typed, a few maps, but on top of them sat two pairs of binoculars, a pair of rancid-looking trainers, an iPod and a laptop. Having donned my pair of socks to avoid fingerprinting my ID all over the boat, I found the on-button – always a good start and not always a given considering my computer skills – and while I waited for it to power up, I took a photo of the whole mess on my phone. After the flash had subsided, I waited for my eyes to readjust, then dismantled the mess, setting all the objects on the floor so I could get at the papers. The laptop was a state-of-the-art thing as thin as an After Eight mint and loaded within seconds. It was password-protected and there was no chance of me cracking the password unless it was 'Password'. I turned the thing off. The map was of southern England, with the Kennet and Avon highlighted in blue felt-tip. I set it aside for the moment because I had glimpsed something scary as I lifted it. Underneath it lay a baby-blue plastic folder. It was open and from it had spilled sheets of A4 with six-by-four colour prints stapled into the corners. I took another photograph of how they were arranged before touching them. The memo at the top had a picture of Verity attached. It was a little grainy and looked as though it had been taken late in the evening and through the windscreen of a car: Verity standing next to her boneshaker bicycle outside the Bell in Walcot Street. She seemed to be talking to someone outside the frame. I flipped up the photo and read the brief but chilling note, printed in a tiny font on the single sheet of A4.

One laptop, Dell Alienware, recover and destroy. Three
USB sticks, blue Scandisk, 128GB, recover and destroy.
All devices in Verity Lake's possession capable of holding
data, mobile phones, mp3 players, digital radios or
cameras to be destroyed. Ms Lake must be left in no
doubt that extreme measures will be taken if further
images surface. How you impress this on the lady I leave
up to you but I suggest you leave a lasting impression.
Destroy this communication.

I pulled out the next sheet. Attached to the top left-hand corner
was a photograph of me standing next to the Honda Jazz,
taken in a supermarket car park. I was looking at a piece of
paper in my hand. The picture had again been taken through
a car windscreen. This time, however, the photographer had
been crouching low behind the steering wheel and enough of
the shape of the wheel was visible, albeit out of focus, to
suggest that it was a sports car, and I was willing to bet that
the logo beside the speedometer spelled Targa 4S. Which
would make it a Porsche. I flipped up the picture and read.

Chris Honeysett, a PI posing as a painter, or vice versa.
Motives unclear. Honeysett appears to be trying to locate
Lake who once worked as an artist's model for him. H.
has a good record of finding mis pers, hence keeping
close surveillance on him may be one way of finding the
girl. If H. is involved, then he needs to be dealt with
precisely as the girl. A search of his home computer
revealed none of the images in question.

In a minute I would need another swig of whisky. The next
sheet had a long-lens photo of a group of scruffy characters
which I recognized as Claw Hammer, Lead Pipe and the dippy
Sam who had fancied himself as Verity's boyfriend and business partner, who had nearly got himself cooked medium-rare
in his burning camper van. I turned to the note.

Various traveller scum Verity hung out with. One of them
is definitely involved, but Verity was the brains since this

lot have not even one between them. Deal with them any
way you like, perhaps get uniform to bust them on drugs/
theft robbery charges.

This was the last sheet in the folder, nothing on the characters
from *Moonglow*. Perhaps *Moonglow* was just part of my own
bit of paranoia which, after this discovery, would be quite
superfluous – I had enough to be scared of now. I stared at
the sheets of A4; I turned the folder over and over. There was
no indication of who might have issued this. I had seen
many a police memo in my time and nothing here looked like
official Avon and Somerset business. I had also never heard
of a Police and Criminal Evidence Act procedure that said
'deal with them any way you like', and while police may think
of travellers as scum, they tend not to put that in official docu-
ments. I went to the shower cubicle for another fortifying swig
or two of Scotch before returning to the folder. The question
that made me break into a sweat – unless it was the six fingers
of whisky I had just consumed – was: Who did these guys
answer to? Was it DI Reid or was it DSI Needham? Reid,
being in Bath himself, would not need to hand out instructions
like these on sheets of A4 and Needham would not be stupid
enough. Until now I had trusted Needham and thought of him
as a bit of a nuisance but also a proper by-the-book copper I
would not hesitate to approach as long as I had first hidden
my Webley, about which he has a bit of an obsession. It was
Reid, I decided there and then, and Reid had handed the memos
to the *Spirit* crew because he himself had received them.

It was time to reassemble the mess on the bench
exactly how I had found it, using the pictures on my phone.
Unfortunately, I had not been very good at charging my mobile
on the boat and leaving the camera on standby had drained
the last milliampere from its battery. No matter, I would do it
from memory.

I don't know if you have ever drunk a quarter of a bottle of
Scotch, taken something apart you shouldn't have in a place
you ought not to be and then tried to restore it with a torch in
your mouth and socks on your hands, but I cannot honestly
recommend it unless you are blessed with complete fearlessness,

a photographic memory and strong teeth. I shuffled the stuff back the way I thought it had looked, laptop off, on the right, rancid trainers over there and binoculars just there. I had just gratefully taken the torch from my mouth when, out of nowhere it seemed, voices appeared beside the boat. I snapped off the torch. 'Yes, you did, you made a complete arse of yourself by getting pissed; you could have waited until we got back,' said the first voice with considerable anger.

The other voice sounded as drunk as I felt. 'You're making a molehill out of . . . no, a mole, a mole . . . of a hill. Anyway, we're here and no harm done. All aboard.' The noise of inebriated feet stomping and sliding on the bulkhead above me was loud in my ears. The crew were back and my mind was a dark blank. The boat gently swayed as the plods heaved themselves aboard. I staggered through the dark cabin to the only place I knew could hide a grown-up person: the head. I managed to find the door, searched for the door handle with fluttering hands and opened it just as the drunker of the two officers managed to get the door to the cabin open. 'Core, it's stuffy in here,' he complained a few inches from my ear before I managed to shut the door and sink on to the tiny toilet inside.

I now had a sheet of varnished plywood between me and the two who talked with loud alcohol-fuelled voices, and it didn't exactly make me feel safe. What were the chances of two blokes who had been drinking not wanting to use the toilet before turning in?

'God, this place is a tip. Get your stuff off my bunk. Why do I always find your bag and stuff on mine?'

'Because yours is the lower,' said the drunk indignantly, 'and I can't see inside my bag when it's up there, can I?'

'Then kindly put it away afterwards, not leave me to do it.'

'Yeah, yeah, takes two ticks, give me a break.'

I heard rummaging and puffing and straining, and then the less drunk officer suddenly burst out, 'Mark, you total dickhead! I let you use my iPod and you leave it lying on the floor.'

'I did not!' protested Mark.

'Yes, you did and I just trod on it! If it's broken, you'll buy me a new one and double quick; this job is boring enough – without music, I swear I'll go mad.'

'I put it there with the binoculars – must have slid off the bench. This wretched tub never stands still. Someone farts on the towpath and it rocks like a seesaw. I'm sick of it. I'm sick of the whole thing.' There was a pause. 'You know what, Nick?' said Mark, suddenly sounding a lot more sober. 'I think we've backed the wrong horse.'

'Shut up! I don't want to talk about it. What's done is done.'

'Is it, though? You don't want to talk about it because you know I'm right. *Do this little job for us and when it comes to the disciplinary hearing I'll make sure you two will be all right*. Well, I think if this goes tits-up, we'll get heaps more than a reprimand. That lot will end up in the slammer for years for their filthy habits, and whoever poured petrol through that kid's letter box is gonna get life. And we'll end up as accessories to the whole disgusting bunch. God, I thought paedophiles were weird but this lot are worse.'

'It's too late now. We'll just have to make sure the girl and anyone with her doesn't get a chance to publish the photos. If they hadn't messed up when they handed over the money, none of this would have happened and we'd be enjoying our suspension from duty in the pub. But Reid says she was very pretty and sweet, which is why they simply believed her. Weird, when they're not into girls at all.'

'If they'd have killed her, they would never have found out where the pictures were and someone else could have turned up demanding more money. Or someone could have found them and handed them in at the nearest cop shop. They let her go to see where she'd run to.'

'Yeah, and then promptly lost her. And now this idiot painter is our best bet to find the bitch and he goes off in a bloody boat at two miles an hour. Only he's not looking very hard; that's our problem. If he's given up, then we have some serious work to do. Shit, I'm turning in; early start tomorrow – we don't want to find the Honey Monster has done a runner at dawn.'

'God, I need a piss,' said the drunker one, not unexpectedly. Next to my face, the door latch lifted.

'Don't use the head!' said Nick. 'The cassette is brimming, you'll just flood us with piss. Go over the side, for God's sake.' The door latch fell and the grumbling drunk clambered out of the cabin on deck. 'And don't fall in, because I'm not going to pull you out,' he added more quietly.

To remind myself that I was stuck in the toilet of not just any sort of drunks but of two rogue police officers, I called them DC Mark and DC Nick in my mind. The boat started swaying a little as DC Mark aimed his stream over the side. By the sound of his swearing, it was not going to plan. He was also talking again but it was indistinguishable.

'On second thoughts, please do fall in,' said his colleague, grunting and sighing as he made lying-down noises.

Mark clattered back into the cabin. 'Moon's out. Makes everything look pretty,' he announced.

'Not you, you ugly old git. Shut up and get in your bunk; I'm tired.'

Not having a wristwatch and with my phone's battery flat, I had no way of knowing how long I had sat there since both had retired to their bunks. The darkness of a stranger's toilet offers no help in marking the passage of time. You may quote me on that. It was worse than life drawing. I thought it had been ages, but had it? What if it was really five minutes and one or both were still awake?

It seemed an absolute age until eventually I heard faint snoring noises. At least one of them was asleep. I put my ear to the door. Was it one snore or two snores? After another age there was sudden loud snoring. The problem was that now I could no longer hear the soft snoring. Was the loud snoring of the one masking the soft snoring of the other? Or had the soft snorer moved and now snored more loudly? What if the loud snorer had woken the soft snorer with his snoring? Should I wait a bit longer? But what if the snoring stopped? I would be back to square one and could end up being faced with two sleepless DCs. Was one snorer better than none? I thought I was still getting drunker and was now worried I'd fall asleep. And start snoring myself.

Eventually, and to make matters worse, I felt the urge to use the toilet myself but couldn't, even though I was sitting on one. This was the clincher: I just had to get out of there. If they woke up, it would be dark and they couldn't see who

I was; I would make a run for it. I felt for the latch on the door. Still wearing socks on my hands, my fingers were less than sensitive and I knocked against it, provoking what sounded to me like a loud click. I was now beyond worrying about fingerprints and took them off. The movement of lifting the latch on the door took a full minute. Very, very slowly, I opened the narrow door, millimetre by millimetre. Having been in complete darkness, the inside of the cabin, illuminated faintly by what moonlight filtered through the curtains, did not seem so dark. I could make out the shape of DC Nick (lower bunk) right in front of me. He breathed steadily in my direction. The loud snoring came from DC Mark (upper bunk), of whom I could see one pale foot, dangling over the side. Both, I judged, were asleep. So were my legs, from having sat motionless in the cramped cubicle. I did not notice this until I tried to stand up and nearly keeled over. I braced myself against the creaking doorframe of the cubicle. It was like having frozen rocks for feet and splintered bamboo canes for legs. When eventually a semblance of feeling returned, it was not a pleasant sensation. I wriggled my toes. PC Nick grumbled. I lifted one monstrous lump and flung it in the direction of the exit, then the other, but I couldn't keep my balance. I swayed and then tilted forward until I caught myself against the bulkhead. PC Nick snuffled, grumbled and turned his back on me. I stood, frozen like a lean-to, fluttery of heart and wriggly of toes, until I had regained full command of my limbs, then opened the door in super slo-mo. Cold night air rushed in to replace the fug in the cabin and a shaft of moonlight fell across the floor. I squeezed myself through the narrowest opening I could manage. Pulling the door shut behind me produced a loud snap. I hadn't taken two tentative steps towards the guard rail when the lights came on inside the boat. I put one foot on the railing and jumped on to the towpath, sending the boat rocking and swaying. Behind me, the cabin door opened and I heard swearing and fumbling as I plunged into the vegetation beside the path and fought my way through to the field beyond. Keeping low, I loped away towards the pub, taking advantage of the time it would take them to put on clothes and boots before they could pursue me, allowing me to put distance between me and the Spiriters. It was very quiet out there and I was drunk and the noisiest thing around, but I did not stop running and stumbling and swearing until I had found *Dreamcatcher* and locked the door behind me. Sitting by an open window, I listened out for anyone approaching but heard nothing but tiny night noises until I fell asleep where I sat.

It was very late in the morning when I woke, with a crick in my neck, where I had fallen asleep sitting on the sofa. Out there it was another sunny day as our Indian summer luck was holding; in here I could hardly straighten my neck and my head protested at the slightest movement in no uncertain terms. My insides were threatening to become my outsides. A classic hangover demands a classic cure and robust handling. On my last shopping excursion I had stocked up on tubs of pickled herring and now was the time to break them out and send them into battle: bread, thickly smothered in salted butter, sprinkled with rings of pickled onion slices, a herring fillet bedded down on top, strong tea and three paracetamol is the Honeysett-endorsed breakfast for the morning after too much free spirit. This is not a miracle cure, but it restored my brain to working order, and I had a lot to think about.

I also had a painting to do and deliver; with half the day already over, I had to work fast. For fast work, pen and ink and watercolour is the perfect medium. I pitched up in the middle of the beer garden with my camping stool and travelling easel and dashed off a wild drawing of the scene, with the amendments John the manager had requested. When I showed it to him, he was delighted. 'It's going to be good, I can see that. Moules marinière on the specials menu today. It's nearly lunchtime. I'll bring you some out; you can tell me what you think.'

Great, I thought and went to work. The mussels arrived just as I had finished the faint pencil sketch. I managed to eat them without dribbling any juice on my sketch, declared them very authentic and then went back to work. This time, as I splashed watercolour about, I had more of an audience. I concentrated hard on my painting but out of the corner of my eye I did see the *Moonglow* crew watching, easily spotted because both wore sunglasses even when the sun went in. People came and went to take a look over my shoulder; some stayed for a bit, sometimes making admiring remarks to their friends, then leaving again, but one or the other of the *Moonglow* crew was always there for the two and a half hours it took me to finish the painting, which made me increasingly nervous. When I closed my paint box and rinsed my brushes, I looked up and they were gone.

While I had been painting, I'd had time to consider my situation – and Verity's. If DCs Mark and Nick were using me to get at her, then me looking for her could only put her in danger unless I managed to lose *Free Spirit*. I didn't even have a plan for the *Moonglow* crew. I had seen nothing of the Free Spiriters, but I knew they were there somewhere.

The painting was duly delivered to John who came out of the kitchen wiping his hands on a tea towel, then took me by the arm to stand outside so he could compare it to the real thing. 'Helen is going to love it. It's very good. I have called a framing workshop in Pewsey and they promised to have it framed by tomorrow afternoon.'

I walked back to *Dreamcatcher* with my fee in cash in my pocket, feeling reasonably happy. When I got to the boat, however, I saw that the stern door had been forced and stood wide open.

# TWELVE

My reasonable happiness evaporated when I saw the door wide open and the wood around the lock splintered. While I had been earning an almost honest dollar sitting in the beer garden, someone had been on the boat. And it looked as if they had taken their time trashing the place. Floorboards had been taken up in several places and wood panels on the bulkheads loosened, presumably to insert an inspection camera to search any cavities. My bed's mattress had been slashed in three places and the engine cover on the stern deck had been opened and not closed again properly. The lock to the gas locker on the front deck had been broken. I had in my time seen several places that had been ransacked, some by cops and some by robbers, but neither cops nor robbers had ever conducted such a bizarre search in which drawers remain unrifled and cupboards unemptied; not a book on the shelves or a garment in the little wardrobe looked as if it had been moved. In the galley I opened the cutlery drawer and my revolver lay, dull, heavy and deadly, among the knives and spoons. What self-respecting criminal would have left it behind? And what police officer, however corrupt, would not have confiscated it, if only to throw it over the side? My headache threatened to return as I sat and pondered what could have provoked such strange behaviour on the part of my burglars. Something Jake had said about Neil, the previous owner, swam back into my mind. Sitting outside on the railing for a better signal, I called Jake. It was answered with angle-grinder noises so I knew I had the right number, but I could only hear what he was saying once he had walked away from it, presumably outside the workshop. '. . . to be a huge job. But it's ready now.'

'I'm sure you're right but I have no idea what you just said.'

'Annis's Norton, you nit – it's ready. How's the boating? Not broken down, have you? I told you I wouldn't be able to come and fix it.'

'No, it's not that. It's something you said. About Neil – how he had changed. Did you say he was very tidy when you knew him?'

'Tidy like a Zen monk with OCD.'

'But when you saw the boat after his death, it looked like a tip?'

'Yes, stuff flung just anywhere.'

'But you didn't think it was the police, you know, looking for clues to his death?'

'They weren't looking for clues; they thought it was an accident. The police officer who led me around it kept saying "bit of a mess he left" and things like that. I got the impression they found it like that.'

'Could it have been the result of someone else's search? A burglary?'

'That was my suspicion at the time.'

'That was your suspicion? But you didn't think to mention it to me?'

'I didn't want to worry you.'

'That's so thoughtful. Well, I'm a tinsy bit worried now because someone broke into the boat while I was a hundred yards up the towpath painting, and they gave it the once over with a crow bar. You didn't think Neil died in an accident, did you?'

'I was not convinced.'

'And you thought sending me out on this boat might jog people's memory or something? Well, I think it has.'

At the end of our conversation my headache was back. I decided to make it worse by making some Turkish coffee, light a cigarette and call up the voice of reason.

'Hi, hon, how's your commission going?' asked Annis. For once it didn't sound as if she was in the millionaire's swimming pool.

'Done and dusted.'

'Paid for?'

'Cash in my pocket.'

'You didn't get paid much, then? Don't spend it all on balsamic vinegar again.'

'I'll think about it. Not in the pool?'

'I'm working outside on the colonnaded terrace. Are you coming to visit, now you're done? I've got fresh sheets on my bed.'

'Did the butler change them for you?'

'No, I found out today they've actually got a kind of maid; they must have hidden her below stairs up to now. She's called Aisha and, as far as I can make out, speaks eight words of English and two of those are "no understand". And she has melancholy brown eyes.'

'If you could see my eyes now, you might call them melancholy too.' I told Annis my news, starting with me breaking into *Free Spirit*.

She called me an idiot and a lunatic. 'Where were the detectives while you broke in?'

'They had been picked up in a Bentley and wafted away.'

'A Bentley,' she said flatly. 'A burgundy-coloured Bentley?'

'Yeeees. You're spooking me now. How did you know it was dark red?'

'Well, Reuben happens to have a wine-red Bentley. And last night he drove off and came back a couple of hours later with two passengers on the back seat. I'm in the gatehouse and I see what drives in and out, though there are other ways in and out of the estate. But Reuben likes to do a ton on the drive to and from the house to show off. Did you see the driver?'

'Only from a real distance and it was dark.'

'Was he a tall man, would you say?'

I thought for a moment. 'No, quite the opposite.'

'Reuben is tiny. Hon?'

'Yes?'

'This is getting weird.'

'Does Reuben know you and I are connected?'

'I certainly haven't mentioned it. He just got my name from Stoneking when he saw my mural in his pool and then looked at my website and rang me. No reason for him to know. But how is he connected with the guys who are tailing you?'

'I've had the impression all along that some pretty rich people are involved. Rich and ruthless.'

I told Annis what I had read in the folder. 'That's scary stuff,' she agreed. 'But there's no mention of me. Perhaps they

don't know you that well. Have you considered calling
DSI Needham?'

'I have. But . . .'

'You think he could be involved too?'

'I don't know what to think anymore. But he's away, anyway,
teaching at Hendon Police College for a couple of weeks; he
won't be back yet.'

'I can't imagine him being involved, but then nothing is
impossible. You can't tell from looking at them. I think the
best thing you can do for Verity – until we know who is doing
what to whom – is to stop following her.'

'I'm glad you said "we".'

'You'd be lost without me. I think you should get out of
there, pronto, and make your way up here, park your boat and
come visiting. I'll smuggle you in.'

'I will. I'll leave here first thing in the morning.'

'Let me know when your ship is parked somewhere and I'll
come and find you.'

The rest of the evening was spent knocking things on the
boat back into shape. The door still closed and locked, but I
was appalled at how easy my burglar had found it to get inside.
I brooded over this violation of my floating island. It had
happened in broad daylight and by the look of things had
taken quite a while. Someone had obviously been confident I
would not turn up and disturb them, probably because they
had an accomplice watching me do a painting of the pub. My
sunglass-addicted pair on *Moonglow* sprang to mind, one of
whom had patiently stood and admired my work, probably to
warn the other should I nip back to the boat to fetch something.
What were they looking for? Had Neil in fact lived off something less harmless than his small army pension? But Jake had
said that he had changed suddenly and planned to leave the
boat and even the country. What had he got himself into? I
stared down the boat, absentmindedly stabbing my fork into
a tin of sardines that had become my supper, and wondered
what they could have been looking for. Drugs? How would
someone who contentedly lived the simple life on the waterways suddenly get into drugs and get himself killed over it?
What worried me even more were other questions: Had the

people who had broken into *Dreamcatcher* found what they were looking for or would they come back? And if they had killed Neil for it, would they be willing to kill again?

Despite rebuilding my early warning system of pots and pans by each door and keeping the lump of the Webley under my pillow, I spent a restless night, waking often, listening, worrying about what might have woken me and imagining the boat surrounded by dark murderous figures, variously carrying crow bars, long knives or petrol cans. My eyes were wide open to greet the first inklings of dawn in the sky. The morning was cool and fresh, the sky overcast and the air smelled of rain to come. A reluctant dawn chorus was all I could hear. The towpath was empty of people. For breakfast I made do with a mug of coffee which I parked on the roof of the boat, then I hastily cast off and started the engine. Its rattle, clatter and putter sounded apocalyptically noisy in my ears and certainly must have woken up my direct neighbours, but I would try to sneak past the enemy who I hoped had drunk as much as the night before and were not easily roused. Pushing against the bank with my boat hook, I shoved off, steering as close to the opposite bank as I dared to keep as far from the moored boats as possible. It would be idiotic to sneak away only to run aground in full view of the opposition. The ancient Lister engine puttered quietly as I crept away at two miles per hour. I saw dark and sinister *Moonglow* lying lightless and eventually drew level with *Free Spirit*, involuntarily holding my breath as I slid past. Until the canal eventually bent right, I kept more than just one eye on the receding line of boats but saw no movement or tell-tale puffs of diesel smoke emitted by hastily started engines. I breathed a deep sigh of relief as I left Honeystreet, the Barge Inn and my shadows behind.

Naturally, as you may have realized, if I had had any sense, I would have slipped away in the opposite direction and plunged down Caen Hill and run towards Bath at full throttle, but, as you also will have noticed, I do not easily fall victim to sensible ideas. I had found an ancient road atlas on board. It was fifteen years out of date, but I presumed that towns and villages had not been moved since it was printed so it would probably do, and I had indeed located the whereabouts of the hamlet of Ufton, which lay near the deceptively named tiny village of Great Bedwyn. Ufton lay close to the canal and so Bearwood Hall could also not be far away. I was hoping to get there in two days if I stuck to the speed limit and nothing unforeseen occurred.

Now that I was putting some distance between me and the opposition, I begrudged every occasion I had to slow down for moored boats and eventually also traffic and early-bird anglers. I particularly resented the anglers because they reminded me that I had let a big fish escape my net only to bring someone into greater danger than she was in already. I cruised, always as fast as I dared, past lush hills and still green woods. When I reached Pewsey and Pewsey Wharf, I slowed down to regulation speed to make sure that no one paid me enough attention to remember me later, should the Spiriters or Moonglowers ask about me. At Honeystreet, just after leaving my mooring, I had passed a turning point, which meant that my shadows could not be completely certain that I had not turned and run in the opposite direction. Perhaps if they did not catch up with me for a while, they might decide to look downstream for me.

Beyond the wharf I entered lush farmlands to either side, with Salisbury Plain stretching out to my right. On this reach of the canal I came upon a long, old-fashioned-looking barge with a wooden sign proclaiming it to be a 'fuel boat'. Various hand-painted signs advertised diesel, butane gas, coal, logs, kindling and services such as 'pump-out' for your boat's head. I had never heard of such a marvellous thing afloat and greeted it with delight. It was at that moment moored up behind a narrowboat customer. I tied up behind the fuel boat on the towpath side. I had no idea how much longer I would have to spend on my boat whichever way I travelled, and the evenings were getting cold now; mornings on the boat felt positively icy. With unseemly haste, I carried off a sack of coal and kindling and threw enough logs on the roof to last for a good while.

The woman who took my money had brawny arms, a deeply tanned summer skin and fingernails black-rimmed with coal dust. 'Keep the change,' I told her, eager to get going again.

'My, my, you really are in a hurry to catch dreams,' she said, folding the money into a pocket of her dungarees. 'Slow down!' she called after me. 'Take it easy. And remember, it's always quicker to walk!' She laughed as I swung the last net of logs on to *Dreamcatcher*'s roof and quickly cast off. So much for not leaving an impression.

Being a novice and having only the vaguest idea what I would find around the next bend, the first lock came as a shock; I had sort of forgotten about this feature of boat travel, and by the looks of it we were going uphill again. There was now sporadic traffic on the water but it was late in the season; there were no more hire boats out here and for long stretches I met no one at all. This meant that I had to negotiate locks by myself and had no one to ask what might be around the corner. *More locks* was the short answer. This run of the canal was very rural, the harvested fields either side dotted with baled hay, though the railway line skirted it for several miles; the trains running past seemed to go with the speed of Japanese bullet trains compared with the progress I was making. It had been getting increasingly overcast; now the rain started – nothing spectacular, just fine, grey, constant and irritating rain, making everything cold, hard and slippery. (The reason you see only sunny pictures of canal holidays is not because people have sunny canal holidays but because they don't want to get their cameras wet.) My progress was desperately slow and some of the lock paddles were so rusty and old that my muscles soon ached with the effort. I had just managed the tedious routine of closing the lock paddles again when behind me a train driver sounded his two-tone horn. I turned around. At a carriage window, two children waved vigorously. I raised my windlass and waved vigorously back until it slipped from my wet grasp, flew away from me in an ungainly arc, clattered against the gate and windmilled down into the dark waters of Lock 54 with a banal splash that did not do justice to the catastrophe it heralded.

Without the windlass to lift and lower the paddles, I would not be able to go through any more locks. I stood and stared down into the dark waters, with rain dripping down my nose, wondering what on earth I was going to do next. Not even the slightest inclination to dive into the lock stirred in me as I dripped and shivered in the sudden chill that blew at me from the north. What I needed, I decided, was an angler. Or else a windlass boat that sold the heavy metal cranks and other things that boaters might irretrievably lose by carelessly dropping them overboard. Did someone sell them? Or did they come with other amenities of the boat such as engines and propellers?

As you might expect, not a single boat was to be seen, and with my luck the next one along would be one or both of my devoted followers. I trotted back to *Dreamcatcher*, cast off and churned away as I pushed the throttle hard forward. Then I reversed hard and stopped again. The stern thingy greaser! I hadn't done it since, well, the last time, and could not remember when that was. I lifted the hatch cover and dived down into the engine department. I gave the thing three turns just to be safe. When I emerged again, I found that in the two minutes this had taken *Dreamcatcher* had drifted and was now almost at right angles to the bank and in danger of grounding. Within the space of five minutes, it seemed, my complete amateur status had marvellously manifested itself. There was only one answer to this. Blind panic. I revved back and forth, poked the bank with the boathook, swore, revved some more and finally chugged away, damp, sweating, feeling stupid and full of foreboding.

As I chugged along, aware that the sight of the next lock would reveal to me the length of my new prison, I had no eyes for the beautiful Savernake countryside that was now being watered quite vigorously from above. I had stuffed a hat on my head but my hair was already so wet that it did little to alleviate my misery. Skippering a boat in autumn rain was worse than riding a motorbike, where at least you would be wearing the appropriate gear. I was ill-equipped for the wet and not a tumble dryer in sight. The blustery wind that had blown in these rain clouds to plague me also made steering a challenge. I soon learnt that a sixty-foot-long object floating slowly on water is easily blown off course if a decent blast of wind gives it a broadside. Unexpected relief, however, loomed ahead. What I first took to be a bridge turned out to be my first tunnel. It was long – over five hundred yards long – low, lined with brick and only wide enough for one boat. I could see the proverbial at the end of the tunnel but nothing inside. I turned on my headlight which was reassuringly bright in this Stygian interior, gave a couple of blasts on my horn to make sure no one entered on a collision course from the other end and took it very slowly. The diesel fumes swirled around me and the engine's putter was amplified by the echoing vault. Every so often I checked behind, half expecting another head-light to appear, but the tunnel stayed empty. It was a relief to be out of the wind and rain. Even going at half speed, it only took a few minutes to make the journey from end to end, but when I cleared the tunnel, the weather had miraculously and dramatically changed again. The wind still blew but the rain had stopped and the clouds were breaking up, allowing the sun through again. It may be an obvious thing to say, but a bit of sunshine can make a lot of difference to a wet man's mood. And it got better.

In my life, luck and misfortune seem to strike a delicate balance and, as we know, sometimes one man's ill luck is another's gain. I chucked the hat down the stairs and let the wind blow-dry my hair. Just half a mile after emerging from the tunnel at the summit of the hill, I saw a single narrowboat ahead, moored on the towpath side to starboard. What was more, I could see a thin curl of smoke coming from the chimney which almost certainly meant someone was at home. I would ask for advice about getting a new windlass. As I approached, however, I recognized the boat, and when I got close enough I could read the name on the stern: it was *Morning Mist*, Vince's old tub.

As I slowly glided up to the bank behind *Morning Mist*, I recalled the strange look Vince had given me at the Black Horse Inn the night before he took off without warning. I decided that our acquaintance was so brief that it really was none of my business, but he had been so helpful in the past that I was sure Vince would give me sound advice about my misfortune if I asked him. I quickly moored up and went to knock on his roof.

It took some time, but eventually the door opened a crack

and half of Vince's face appeared in the gap. 'Oh. You found me, then,' he said flatly and with a marked absence of enthusiasm.

'Hi, Vince, you all right? Good to see you again.'

'Yeah, hi,' he conceded, still giving me no more than half a face. He eyed me with a suspicious frown.

'Erm, I had a bit of a mishap back there and I thought you could give me some advice . . .'

He frowned. 'Mishap, eh?' Vince's better nature won over whatever made him wary of me; he made up his mind and squeezed sideways through the door. Behind him, the interior looked dim and the chicken coop smell followed him out on to the stern deck. 'Like what?'

'I managed to drop my windlass in the lock.'

Vince's face softened into a smile. 'You didn't, did you?' He scrutinized my face. 'And that's all you want from me?'

'Not sure what you mean. I wanted to ask if you know how I can get my hands on another one, or how I can get it out of the damn lock.'

'You haven't been looking for me, then?'

'No, just pure luck.'

'But I heard you on the phone, at the Black Horse. You're a detective and you mentioned an iguana?'

'Yes, apart from being an impoverished painter, I also dabble as a private eye. I once managed to find an escaped iguana called Knut and for some reason it made the papers. The story has been following me around for years.'

'And you're not looking for an iguana now?'

'Lor', no, I'm looking for a girl called Verity.' I began to get an inkling of the source of Vince's chicken coop-flavoured anxiety. 'So unless you have her hidden in your gas locker, you're safe from me.'

Vince breathed an obvious sigh of relief. 'Well, that's all right, then. Good to see you again. I've been trying to recreate your spaghetti dish . . .'

'Carbonara.'

'Yeah, that one, but it turned out a total mess.'

'I'll write down the recipe for you.'

'Great. Now let's get your windlass back. You're not the

first to have dropped stuff overboard, and I go well prepared. Back in a tick.' He disappeared into the bowels of his boat, still carefully closing the door behind him, but re-emerged only a couple of minutes later, carrying two large red-and-black horseshoe magnets fixed together with wire and fastened to one end of a green nylon line on a plastic reel. 'Let's go fishing.'

'I don't fancy walking, let's take my tandem.'

'Never ridden a tandem before.'

'Really? Neither have I.'

It showed. We wobbled. Twice we barely avoided cycling into the drink, an experience I thought I had sufficiently explored not to need repeating. There was now occasional traffic on the water and the unusual sight of two middle-aged men wobbling along on a pink tandem made people give us friendly waves. I firmly resisted waving back at them. We took the tunnel at full speed with me ringing my bell all the way for the pleasing echo it got.

'Do you remember where it went in?' Vince asked. We were staring down into the murky depths of Lock 54. The mossy sides of it looked slimy and uninviting.

I pointed at where I thought it had gone under. 'About there.'

Vince unwound the line a few feet, then swung the heavy magnets out, away from the side and let them plunge under water, allowing the reel to run in his hands until it stopped, then he laboriously wound it up again. At the end of the magnets hung an old tin. The soggy label was still legible. 'Vegetarian Ravioli,' said Vince with deep disappointment in his voice. The next cast lifted a mobile phone from the bottom, a Nokia C3. 'This lock is full of crap, innit?'

Third time lucky. 'Oops, this is heavy, I think we got it.' He gently lifted my dripping hand crank from the lock.

'Genius, Vince. I can't tell you how stupid I felt chucking it in the lock. How can I repay you?'

'That's easy,' said Vince.

Half an hour later I was ushered into the dim inner sanctum of *Morning Mist*. It was warm inside the boat, much warmer than outside. The smell was strong to someone unused to it but not completely unpleasant. Where in most liveaboard narrowboats you might have found a sofa, TV screen, book-shelves and so forth, here stood – on long, custom-made metal shelving – terrarium after terrarium full of exotic reptiles. Vince pointed out some of the specimens. 'That's Vinny the viper, and next door that's Cammy' – he tapped a fingernail on a chameleon's glass prison – 'that's Lizzy the lizard, that's Puff the adder . . .' There were frogs and tortoises and some tiny turtles in an aquarium. Next came a large iguana.

'Don't tell me,' I begged. 'It's Iggy, right?'

'Close. It's Pop.'

But the *pièce de résistance* came at the end. Near his fuel burner, which was chucking out tropical heat waves, was a giant terrarium, seven feet long and four feet deep. Inside was what had given Vince the jitters when he heard me mention Knut the iguana on the phone. 'I thought you were some sort of reptile specialist,' he said, 'hunting down illegally owned animals.'

'Well, that one is certainly illegal,' I agreed.

'I know. Meet Chomsky the crocodile.'

The croc in question was probably three feet long and looked as ill-tempered as crocs get when confined in a space smaller than, let's say, Australia. 'I got him when he was tiny, but he's growing like mad and getting too big for his terrarium now. He's also eating me out of house and home.'

'You haven't got a big brother called Hagrid by any chance?'

'Ha, yeah, I know. And I know I have to give him up, but it's not easy. I can't just set him free in the countryside. And one or two others of my friends are illegal immigrants as well. I'm scared of what they'll do to me if I own up to them.'

I looked down at Chomsky. 'How big do they get?'

'Regulation croc size. Big enough to eat a chap.'

'Hello, Chomsky, I'm Chris and I taste terrible.' I turned to Vince and gave him a look that was meant to be severe and sympathetic at the same time. 'Call Bristol Zoo. Tell them about your predicament; tell them you have been *a bit silly and are very, very sorry* and that you need help and that you want the best for him and for anything else that should not be crewing this boat. With any luck, they'll be more interested in caring for the animals than prosecuting you. Try it. Test the waters.'

'Yeah.' He nodded sadly at his crocodile. 'You're right. I'll try it.'

'How have you been feeding them, anyway? Do they eat cat food?'

'No, and that's my problem. I have two fridges going to keep their food in. That's why everything I eat myself is out of tins or powdered – no space, see? But I've got total engine failure and can't charge my batteries. I'm waiting for a mechanic but he won't be here for another day or so. My solar panel has always been useless and my batteries are pretty much completely flat now.'

'Bring them over, we'll charge them on *Dreamcatcher*.'

'Oh, mate, that's a relief, I'm ever so grateful.'

Vince staggered back and forth with his batteries. I left him to it while I rummaged in the galley for a lunch idea. Vince had connected three of his batteries in place of mine and started *Dreamcatcher*'s engine to charge them, while three of mine were powering his floating zoo. I was quite resigned to this taking all day, so relieved was I to have my windlass back and not to be by myself if my shadows caught up with me. By the time Vince came down the stairs into the boat, I had decided to tell him the whole story. Perhaps when he got going again, he could keep an eye out for Verity and warn her that the canals were not as safe as she had thought. But when I looked up, Vince gave me the strangest look yet. He came and stood close to me and then gently laid a package on the worktop. I looked at him, slightly puzzled. 'Look familiar?' he asked.

'No.'

'Didn't think you would have let me move the batteries if you knew it was there.' The package consisted of a large resealable freezer bag which covered a brightly coloured child's plastic pencil case. 'Under your number three battery, someone cut a hole in the spar it's standing on and put this inside. Have a butcher's at it.'

'It's not bloody heroin, is it?'

Vince shook his head. Now he knew it wasn't mine, he was enjoying himself. 'Much prettier.'

I opened the bag and squeezed the pencil case. It was heavy

and felt like a bag of screws. I unzipped it and looked inside. 'Blimey! It's Neil's retirement plan.' The case was half full of cut diamonds, all more or less the same size, like a bag of dried chickpeas. For the moment I was lost for words since too many thoughts crowded my mind. 'Where did they come from?' was an obvious one and also 'Who do they belong to?' but 'Who is going to walk away with them?' might become an interesting question.

'You think that's why the chap who owned this boat before died?' asked Vince quietly.

'He probably died in a fight in the lock. Perhaps he fell during the fight and knocked himself out and fell in. They wouldn't have drowned him until they knew where the stash was, I don't think.'

'Maybe,' said Vince, unconvinced. 'Or they thought they would find it without his help. Either way, I don't think they will let it go, do you?'

I didn't. 'I don't know anything about diamonds, but Neil was going to move to Spain and presumably buy a house there with these. And live happily ever after.'

'I wonder how he got hold of them. Do you think he stole them off the crooks?'

I zipped up the pencil case, put it back into the plastic freezer bag and carefully sealed it again. When I had filled the little sink with water, I dropped the bag in it. It floated.

'Flotsam,' I concluded. 'It fell off a boat and he fished it out of the canal. And somehow the owners knew he had picked it up or saw him picking it up. And they've been looking for it ever since. Those guys who are following me?'

'Which ones, there are so many?'

'The *Moonglow* crew.'

'That dark floating coffin?'

'Yes. I'm pretty sure they're after this little stash of carbon.' I fished out the package, dried it off, opened it again and stared at the glittering things. 'They searched *Dreamcatcher* back at the Barge Inn, looked behind the wood panelling and under floorboards. And that explains why they didn't touch any of my stuff. They guessed quite rightly that I had no idea about the diamonds and that it had to be hidden in the fabric of the boat. Let's hope they continue to think it hasn't been found.' I picked out one of the diamonds and, holding it tight between thumb and forefinger, drew it across the window. It left a scratch. 'Real diamonds,' I concluded. I was suddenly getting quite nervous about the baubles and sealed them all up again. 'They didn't come past us while you were out there shifting the batteries, did they?'

'Not that I saw but I admit I didn't pay attention to boats.'

I hastily drew the curtains on the window and looked around for a new hiding place. What to do with the stuff? 'Shame you haven't got a python, we could stuff them in a chicken and feed it to her – they'd be safe for a bit.' While I peeled potatoes, Vince and I went through possible hiding places, most of which were on the preposterous side.

A pan of plump sautéed sausages were kept company by a handful of finely sliced onions, a glug of wine and a bit of stock, left to braise while I boiled the potatoes. When they were nearly ready to be mashed, I cracked open a jar of Polish red cabbage and quickly heated it through.

'You make it look so damn easy,' admired Vince as he sat down in front of his mountain of mash, potatoes, gravy and cabbage.

'It is,' I said distractedly, while still puzzling over what would be the safest place to stash the diamonds. *At a police station* was the logical answer, but at the moment I had no desire to spend a day explaining myself in an interview room, and while there was the tiniest chance of walking away with all of/half of/some of the diamonds, I would hold on to them. Then it came to me. *The best place to hide a thing from someone who is searching for it is in a place that someone has already searched.* 'Got a housewife, Vince?'

'Needle and thread? Sure. What colour thread?'

'Sort of mattress colour.'

'Eh?'

Half an hour later I had sewn up my slashed mattress with the diamond package inside.

'But what kind of crook carries around diamonds?' Vince mused as we sat on the stern deck of *Morning Mist* and sipped coffee, away from *Dreamcatcher*'s chugging diesel engine.

The sun was back, though there was still enough wind to remind us that it was really autumn. Leaves were turning. I would light the stove tonight.

Few boats had come past us and we had seen no sign of *Free Spirit* or *Moonglow*. Of course, if I had thought about it back then, I could have slowed up *Free Spirit* considerably had I chucked *their* windlass in the drink. 'All sorts of criminals use all sorts of things apart from money. Large drug deals are often struck with precious stones or stolen works of art as collateral. Plus it's an international currency and won't go out of date.'

'It's crap, though, isn't it? You can't go into a car dealer's and pay with a couple of diamonds.'

We spent the afternoon watching the slow traffic, drinking too much coffee, smoking and talking about reptiles, diamonds, crooks and boats until the sun disappeared behind the trees and it became too chilly. Vince went to feed his charges and I went to cook us a meal and to light *Dreamcatcher*'s solid fuel stove. I promised to call Vince when supper was ready. The stove in *Dreamcatcher* was a small pot-bellied lump of cast iron with ornate clawed feet like a roll-top bath and had a stove pipe that kinked first this way then that before it went through the roof. Up on the roof lay the chained-up lum-hatted pipe, removable for passing through low tunnels. I stuck it in the hole without looking inside – the *Moonglow* crew would have – and went to build my fire. Some of the less useful pages of the road atlas went in, followed by kindling, two logs and a smattering of coal. Then I lit it. The paper burnt merrily, the kindling caught and I was confident I'd have a roaring fire soon. I closed the front hatch and turned my attention to my provisions, but moments later I heard Vince call my name repeatedly, coming nearer. He clattered down the steps into the boat, all aflutter.

'It's Chomsky, he's escaped!'

'What? How?'

'I . . . I must have forgotten to close the terrarium after I showed him to you. And both bow and stern doors were open for ventilation. While we were sitting having coffee, he legged it.'

Smoke seeped from several gaps in the coal burner. I opened

the front door a bit. Smoke billowed out. 'Would he have jumped in the water?' I asked. 'And swum off?' I added hopefully. If he had, our chances of getting the croc back would be nil. 'Could you just leave him to it? Could he feed himself in the canal? Eat fish?'

'Yes,' he admitted. 'Fish, ducks, swans, dogs, small children. Later bigger children. He would not survive the cold; we have to find him.' Outside, the sun was setting. 'We'll have to hurry.' He coughed. 'Your stove is smoking.'

We rushed outside but we didn't get far. Waiting for us, or rather for me, was a familiar face. It was Mickey, Mr Lead Piping from the traveller camp, only this time he had what looked like a filleting knife which he pointed at my chest while grabbing me by my jacket. His eyes were wild with whatever drugs he had recently snorted and his mouth worked weirdly. His black T-shirt looked damp and his skin was covered in a sheen of sweat. Mickey had waited for me squeezed into the corner of the stern deck beside the rear door and grabbed me before I saw him.

'Steady on,' said Vince who retreated to the tiller and looked as terrified as I felt.

Mickey was not alone. On the towpath, holding their bicycles, loaded with rolls of camping gear and bags, stood Sam, the dippy chap whose caravan had gone up in smoke and who had deluded himself that he and Verity were going to sail off into the sunset together. He looked fine, considering he had nearly died, though his hair was much shorter now, suggesting he might have lost some in the fire. He looked drunk and even dippier than before.

Unlike his mate Mickey. Whatever he had imbibed made him look too awake to live. He brought his face close to mine. With it came a memorable smell of rotting gums. 'I've had enough now,' he babbled at me, 'totally enough I think you know exactly where the little bitch is hanging out and where she's stashed the dosh and you're going to tell me because I ain't gonna mess about, you get me? Totally not.' This came out in one gush without punctuation but with considerable force and a soupçon of spit. The knife had pierced my T-shirt and I could feel that he had already drawn blood.

Sam stood unhappily on the towpath, hunched in a camou-flage jacket that was too big for him. 'Mickey, no, if you stab him, we'll never find Verity.'

'Shut up!' snapped Mickey. 'I'll stab him a bit at a time, until he tells us.' He leant past me to hiss at Vince. 'And you don't move, right?'

'I'm not moving,' I heard Vince say behind me. His voice was strangely calm and I could see why. As Mickey leant away from me, I could see past him towards the front of the boat and at the other end appeared the knobbly front end of a young crocodile. Chomsky had used the tarpaulin-covered tandem as a ramp to climb up on the roof and was now making his way towards us, eyes glittering.

Mickey turned his attention back to prodding me. 'Right, where is the little bitch? She owes us a wodge of money big enough to keep me in style for years. It was me who pinched the sodding laptop bag in the first place.'

'I'm afraid,' I said as slowly as I dared to give Chomsky time to cover some ground, 'I have no idea where Verity is.'

'Yeah, right,' spat Mickey, getting restless on his feet. 'That's why you got yourself a boat to run up the canal with, is it? We *know* . . .'

'Mickey, mate,' interrupted Sam. He had at last spotted Chomsky in the twilight, making progress across *Dreamcatcher*'s roof.

'Shut up, Sam, it's now or never. It's now, mate, he's gonna tell us.'

'I do know Verity bought a boat,' I admitted.

'We know that, we know, but what is the damn thing called? And where is it?'

'It's called *Time On My Side*.' Chomsky had a hungry gleam in his eyes as he advanced on Mickey from behind. Mickey's right hand, which threatened me with the knife, was held high, his elbow pointing directly towards the croc.

Sam tried again but his drunkenness and astonishment played havoc with his eloquence. 'No, mate, really, it's not that, it's—'

'Shut up! It's your fault in the first place she got away with all our money, you stupid git!' Sam gave up. He shrugged and let one of the bikes fall sideways with a clatter and began wheeling the other away along the towpath. Mickey looked towards Sam just as Chomsky reached his quivering, sweat-glistening, bite-sized elbow. With a sudden lurch forward, he chomped down on it. I stepped back and hit Mickey on the nose. 'Aaaaah, a crocodile! What the . . . aaaaaaaaaaarrrh!' The knife clattered on the deck as he tried to prise Chomsky's jaws apart with his left hand while a stream of swear words issued from his mouth in a high-pitched voice.

Soon we all worked on Chomsky. To say that crocodiles have quite a bite on them is an understatement and even a juvenile biting you could not be described as 'giving you a bit of a nip'. What Chomsky had in his jaws tasted like food and he was determined to hang on to it. Smoke started to rise from the inside of my boat, stinging in my eyes. Five hands were now prising the animal's jaws apart and all three of us were screaming, swearing and imploring respectively. Eventually, Mickey managed to wrench his punctured arm free with a final scream. I gladly let go and Vince pounced on the disappointed Chomsky, holding his jaws shut. 'Help me carry him back!' he coughed as the smoke got worse.

Mickey, in the meantime, had staggered off the deck on to the towpath and, swearing incoherently, picked up his bicycle and wheeled it away into the dusk at a trot.

We managed to carry the surprisingly heavy and struggling croc back to *Morning Mist* and plonk him unceremoniously into his prison. Who knew crocodiles could hiss with anger?

# THIRTEEN

Autumn had arrived overnight. The air was markedly cooler than before and a blustery following wind chased me westward. Vince had seen me off soon after sunrise. He had promised to give his illegal housemates to a zoo and keep an eye out for Verity on *Time Out*; if he saw her, he would warn her that the canals were not a safe place to hide.

Barring any more accidents, reptile strikes or knife attacks, I would reach Ufton later that day. Annis had promised to pick me up as long as I could make it to a road. In the meantime, I learnt to drive a boat that was blown along by a blustery, unpredictable wind. Sudden showers that lasted for a minute or two flung in more nuisance. After Vince had found the old bird's nest in the chimney, *Dreamcatcher*'s stove was working fine and the inside of the boat was toasty and dry while the skipper was standing in the wind and rain. Recent events had taken the shine off narrowboating. Having to stand in the cold and wet just five feet away from warmth and comfort now seemed like a glaring design flaw to me. But when the sun reappeared and the rain clouds passed away into the east, the charm of the canal worked on me again, enough to be interested in a curious boat moored beside the towpath. It was an immensely long, seventy-foot narrowboat, painted pillar-box red with the words 'Boaters' Lending Library' in foot-high letters on the side. Being sure that Verity, who was never without a charity-shop paperback, would not have bypassed this boat without looking in, I tied up beside it and climbed across.

Books and more books, as you would expect from a library. They covered the walls – sorry, bulkheads – and stood about in orange crates, all of them paperbacks. The librarian was there, sitting in a small armchair beside a tiny table with a mug of coffee and a laptop. She was suitably bespectacled, middle-aged and wore a pink cardigan – what more could you demand from a floating librarian?

'Membership is a pound. Administration fee,' she explained.

But how did it work? 'How long are you allowed to keep the books? It could be a year before people pass you again.'

'Oh yeah, and I move about, too. It's a pound deposit per book. Most people don't bring them back. Some always do, which is disappointing. I buy paperbacks at charity shops for fifty pence and basically sell them for a quid. But as a library I don't need a trading licence, don't have to charge VAT and I don't earn enough to have to pay tax. Just enough to keep me in food, diesel and reading matter.'

I congratulated her on her business acumen and asked if a young woman had recently joined. She was a friend, I explained, and I was trying to catch up with her. I described Verity to her and mentioned the name of her boat.

'Yes, just a few days ago. New on the canals. Valerie, isn't it?'

'Erm, yes,' I agreed. She typed the name into her computer and 'Valerie's' borrowing history appeared. *Treasure Island*, *Robinson Crusoe*, *Dracula*, *Frankenstein* and *Around Ireland with a Fridge*. 'That should keep her quiet for a bit,' said the indiscreet librarian. 'Exactly a week ago. Nice girl.'

I declined to join, claiming I was fresh out of pound coins.

Keeping an eye on my map, I drew level with Ufton in the middle of the afternoon, though the tiny village lay back from the canal about a quarter of a mile in the lee of a green hill crowned with a copse of broad-leafed trees. There were no other boats to be seen. I moored near a humpback bridge and called Annis.

'I think I've been across that bridge. Stand on it so I can see you and I'll come and get you.'

Standing on the bridge, I looked down on *Dreamcatcher* where it sat forlorn beside the narrow muddy footpath. It contained virtually all my painting materials, my gun and a fortune in someone else's diamonds and I was just going to leave it parked there? Was I about to make another monumental mistake?

When Annis turned up in her Landy twenty minutes later, she had an answer to that question. Several, in fact. 'You can buy more painting gear – don't worry about that – and your gun? When has that ever been of any use? You never have it handy when you need it, have you noticed?' She turned into a narrow tarmacked lane: mossy drystone walls on either side with a narrow belt of beeches or oaks, then pasture beyond. Brown cattle grazed in the afternoon light. 'As for the diamonds? If someone comes asking for them, hand them over and stay alive. That's my firm recommendation. And there's Bearwood.'

The Land Rover backfired as though to salute it. Before us loomed an enormous dark hedge. The land beyond it rose so that in the distance I could see a substantial country house studded with countless chimneys, and not far behind that the dark line of trees that gave Bearwood its name. We drove along the hedge for quite a way before we came to the front gate, set between two sandstone pillars topped with stone balls and a security camera each. Not far beyond it stood Annis's temporary abode, the gatehouse – a substantial nineteenth-century building with an out-of-proportion mock turret stuck to one side. Annis got out and punched the security number into a keypad and the gate swung open on well-oiled hinges.

'Everything here is well oiled and electrified,' she said as she drove the Landy off the tarmac road that wound through a vast expanse of grass towards the big house three hundred yards away. She parked on the grass in the lee of the gatehouse, out of sight of the manor. 'Reuben has motion sensors around the big house, activated after dark. You come within fifty yards of the place and an alarm goes off, metal blinds rattle down behind the ground-floor windows and the lawn is floodlit. He's very proud of it and deliberately left it on to impress me when he first had me up for supper. Problem is, every other day the deer get in and set it off, which must be a nuisance.'

'He obviously thinks it's worth it.'

'He's got a stinking amount of money – lots of it hanging on the walls. He's got a Hockney in his bedroom.'

'*Has he*?'

'Apparently.'

'What have you got in yours?'

'Fresh sheets,' Annis semaphored with her eyebrows.

*     *     *

Two hours later the fresh sheets were just a memory, and when we got out of the shower, Annis returned her attention to less pleasant matters. 'Weird things are going on here. There's more than one entrance to the estate; it's a hundred acres or so. Some traffic comes through here and some from somewhere else – I've no idea where the back door to this place is. Reuben always comes through the main entrance here. He drives up to the house like a racing driver; you can hear the Bentley's tyres screech to a halt at the house from here. He loves doing it, especially when he has someone in the car with him.'

I dug out my mobile and the picture I had taken of the Bentley collecting the two detectives. 'Is that it?' I zoomed in as far as it would go.

'Yup, that's it; his plate reads REU8EN.' I squinted at it. If you knew what it spelled, you could just make it out. 'So the guys he turned up with that night really were your bent police officers,' she said.

'DC Mark and DC Nick. And from what I overheard, they have both been suspended and are doing a favour for someone with influence who promised to get the charges against them dropped.'

'I don't think it's Reuben, but he has a lot of posh friends who turn up in posh cars: Mercs and Porsches. But they all come in the back way, which I thought is a bit strange since the other way goes through the wood and isn't tarmacked. Why would you want to bump expensive sports cars over that? Even the deliveries come through the front gate here, though they decidedly go into the house by the tradesmen's entrance. I think it's to avoid being on the CCTV recordings.'

'So what do you think goes on here?'

'I've no idea. He has had me over for supper twice but never when he has other guests, which is about twice a week. And it seems to be the same crowd. I can see the place where they park beside the house from the upstairs bathroom window, and it's always the same cars: silver Merc, dark-blue Porsche, two Range Rovers and a Ferrari. The parking area is brightly lit; you can see the cars clearly from here.'

'No big grey Ford, though?'

'You're thinking DSI Needham? No. You don't think he's involved somehow?'

'I got a bit paranoid out there.'

'What you need is some art therapy.'

The sun had already set when we stepped outside the gatehouse. Cars were arriving by the side of the house; we could see the headlights appearing and turning. Annis led me through the landscaped gardens, towards a pond. It looked big enough to float narrowboats on. Above it stood the colonnaded walkway, the back wall of which now sported an original Annis Jordan mural.

'It looks a bit out of place,' I commented.

'I know.'

'I mean, it's brilliant, of course.'

'I know. Come on. I'll show you the one in the pool house. We can get in from the gardens. But we'll have to be quick before it gets completely dark or we'll set off the alarm.'

The pool house was a converted coach house connected to the main building. It stood on the opposite side to the parking area where another set of headlights appeared as we made our way across the sloping lawns. A moment later we heard a growling engine noise.

Annis pulled me into the shadows under a stand of enormous pine trees. 'That's Reuben's Bentley.' She whispered it as though he might hear over the roar of his exhausts. With its headlights on high beam, the car screamed along the narrow drive towards the house, accelerating most of the way before breaking with an agonized squeal. 'Looks like he's having another soirée. Now you are here, I think we should find out what's going on.'

'D'you think?' I felt I was as close to Reuben and his strange friends as I ever wanted to be.

The door to the pool house was keypad-controlled. Annis entered the number and the lock clicked open. It was quiet inside, not a drip or a hum. Annis's whispering echoed around us. 'I won't put the lights on; someone might see. What do you think? Nearly done.'

Moonlight fell through the enormous skylights into the pool

house, shimmered on the still water and cast a ghostly light on to the mural. It was truly monumental, gloriously colourful, and could only be appreciated fully from the opposite side of the pool where we stood under giant potted palms. Paint pots and bunches of brushes lined a long trestle table in front of the enormous painting. We discussed her work in hushed tones in the fading light until Annis began pulling me towards a door at the other end. 'They didn't give me the code for the door to the house but I watched Popik several times and they are not very imaginative with their pin numbers.' Her index finger poked the keypad: 1, 2, 3, 4. 'How lazy is that?' The door fell ajar. It was dark on the other side.

'Erm, are we sure about this?' I enquired.

'I think the answer to a lot of things lies on the other side of this door. We might find out why all these guys are after Verity and what she has on them.'

'All right, but remember they burn people who make a nuisance of themselves.'

'I'll bear it in mind.'

Behind us we left the door to the pool house open and moonlight and warm chlorinated air followed us down the short, narrow, lightless corridor to another door; it was unlocked. On the other side we stepped into the house proper. We stood in a broad, carpeted corridor full of giant potted ferns in hideous brass pots. Moonlight fell through the enormous sash windows. The smell of chlorine had been replaced with that of cooking. 'Roast lamb?' I suggested.

'We must be near the kitchen. I've not been in this part.' For someone who had never been there, Annis skipped confidently along the corridor.

'What's our excuse if we get caught?' I asked.

'Let's not get caught.' Somewhere far away a door slammed. We took a right and a left turn. 'Ah, this looks more familiar: the entrance hall, I know where we are now; the dining room is over there.' As we reached the hall, from which rose a broad, gloomy staircase past equally gloomy wall hangings, we could see a thickly carpeted, brightly lit corridor lead away. The murmur of voices and the unmistakable clink of glasses came from there. Several closed doors led off the corridor, but the left leaf of a double door stood ajar. Very bright light spilt from it and the voices came from there. We tiptoed closer; as we did, we heard, among the voices, the bleating of a lamb.

'That lamb's not cooked,' Annis whispered.

We crept closer, Annis just ahead of me. Light and heat streamed from the half-open door. Very carefully, Annis put her head around the corner and froze. Then she withdrew it to stare at me, eyes wide. She pushed me forward so I could look in. The room was brightly lit with photographic lights. One video camera stood on a tripod; another was hand-held by a young cameraman. Two men and two women in various stages of undress were standing and sitting on antique chairs. One man was stroking a lamb that had coloured beads braided into the wool around its neck and pink bows around its hind legs. Watching the scene were several people, all holding mobile phones. Among them were Verity's 'aunt', now wearing only expensive black lingerie, a short fat man putting undue strain on his suit trousers and sucking on an unlit cigar, and a handsome young man who wore only studded leather briefs. And behind him, fully dressed in his usual browns, stood Detective Inspector Reid, taking pictures of the scene on his iPhone. I withdrew my head.

'Sheep fanciers,' I whispered. 'And DI Reid is one of them.'

'Zoophiles. And they've got police protection.' Just then a door opened at the end of the corridor and two people stepped into the light. The first, an athletic man with short-cropped hair, was leading a pink piglet on a pink collar and lead; the other, a small man in his late sixties, pulled along a giant white poodle with multicoloured ribbons around its ears. 'Popik and Reuben!' hissed Annis. 'Run!'

'Oi, you two!' bellowed Popik and started running towards us, letting go of the piglet's lead.

'Get them! They mustn't get away!' shouted the other.

We ran. The sound of a door flying open behind us and more angry voices announced that the chase was truly on. Annis was trying to retrace her steps but landed us in a place neither of us remembered. We skidded to a halt, but the sound of feet behind us meant there was no time to lose. 'Sod it!' said Annis emphatically and sprinted away. At the next turn we found a narrower service corridor that again smelled of roast lamb.

'You think they eat them afterwards?' I panted. In the distance I could see a fern in a brass pot. 'I think the pool-house door is somewhere down there.' We ran towards it and I was right. We piled through the door and out of the next into the pool house, past the moonlit mural and out on to the lawn. It was after dark and we hadn't gone five yards when the lawns before us became floodlit and the steel shutters on all the ground-floor windows rattled down with an ominous sound, like a drawbridge lowering across a moat. We sprinted towards the gatehouse, followed by raised voices and barking dogs. By the time we fell against the Land Rover, I had barely enough breath to speak. 'What's . . . the code . . . for the gate?'

'Five, six, seven, eight.'

'Lazy . . . bastards,' I panted as I punched in the numbers. Four men and two dogs were approaching fast down the harshly lit lawn. I flung myself into the passenger seat as Annis reversed on to the tarmacked drive. 'We'll never . . . outrun a Bentley . . . in this heap!' The Landy agreed and backfired.

'I can go places a Bentley can't.'

'Didn't you say the dog shaggers had Range Rovers?'

Annis was too busy screeching out of the gate and down the narrow, unlit lane.

I reached across and flicked on the headlight, then looked back. 'No sign of any cars,' I announced. Two headlights emerged from the gate, swiftly followed by two more. 'Spoke too soon.' We left the hedge behind and entered the narrow lane, bordered by drystone walls. Annis crunched up through the gears; the engine whined and backfired a couple of times. We slowed down. 'Why are you slowing down?'

'I'm not. It's conking out. Did it twice on the way here. I think the engine's had it.'

'Great timing.'

Annis slewed the wheel around to the left and with the last momentum parked the Land Rover across the narrow lane. She took the keys from the ignition as a memento. 'Bye-bye, Landy; it was good,' she said and got out. I found myself on the wrong side of the thing, caught in the headlights of two sports cars. I vaulted (OK, scrabbled) across the bonnet and ran after Annis who was already standing on the other side of the wall, urging me on. 'We'll go cross-country; I used to be good at that.'

I followed her across the tufty meadow; she set an ambitious pace. 'Which way is the canal?' I asked. 'We'll take the boat.'

'Your boat? It goes four miles an hour.'

'It's on the water. It's like having your own moat around you. And it's got my gun on it.'

'I love that gun,' Annis panted. 'It's that way to the canal.'

Looking over my shoulder, I could see the dark line of the drystone wall silhouetted against the headlights of the cars. More headlights were approaching. I saw a dark figure climb across the wall and soon we could both hear excited barking. Another drystone wall loomed ahead, on the other side a meadow full of dark shapes. Sheep. A few started trotting about as we ran past and I had not even enough breath to shout 'Mint sauce!' at them. With her unfailing sense of direction, Annis brought us out on to the road that ran across the bridge where she had picked me up. We jogged along. Headlights appeared behind us just as we slithered down the slope beside the bridge. Without the light of the moon, we would have been lost. 'Cast off; I'll start the engine.' Old-fashioned diesel engines do not like to be rushed. 'Come oooon, come oooon,' I urged while I waited, then the engine coughed and started just as Annis jumped aboard.

'Never seen a boat tied up with a granny knot before. We're lucky it's still here.'

A car screeched to a halt on the bridge as I pushed the throttle forward and we got under way. *Dreamcatcher*'s single headlamp illuminated very little. 'Is that full beam?' Annis asked.

'It's just for going through tunnels; you're not allowed to move on the canal after dark,' I explained.

'Then what's that thing behind us doing?'

'What?' The twin headlights on *Free Spirit* were not much better than ours, but their engine was thirty years younger and the enemy gained on us with alarming speed. 'They must have called them and told them we were coming. We're lucky they weren't already on our boat.'

'Can you not go faster?'

Black diesel smoke belched from the exhaust as I pushed the throttle all the way. 'Full speed ahead. That's all there is.'

'I think even now I could hop faster on one leg!' complained Annis. 'What's that on the right – a turn-off?' She pointed to the dark opening on our right.

'It's just a winding hole for turning around.'

No sooner had we passed it than bright lights appeared inside it. Two searchlights, four side lights and a bar of blue beacons came to life. A police siren wailed and out of the winding hole shot a police launch, a huge RIB capable of doing twenty-eight knots to our five. In the prow stood the familiar shape of DSI Needham, made even bulkier by a bright yellow life jacket. He had a loudhailer and bellowed into it. 'Cut your engine, cut your engine! We're coming alongside!'

But for once it wasn't us he was shouting at. The police boat swooped alongside *Free Spirit* to allow four uniformed officers to jump across, tazers drawn, shouting. That accomplished, the police launch rapidly approached our stern as I frantically tried to slow the sixty-foot *Dreamcatcher* before it crashed into the lock gates in front of us. Eventually, both boats stopped swaying enough for the superintendent to heave himself aboard. 'I seem to remember telling you to keep your nose out of this,' was his opening shot at me. 'Evening, Ms Jordan,' he added in a perfectly normal tone in Annis's direction before continuing to berate me. 'You couldn't leave it alone, could you?'

'You were away teaching and I didn't trust Reid. They're sheep shaggers, Mike, and Reid is involved.'

'I had long suspected Reid was bent, and I wasn't away teaching, I was giving Reid and his two stooges rope to hang themselves with. We've been following you and them all the way. At Bearwood Manor, did you by any chance see a fat man sucking an unlit cigar?' I nodded. 'That was retired Assistant Chief Constable Schofield.'

'Reid was there, too.'

He nodded sagely. 'All being rounded up as we speak. Now,

is there any chance at all you might make me a cup of decent coffee that doesn't come out of a Thermos and has real sugar in it?'

'Sure, just let me park this tub.'

'*Moor* it!' Needham and Annis said in unison.

'There is something else you should know,' I said when I handed him a mug of coffee the way he liked it: strong and sweet. 'There's a couple of guys on a boat called *Moonglow* who have been following me.'

Needham gave tiny nods while blowing on his coffee. 'Yeah, yeah, yeah. I think that's them now. Behind you.' All I saw was a procession of feet and pools of torchlight coming past the window, although there were at least six pairs of feet. 'Manchester drug dealers who move around on the canals to avoid our number plate recognition and motorway checks. We scooped those two up a couple of hours ago.'

'How did you know about these guys?'

'We watched them following you and compared their mugs with our database. Both are known to us. Terry Shard and Keith Mead, a rap sheet as long as my arm and known drug dealers. When Neil Jenkins, who used to own this boat, died in Lock Thirteen in Bath, their fingerprints were all over the boat. So where are the diamonds, Honeypot?'

'I'll get them.' I opened the cutlery drawer. My gun stared up at me. I shoved it to the back and picked up a knife to slash the poor mattress with again. When I eventually handed him the package, he reacted as though he had seen it a hundred times and just stuffed it in his jacket pocket. 'They hadn't found it back in Bath and then the boat disappeared from the canals. When they heard it was pottering about on the Kennet and Avon again, they flew into Bristol and grabbed a boat to go after you. So where had Jenkins hidden the diamonds?'

'Under number three battery.'

'Ah.' He patted the bulge in his jacket. 'Two hundred and fifty grand, apparently.' He drained his mug. 'You didn't find Verity Lake, did you?'

'Nope.'

'Would you tell me if you had?'

'Not sure.'

'You don't change, do you?' he said and pushed out of the door on to the stern deck. I followed. Lots of lights had appeared; a police van and two more police cruisers with blue beacons flashing stood on the bridge. *Free Spirit* had been moored. Needham was still wearing his life jacket. 'I think you can take your life jacket off now,' I suggested.

'Yes, bloody uncomfortable.'

'You do know the canal is only four feet deep, don't you?'

'Now he tells me.' He impatiently shrugged out of the thing before climbing on to the towpath. 'You are cordially invited to visit me at Manvers Street station at your earliest convenience, Mr Honeysett,' he said and steamed away towards the lights.

I slept beautifully that night, without fear of intruders, and at the entirely civilized time of ten in the morning I served mushroom omelettes in patchy autumn sunshine on the stern deck. 'I could get used to this,' said Annis, throwing bits of toast to the ducks. I don't suppose I'll get paid for my murals now, or we could have afforded to buy the boat off Jake. And I don't suppose I'll get my paints back, either. And the Landy has finally died and I'll need a new one.'

I dug around in my jeans pocket and dropped a couple of diamonds on to her empty plate. 'We'll go halves, shall we? That should ease the pain.'

'You old romantic, you. Thieving old romantic.'

'My recovery fee.'

We took our time pootling back towards Bath, stopping off at many pubs and beauty spots on the way as the weather turned cold and the smell of smoke from boats' wood burners flavoured the air. The season had turned at last, and when we finally approached Bath, it was truly autumn and grey skies threatened rain.

I pointed out the Raft, the floating café in Bathampton. 'Nice caff that,' I said as I slowed to a crawl. 'Excellent cappuccino.'

From the opposite direction a dredger barge came towards. I politely tucked *Dreamcatcher* in behind the floating café.

'Hon?' Annis poked me in the ribs. 'The angler we just passed?'

'What about him?'

'Well, he's wearing a pearl necklace, pearl earrings and pink lipstick.'

'What?' I looked back. About twenty yards behind on the towpath sat one die-hard angler. Even from here I could see a familiar pearl earring. 'Take the helm!'

In my haste to get my hands on the angler, I nearly slid into the canal as I clambered ashore. They say anglers are mesmerized by staring at the water but not as mesmerized as I was as I carefully crept up on the angler. He was both Janette's BMW-driving middle-aged girlfriend *and* Henry Blinkhorn. He was wearing an angling outfit with many pockets but also heavy make-up, thick lipstick, false eyelashes, pearl earrings and necklace. All that was missing was the wig. In its place, Blinkhorn showed just a sparse crown of steel-grey hair.

Well, it worked in *The Great Escape*. 'Henry!' I said jovially as I stood behind him. He turned, smiling up at me, then his smile fell as he recognized both me and his mistake. His hand flew to his throat where it closed on the strand of pearls. I gently laid a hand on his shoulder. 'My name is Chris Honeysett. I'm a private investigator. And I'm making what is called a citizen's arrest.'

I was prepared for long explanations when the police turned up, but one of the officers remembered the case of the disappearing fisherman. 'Well spotted, sir,' he congratulated me.

'Yes, well spotted, Honeypot,' teased Annis as we resumed our journey. 'I think we'll go halves on the "dead man fishing" too. Don't you think? It's only fair. And I do need a new Land Rover. And paints, of course, and brushes, and I left loads of clothes behind! *Loads!* In fact, I'll need to go clothes shopping straight away. Can't this thing go any faster? Come on, put your foot down. We'll go halves if you get a speeding fine.'

And thus ended my narrowboat adventure. We did not get a speeding fine but we did nab Henry Blinkhorn and his wife

Janette (who both got rather more than a fine – four years, in fact) and collected my – sorry, *our* – two per cent, which among other things paid for the invisible Honda Jazz and a new ancient Land Rover for Annis. We had seen the last of DI Reid and his equally corrupt cronies and the whole animal-fancier club was rounded up. I had to look for a new life model since Verity definitely wouldn't be back. She pretty soon gave up on canal life and did what Neil Jenkins had hoped to do with his ill-gotten diamonds: she moved to Spain from where she sent us a couple of postcards. One of my own ill-gotten diamonds now sits in a rather splendid ring we had made for Annis. The other I chucked in a drawer.

For a rainy day.